afterburn

Also by Zane

Addicted
The Heat Seekers
The Sex Chronicles: Shattering the Myth
Gettin' Buck Wild: Sex Chronicles II
The Sisters of APF: The Indoctrination of Soror Ride Dick
Shame on It All
Nervous
Skyscraper

Edited by Zane

Chocolate Flava: The Eroticanoir.com Anthology

afterburn

a novel

zane

ATRIA BOOKS

New York   London   Toronto   Sydney

ATRIA BOOKS
1230 Avenue of the Americas
New York, NY 10020

ISBN: 0-7434-7097-4

ATRIA BOOKS is a trademark of Simon & Schuster, Inc.

Manufactured in the United States of America

For Deotis, Jewell, Kevin, Lynn, Michael, Richie, Bradley,
and all those who left us too soon

For Aunt Jennie, who left us the day I completed this book

Life is like a coin.
You can spend it any way you wish,
but you can spend it only once.
—Author Unknown

From the Journal of Yardley Brown
June 1, 2004

As she lies sleeping, I can't help but be grateful that I finally know what true love is. I thought I'd found love before, thought that I'd embraced it, but I was wrong. Sheila, Roxie, all the rest of them, they had come into my life and turned it into chaos. Now I'm finally at peace with myself and my ability to give a woman what she really wants and really needs.

Not to seem like I'm reducing it to a sexual thing, but she does something to me. I can't contain myself when I'm around her. My dick gets hard every time I think of her. I spend half of my days and all of my nights—the ones when she isn't here with me—fantasizing about what the next time with her will be like.

Sometimes I wish that I could place my dick inside of her and sleep there, feeling her pussy pulsating around my shaft, letting me know that we are as one. But it is more than sex; it is love. The kind of love I've searched for my entire life. The kind of love that I want to feel for the rest of my life.

Yes, I mean it. She's the one. My only fear is that she's been damaged so much in her past that she'll fight me tooth and nail and refuse to totally open up to me; the way I need her to open up to me.

To think that we wasted so much time—almost two years—wasting time trying to make relationships work with other people, when we belonged together all along. I guess it's like my mother always told me. Things don't happen when we want them to happen; they happen when they're supposed to happen.

Learn as if you were going to live forever.
Live as if you were going to die tomorrow.
—Mahatma Gandhi

One

Rayne Waters, Age 15
Birmingham, AL
June 1990

I was lying in my bed dreaming about Prince laying me down on his basement bed; like he did to Apollonia in *Purple Rain*. I'd fallen asleep staring at the poster of him I had taped to my bedroom ceiling; a nightly routine for me. It was the one where he was lying on his stomach with his ass cheeks exposed; enough to tease the millions of teenage girls who idolized him like me.

"Rayne, wake up! Wake up, dammit!"

Momma's high-pitched, irritating voice pierced into my blissful sleep. I willed both it and her to go away. Lost cause. Momma shook my shoulders and yanked me halfway off my twin-sized canopy bed.

"Rayne, you know you hear me! Sit up, missy! Time for a talk!"

Trying to sleep was out of the question so I propped my back up on a pillow. "Momma, it's the middle of the night. Can't this wait?"

"No, it can't wait."

Her breath almost knocked me out when she plopped down

beside me, landing her hip on one of my kidneys. I moved over slightly. She was drunk again; no huge surprise. Momma spent at least five nights a week at the Eagle, a cruddy bar less than a mile from our apartment.

"Baby, I should've done this a long time ago, so listen up!"

"Done what, Momma?" Various scenarios raced through my head. Then I remembered my less than stellar grades. "Is this about my progress report? I'm gonna pull that D up in math. I promise."

Momma let out this hideous laugh. "This ain't 'bout no damn school! Fuck school!"

Humph, I wonder how many members of the PTA would want to jump on Momma's back for telling her child to "fuck school." She wasn't exactly June Cleaver but she could've at least been supportive of my education. I was really trying hard in school and was having issues with a couple of classes; mainly because of my staying up half the weeknights waiting for her to come home. I'd hear all these creepy noises in and around our apartment and we didn't exactly live in the safest area of Birmingham. I realized Momma was doing the best she could, considering my father—who she refused to name, if she even knew his name—had never been a part of our lives. Momma worked as a waitress at this dump where they couldn't even give me free food to eat. She used to try to get me to come by there after school to eat at her employee discount rate, but after a couple times of struggling to chew their meatloaf and ending up on the toilet for three hours, I decided my digestive system was more important than saving money.

On the flip side, I'd gained a lot of weight from eating fast food. I tried to tell myself that I could lose it at any given time. After all, I was young, and that had to count for something. I wasn't obese, so I simply let it flow and ignored the few assholes at school who made comments. I'd tell them, "God didn't intend for everyone to be a bag of bones!"

Momma slapped me on the leg and the pain shot up my spine. The room was flooded with an unwelcome burst of light after she reached for the ceramic lamp on my nightstand. "I wanna talk to you about fast ass boys!"

"Momma, why are you yelling? I'm right here."

Once my eyes adjusted to the light, I noticed her mascara and lipstick were smudged. She was so beautiful, even in disarray. She had the smoothest caramel skin, and men lost their minds over her gray eyes; the ones I shared with her.

"What about boys?" I asked. "I'm not even dating."

She pulled the bottom of my nightgown down further over my legs, like there were a bunch of perverted old men standing around my room or something.

"That Henry boy," she said in disgust. "I've noticed he keeps coming 'round here, sniffing your drawers."

"This is crazy, Momma," I stated in protest.

Henry Wilkes was *ugmo,* which made him twice as jacked up in the face than ugly. Chance Martinez, my best friend, and I had made up the word to describe him. He was still my friend because you have to take friends where you can get them and most of the boys in the school were so stuck on themselves that they made me sick. The majority of the girls were too busy sizing each other up in competition to be friendly.

"Momma, Henry and I are friends. I don't like him. He's not attractive, at all."

"Forget being attractive. Does he have any money?"

She was tripping. Did she not realize that no one at my school had money? If they did, they sure as hell wouldn't be playing house in our neighborhood. We didn't have two nickels to rub together and it was my guess that Henry and his family didn't have two pennies to rub together.

She stared at me like she was awaiting a response, one

that should've been obvious, so I replied, "Don't think so. Why?"

Her voice went up three decibels as she catapulted off the bed and threw her hands on her hips. "'Cause if he ain't got no money, he needs to keep his little ass from 'round here!"

"Henry's my partner for a science project. That's why he's been coming over lately."

I figured that was the end of the conversation so I laid back down. Momma pinched me on the shoulder and I shrieked out in pain. "Ow, Momma! Why'd you do that?"

"Sit up and listen to me, dammit! I've been whoring all my life and I'm a good whore. You better learn how to be a good whore, too!"

Momma was about to give up too much information so I tried to ward her off. "Momma, please go to bed. You're drunk."

"I ain't drunk."

We both realized she was lying.

"I know what the hell I'm saying. Don't ever fall in love, Rayne. Not ever. Bastards will chew you up like a wad of tobacco. Believe that." I didn't feel like hearing her mouth, but at least she'd finally lowered her voice some. "Men care about two things. Money and pussy; in that order. You need to concentrate on the money and intake dick for financial purposes only."

I suppressed a laugh. If she'd been following that philosophy, we would've been living large. She was tripping, *hard*. I couldn't imagine how many drinks she must've had. The bartender at the Eagle must've made some seriously strong drinks that night.

It wasn't a secret that Momma loved spending time with men. Quite often, I'd wake up and find strange men scrambling eggs in the kitchen—the main staple we kept in the house—in the buff or close to it. Even so, the whoring comment had thrown me for a loop. She'd never come straight out and used the word "pussy" in front of me before, either.

"That's not true, Momma, about men caring about two things. Some men care about more than that."

She grabbed both sides of my face and stared into my eyes. "The hell they do. Loving a man will destroy you. He'll destroy you. He'll take your self-esteem. He'll take your dignity. Then he'll walk away and leave you with a stack of bills, bad credit, and possibly one or two babies." I wondered if she was talking about my nameless father. "Men are selfish and aren't capable of loving anyone but themselves."

"I've seen plenty of men in love. Men that treat women with respect," I told her.

I glanced at my alarm clock. Five A.M. *Why couldn't she simply go to bed?*

Momma rolled her eyes at me. "Where? Where have you ever seen men in love? On cable? At the movies? Fantasyland, perhaps? That shit ain't real. Name one fool—just one—you actually know who's in love."

Normally, I'd hate being put on the spot, but I had an answer for that one right away. Chance had been my best friend since first grade. If there was one thing I was absolutely certain of, her parents were madly in love. Chance was the third of six children and every experience in their home was like the Latino version of *The Cosby Show*. Even though they were a far cry from rich—more like barely making ends meet—everyone was always happy, smiling, and content; especially the parents. Yes, they were definitely in love. I was sure of it.

"Manuel Martinez. Chance's daddy. He adores his wife," I stated avidly. "They're incredibly cute together."

Momma laughed so hard, I thought she was going to choke on her own tongue.

"What's so funny, Momma?"

"Rayne, I hate to burst your bubble, but *puleeze!* Manuel's ass ain't in love. He's hanging in there because of all the damn babies that heifer keeps dropping. I've fucked Manuel a dozen times."

I almost choked on my own tongue at that point. "You had sex with Chance's daddy?"

"Shit, everyone's had sex with Chance's daddy."

I sat up higher on the bed. "Like who?"

"Never mind all that. Let's just say that Manuel has stuck more money in panties and seen more sluts working the pole than any man in Birmingham."

"Working the pole?"

"Yes, the pole!"

I looked at her in confusion.

"Shit, I'm glad you don't know what I mean 'cause your ass better not end up working the pole at some sleazy strip club."

"Ah," I whispered, getting her point.

"Listen to me, Rayne. Men ain't no damn good."

I laid back down. "You said that already."

It couldn't be true. Mr. Martinez was always so lovey-dovey. If a man like him would not only cheat but frequent strip clubs, what kind of man wouldn't? No, I wasn't buying it. I had to defend such an honorable man. Momma had to be mistaken, delusional, or something.

"I don't believe you had sex with him, Momma."

"Are you calling me a liar?" Momma's gray eyes turned almost jet black, like they always did when she was angry. "Are you calling me a liar, Rayne?"

I wasn't about to back down from her; even though her body language was giving off the indication that she'd haul off and slap me if I responded "yes." Instead, I said, "You're mistaken or confused. Maybe you have him mixed up with someone else."

Her knees started wobbling and she sat back down on the bed. If she hadn't, she surely would've fallen at any second.

"Okay, missy, I'll put it this way. If I ain't never let him have the coochie, how do I know he has a tattoo of an anchor on his ass?"

"An anchor?" This was simply too much for me.

"Yeah, Manuel used to be a sailor. That's probably why he's so damn freaky now. Military men are the *nastiest of all*." She emphasized the last portion of her statement and the liquor on her breath was so strong, I almost passed out.

"I've heard enough, Momma. I can't take any more of this," I stated sternly and covered my head with my comforter before she could start breathing on me again. "Can I please go to sleep? I'm going to Six Flags tomorrow, in Atlanta. Remember?"

"With who?" Momma asked. Once again, she'd forgotten something I'd told her less than twenty-four hours earlier.

"Chance."

"Manuel going, or is he staying here so he can fuck some stripper tomorrow night?"

I sucked in air and ignored that. "No, Ruiz is driving us."

Chance's older brother, Ruiz, was one of the finest men on the planet. I'd fallen in puppy love/lust with him when Chance and I were in the sixth grade and he was in the tenth. I was nothing more than a baby sister to him but that didn't change the fact that I wanted to be his girlfriend.

"Tell Ruiz he can't have none, either."

Ruiz can have anything from me, I thought as a sly grin came across my face.

"Not unless he's giving up some cash and I know his ass is broke," she continued with her bashing. "Broke daddy, broke son."

Seeing an opportunity to catch Momma in a lie, I inquired, "If Mr. Martinez is so broke, why'd you have sex with him? What about your intaking dick for financial purposes policy?"

I should've kept my mouth shut because I wasn't prepared for her answer.

"'Cause Manuel eats a mean pussy, that's why! I've had a lot of sweet pussy lickings in my day but *damn!* Manuel can make a woman want to——"

I let out a slight scream——making her pause in midsentence—— and clamped my eyes shut, willing Momma to get up and go into her own bedroom.

"Baby, I'm gonna let you go back to sleep." She pulled my comforter down to my waist and started rubbing my back gently. Even she realized that she'd gone too far. "If I don't see you, have fun at Six Flags. I might still be in bed when you leave."

I kept my eyes shut, trying to mask my anger. "Goodnight, Momma."

"You need some money? I've got a little something hidden under my mattress; some tip money."

She must've really been feeling guilty about her admittance of an affair with my best friend's father. I always had to beg for money; she *never* offered it.

"No thanks, Momma," I responded.

I'd recently started a job at a bookstore——working part-time until school let out in a couple of weeks for the summer and I could work full-time. I'd saved up for Six Flags and was looking forward to having a good time and looking forward to peeping Ruiz's muscles all day. I was hoping he'd wear a tank top and shorts so I could see some skin. I'd picked out the perfect outfit to wear; one that was teasingly revealing but not too obvious.

"Sorry I woke you, Rayne," she said, continuing to rub my back. "This talk about the birds and bees is long overdue though."

"Thanks, Momma. I appreciate it."

Nothing could've been further from the truth but I didn't want her to feel too bad. She was still my mother——the only relative I'd ever known since my grandparents died long before I was born. However, Momma couldn't teach me anything about sex that I didn't already know. Sure, she may have been able to embark on perversion but I wasn't interested in those kinds of acts. I hadn't gone all the way—mainly because Ruiz had never tried me—but I knew what to expect when I did. I had zero intention of becoming a whore and definitely not a *proud whore* like Momma.

She seemed to read my mind. "Are you having sex, Rayne?"

"No, Momma. Not yet." I threw the "not yet" in there intentionally. I wanted to put her on notice that I wouldn't hesitate to do it when I was ready.

"I didn't think you were, but I needed to know. When you do start, I gotta get you on the pill. I ain't even tryin' to be a grandma. I'm too sexy and way too fine for all that."

I giggled. "You don't have to worry about that."

"Baby, I'm too tired to crawl in my room. Can I crash in here?"

"Sure, Momma," I quickly answered. If it took allowing her to sleep with me—liquor breath and all—to get her to shut her trap, it was well worth it.

I scooted over farther on the bed, pressing myself up against the wall, as she slipped off her three-inch pumps and climbed underneath the comforter with me.

We both stared up at Prince. *Sexy motherfucker.*

"You know Momma loves you, baby?"

"Yes."

"Good. That's real good."

She started humming "Sexual Healing" by Marvin Gaye—her favorite song—until we both drifted off to sleep as the sun was coming up. By ten, I was on the highway with Chance and Ruiz, headed for Six Flags.

Two

Yardley Brown, Age 16
White Oak, MD
September 1990

I wanted my sixteenth birthday to be special; I really did. However, can you say overkill? Felix, Dwayne, and Mike were my boys and all, but I wasn't even trying to go the direction they took my birthday party in.

I'd invited Roxie to the party. My parents were out of town and it was the perfect opportunity to get to know her better. Roxie was a year older than me but hanging onto her virginity like it was the eighth wonder of the world. I couldn't say I blamed her. As fine as she was, she could afford to be selective. Every boy in our high school wanted to crawl in between her long, sienna legs and dig her back out.

Roxie had this long, wavy black hair that I yearned to run my fingers through. Her huge dark brown eyes gave me a hard-on every time I gazed into them. Roxie was in my Physics class and I couldn't concentrate on our teacher most of the time. I was too busy daydreaming about her.

It was her clothes. Her hair. Her smell. She wasn't trashy like a lot of the girls in school. The majority of them wore skirts riding up their asses—even though it was against the dress code that no one enforced—and always had makeup caked on their faces. Roxie's eyelashes were naturally long and thick, unlike the girls whose eyelashes stuck together while little balls of black gook dropped onto their cheeks from using too much mascara. Roxie was different. She had class and she was my woman. . . .

. . . In my mind. All I needed was the space and opportunity to convince her. That was why I'd invited her over to Mike's for my birthday party. I'd hoped to convince her to go home with me since my parents were gone for the weekend. We could have the place all to ourselves.

There were fine girls on top of fine girls that night. I was trying to figure out where they'd come from. They surely didn't attend the same school as me. We'd expected a lot of girls but we'd hit the lottery. Surely, it had something to do with Felix recently becoming single. Even back then, Felix could've beaten out any brother in the Player of the Year Competition. That included men twice his age.

Felix and Donna had dated for three years, much to the dismay of all the girls trying to bed him. Donna had dropped Felix faster than most people could blink when she'd caught him in the boys' locker room doing the nasty with her twin sister Dana. Felix had always wanted both twins and his hard work and perseverance had paid off. However, he didn't bother to get Donna's permission first. Donna had beaten her sister's ass and then they'd made up and blamed it all on Felix. He was hurt—for two days— and then was ready to move on.

You'd think that I would've learned from Felix's mistakes but we tend to do stupid things when we're young. Never once do we consider that the repercussions aren't worth it. Such was the case when I'd agreed to go upstairs to Mike's bedroom with "a woman of the night."

My boys had decided that sixteen years was way too long for any brother to live without tapping at least one ass. Two years ahead of me in sexual activity, they were tired of me never having any freaky tales to share. They'd decided to scrape together all their available cash on hand—mostly beer money—and purchase my very first piece of pussy.

Angel, who definitely didn't live up to her name, was gorgeous without a doubt. Her skin was dark, like a juicy plum, and she had the largest breasts I'd ever seen in person. Being more experienced now, looking back, I'd say that she had to be filling up every millimeter of a 42DDD bra. She was hot and trampy; like the women in Mike's porno films we used to watch.

"You got a big ass dick for a teenager!"

Angel was sitting on the bed staring at my privates. She called it "a routine inspection." Standing there with my jeans and boxers tangled around my ankles, I felt so violated. Angel's face was close enough to my hard dick for me to feel her breath on it.

"Thanks, I guess," I muttered, stunned by her remark.

Angel lifted up the shaft of my dick and fingered my balls. Not in a romantic way. It was more like a "let me make sure there aren't any bumps underneath them" way. I didn't have any sexual diseases; unless you could get them from whacking off.

She finally quit messing around down there. "Trust me, little brother, you're hung like a horse compared to some of these rabbit-dick men out here. With some of the teeny-weeny ones, I'm not even sure I'm actually being fucked. Know what I'm saying?"

"No, not really," I said nervously.

Angel kicked off her shoes as she leaned back on her elbows. When the room suddenly smelled like musty feet, I wondered if the rest of her was clean.

"So, Yardley, that's a crazy name for a brother. That sounds like some shit from Scotland or someplace like that."

"It was my great-grandfather's name," I told her. "And, as a matter of fact, he was from Scotland."

"Ah, so someone had a little jungle fever? Ain't a damn thing wrong with that."

I ignored her comment. "Can we please get on with this?"

Angel was smacking a wad of gum from side to side in her mouth. "Cool by me. So, *Yardley,* what you wanna do first?"

"I don't know." I wasn't sure I wanted to be there; rather less what I wanted to do first. My mind flashed to Roxie. I lifted my wrist to peep my watch. It was ten-fifteen and Roxie had told me she probably wouldn't be able to make it before eleven. She was stuck with babysitting her younger brother until her parents came home from a dinner dance. The forty-five minute time frame helped me to relax *slightly.* "What do you usually do, Angel?"

She sat up and grabbed my dick. "Since I've completed my inspection and I'm down here anyway, want me to suck it for you?"

My first blow job. *Damn, was I ready for that?*

"Is it going to hurt?"

Angel suppressed a laugh; even though I could tell she wanted to ridicule me.

"Naw, sugar. I'm a professional. If there's one thing I know how to do, it's suck a damn dick."

What a powerful statement. Even though I didn't think it was physically possible, my dick got even harder as the words left her lips. Angel took the gum from her mouth and stuck it on the corner of Mike's nightstand.

"Relax, Yardley."

Angel dove in, drawing my entire dick into her mouth without blinking an eye. I started making noises I didn't realize I was capable of making. After a brief two minutes of "oohs" and "aahs" emitting from my throat, I busted my first nut that hadn't been the result of using my own hand.

Angel couldn't hold it in any longer and fell out laughing. I collapsed on the bed so I could attempt to regain some composure. I damn sure wasn't supposed to come that fast. I never knew it would feel so wonderful to place my dick into a woman's mouth. I didn't think I could handle sticking it in her mouth and her pussy in the same night; a frightening concept to an inexperienced teenage boy.

"I think that's about it for you, sugar," Angel said, obviously recognizing that I could not even hang with her. "It's a shame." She touched my dick and it hurt because it was still sensitive from the orgasm I'd endured. "You have so much potential with that big, juicy dick of yours. What a waste."

Angel retrieved her gum, plopped it back into her mouth, and slipped back into her shoes. *Thank goodness for that!* She snapped her purse open and started digging through it.

"Tell you what. Let me give you my business card and brochure. Give me a call sometime next week. If I'm in a good mood, I might finish the job for free."

I was floored. "You have a brochure?"

"Absolutely! Like I said, I'm a *professional.* How do you think your friends found me in the first place?"

Angel handed me a full-color business card with her picture, along with a matching brochure. The brochure listed Angel's special skills and featured her in various sets of raunchy lingerie. Apparently, she could tie a cherry string with her tongue, she was double-jointed, and she had no problem giving or receiving golden showers.

Sick, sick, sick! At that point, I couldn't wait to get Angel out of the house. Being a graduate of UHT, the University of Home Training, I decided some form of thanks was in order.

"Thanks for everything, Angel. That was very nice." I extended my hand.

She shook it. "Anytime, baby boy." Angel headed for the bedroom door after gathering her belongings.

I pulled up my pants and zippered them.

"I meant what I said. Call me." She held her fingers up to her cheek, spreading them to mimic a telephone, and then disappeared from my line of vision.

After going into the bathroom to take a leak and wash my face, I went downstairs. Angel was gone. However, Roxie was there; attitude and all. I saw her hand before I saw her face, when she slapped me clear across mine. It stung something fierce.

"Yardley, how could you do this to me?" Roxie screamed at me, with dozens of party guests looking on. "How could you?"

Roxie pushed her way through the crowd and out the front door before I could say a word in my own defense. Not that I had a defense. Never had I felt so ashamed and disappointed at the same time. There was no way Roxie would give me another chance. Our love affair was over before it had even begun.

Being his typical self, Mike tried to pretend like Roxie hadn't slapped the shit out of me. It was like it had never happened. "Man, that was quick. Must've been some good booty."

"For what we paid for it, it ought to be good and tight," Felix said.

Dwayne wasn't buying into that pipe dream. "A hooker with a tight booty? Man, get real!"

I was speechless. Mike waved his hand in front of my face, snapping me out of a trance.

"You sweating Roxie?" Felix asked. "Forget that skeezer, man. She wasn't trying to handle her business, so we got you someone who would."

They exchanged high-fives while the girls in the room all huddled over by the sofa like an NFL team. Talking trash about us, more than likely. My little escapade was destined to be the talk of the school for a solid week. Maybe I'd fake sick or something.

I went into the kitchen to grab a beer out of the fridge, leaving the boys standing in the living room guffawing and cracking jokes about me. As the ice-cold liquid hit the back of my throat, the expression on Roxie's face invaded my thoughts. It was an expression of pain. I vowed right then and there never to intentionally hurt another woman in my entire life. Once I did become sexually active, I was determined to treat women with respect and compassion. I'd never prey on them and think of them as nothing but pieces of ass. Unfortunately, by deciding to be as gentle as a lamb, I was setting myself up to be the prey.

Three

Rayne Waters, Age 19
University of Alabama
Thanksgiving Day 1994

I'd decided to stay at school during Thanksgiving. I couldn't deal with Momma and her drinking, which had gotten progressively worse. Chance was my roommate and had gone home to spend the day with the Martinez clan. She'd tried to insist that I join her but I felt uncomfortable being around Ruiz and his new bride. My puppy-love crush had turned into more—much more—during my senior year in high school. In fact, I'd ended up giving Ruiz my virginity. Up until that point—one Saturday night at the drive-in movies—I'd simply done a lot of "dry fucking" with various boys. None of them were manly enough for me to actually "grace with the booty" so I'd refused to give it up. Then came that fateful night when Ruiz was supposed to be driving Chance and me to the movies to see *New Jack City*. Chance came down with strep throat, after making out with these two freaky boys from our rival school behind the bleachers at a football game. Ruiz had called to tell me that he still planned to go see it and asked if I wanted to go see it alone with him.

The way he'd spoken the words—"Rayne, you want to go hang out with me and just little ol' me?"—made my panties wet. First of all, there wasn't a damn thing "little" about Ruiz. He was cut from top to bottom and worked out at the local Bally's religiously. Secondly, my hormones were out of control. Getting any amount of attention from the boy that I'd masturbated myself to sleep thinking about countless times was a welcomed change.

It had taken me forever to decide what to wear. Silly now that I think about it. At a drive-in movie, no one can see what you have on. But I wanted to impress Ruiz, so I threw the majority of the clothes out of my closet onto my bed before finally deciding on a cute pink outfit—a pair of leggings with a baby doll top to match. I pinned my hair up in a bun and let one strand of hair dangle over my left eye. I'd seen a picture of Iman, the famous fashion model, in a magazine with a similar look and attempted to emulate it.

Momma was out doing her regular dirt at the Eagle so I snuck into her room and raided her makeup caddy, applying some rouge, lipstick, and eyeliner the best that I could. I never wore more than lip gloss but I wanted to look older for Ruiz; hoping that he'd forget my real age.

When Ruiz pulled up in his t-top red Camaro and blew the horn, I had to fight to suppress the scream building up in my throat. This was really happening. I was going out on an actual date with Ruiz Martinez—even though I was sure he didn't view it as a date.

We got to the Majestic Drive-In and there were people from my school everywhere. A black or Latino movie coming out back in those days was still considered special so everyone in our school would rush to see it on release day. Otherwise, they'd feel left out on Monday morning, when everyone started talking about how awesome it was. Back then, no matter what the movie was about—even if it was derogatory to blacks and Latinos and made us all out to be drug dealers and gangsters—it was still awesome because "we" were in it.

I was mad that I couldn't show Ruiz off more. If we'd gone to a regular theater, I could've sported him on my arm as eye candy. On the other hand, the drive-in meant that we could be completely alone to do whatever, without people watching us instead of the movie. I did get to show him off briefly, when we went inside to get popcorn, Twizzlers, and cola with cherry fountain syrup. Jessica Wilson, who I knew for a fact also had a thing for Ruiz, almost shit herself when she saw us together. Even though it wasn't an official date, I made it seem that way by giggling at his every comment and rubbing my fingers up and down his arm while we waited in line for our turn.

Jessica was there with Langston, the captain of the football team. While he was fine enough, his head was way too up in the clouds for me to ever be interested. When it came down to it, Langston cared about his looks more than he cared about the looks of the girl on his arm. It was his world and anyone who didn't like it could step. I'd spent an hour talking to him on the phone once. I caught on quick, five minutes into the conversation, that he was only calling to feel me out and see if I would be an easy lay for him.

Boys were so silly; thinking that we weren't up on their immature games. Sure, some girls were still in that naïve stage but most of us knew the deal. Momma had definitely educated me. I'd never gotten over the fact that she'd had sex with Chance's daddy. Often times, when I was over their house visiting, I'd sit there and stare at him, wondering if his wife even suspected that he was cheating. When he'd leave out saying he was going to the store or had to go back to work to do some overtime, I'd think he was headed to one of the local strip clubs instead. Momma's revelation had changed my entire outlook on men. The one man that I would've sworn was faithful had turned out to be banging numerous other women. Lack of trust had become a major hang-up for me before I'd even had my first serious relationship.

Still, part of me hoped that Ruiz was different. Not that I thought he and I would hook up, but he was my fantasy man and I wanted to at least believe that his scruples were better than his father's.

We were back in his Camaro, watching the film, and chowing down on popcorn when Ruiz came out the blue and asked, "Rayne, you have the hots for me, don't you?"

Had he really just asked me that?

"What?" I replied in astonishment.

"I asked if you have the hots for me." He took my left hand into his right and started playing with my fingers.

"Ruiz, you know you're like a brother to me."

I could see his eyebrows rise in the dim lighting of the car. He took his free hand and turned the volume down on the speaker that was hooked onto the driver's side window. "So it's just my imagination that you're looking different tonight to impress me?"

I let out this hideous fake laugh; a nervous one. "Different? What's different about me?"

"The tight pants. The makeup. The high heels you can hardly walk in."

He was right on the money about the heels. I'd almost busted my ass three times on the way to and from the concession stand.

"Ruiz, I always dress like this," I lied. "You probably haven't noticed before; since you've known me so long. Chance and I are both growing up."

He chuckled. "Yeah, but Chance doesn't dress like that. Ma would kill her, if she even tried."

"Well, you know your mother and my mother are two entirely separate people; like night and day."

"Like an angel and a demon," he said.

The sad part about his comment—him obviously referring to my mother as the demon—was that I couldn't argue with him. Mrs. Martinez had the face and spirit of an angel. My mother, while unquestionably beautiful—was a snake.

Ruiz realized that I was saddened by his words so he let my hand go and put his arm around my shoulder. "So you like this movie?"

"It's okay. Seems like it's going to be full of violence."

"Humph, no doubt." He shrugged. "It's about the emergence of crack in America; starting with the hood. Rich people use that pure cocaine shit. We get to use the bottom of the barrel leftovers."

The way he'd said "we" made me curious. "You ever use crack?"

"No, not me, homes. Hell, I won't lie. I've smoked my share of weed in my day and have no plans of giving it up, but I'm not trying to get strung out on crack. That shit's for the birds." He started caressing my arm. "Enough of all that. Why don't you come here and give me a kiss?"

"A kiss?"

He grinned at me. "Yeah, a kiss. I know you've kissed before."

"I've done a lot of things before," I quickly replied, not wanting him to know that I was still hanging on to my virginity like it was worth all the gold on the face of the earth.

Ruiz smirked. "You don't say. Tell me about some of the things you've done."

"Why would you want to hear about what I've done with other boys?"

He took the popcorn out of my lap and sat it on the floor between my feet. "Actually, I'm more interested in you showing me. You've seen what boys have to offer. Now why don't you come check out what a man has to offer?"

Damn, I was scared as shit suddenly!

"Come here and kiss me," he beckoned. "Just one kiss and you can tell me whether you like it or not."

If there were such a thing as being weak in the knees when you're sitting down, then that's what I was; weak in the damn knees. I still wasn't budging so he leaned over and kissed me. At first, I was timid and held back the tongue. Then I asked myself, *What the hell are you doing, Rayne? Isn't this what you've always wanted?*

I decided to let it go and—by the time Ruiz and I came back up for air—Wesley Snipes was shooting his best friend in the movie and it was practically over.

It was the most intense kissing I'd ever experienced. Ruiz was right; men had a lot more to offer than boys. That kissing led to him taking me over to one of his friends' apartments and blowing my damn back out. I'd seen numerous dicks, without a doubt. Boys had whipped their dicks out in front of me, trying to encourage me to feel them up or suck them off; neither of which was happening. But with Ruiz, it had been different. He'd kissed me so longingly that it made me feel desired; desired by the one person I'd always wanted to crave me. It had been like a dream sequence, him undressing me slowly and then undressing himself so I could gaze upon his exquisite form. When he took my left breast in his mouth, licking my nipple with his lengthy, moist tongue, I shivered. Ruiz knew what he was doing so I didn't mind spreading my legs for him when he whispered, "Open up for me."

He figured out—when he was sticking his dick in my pussy—that I was indeed a virgin. It was like navigating a maze, him trying to get his seven inches up inside me. Once we managed to work it out, it was painful in the beginning. Then I closed my eyes and settled in for the ride. What a ride it was; my first time. He sucked every inch of me—*twice*—and I loved it.

After we were done, Ruiz drove me home, and it suddenly seemed like there was some tension in the air.

"Rayne, I don't know what to say," he said about a mile from my apartment.

I sat there, in the bucket seat of his car, trying to find words to express what I was feeling. "Ruiz, I want you to know that I'm glad it was you."

"Glad it was me?"

"Yeah, I'm glad you're the one who took my virginity. It was as it should be."

He sighed and turned the heat on in his car. The early morning chill had kicked in outside. "Rayne, you're my little sister's best friend."

"And?" I asked. "Now I'm Chance's best friend and your girlfriend, right?"

Ruiz didn't respond. He pulled up in front of our building, shifted into park, and glared at me under the streetlight.

I got his drift. "It's okay. I get it. I was something to do tonight; nothing more, nothing less."

He reached for my hand. "No, it's not even like that. I love you."

I bit my bottom lip. *Had he really said that?*

"You love me?" I asked. "Really?"

"Yeah, I love you, like a sister and—"

"Never mind." I yanked my hand away, opened the car door and got out. "Thanks for the movie. Tell Chance I'll call her later."

Ruiz jumped out of the driver's side. "Rayne, let's talk about this. We need to discuss it."

"There's nothing to discuss. It happened." My back was to him and it was going to stay that way because tears were streaming down my face. "Take care, Ruiz," I said as I entered the front door of the building and ran up the steps.

I sat in the stairwell on the second landing, wiping my face with my baby doll shirt. I tripped twice trying to get up that far. Heels and I didn't agree well. I was ashamed. How could I have been so stupid? Then again, if I had to lose my virginity, I did want it to be with Ruiz. I'd expected it to be different, though; not during but afterwards. I'd expected him to be my man, to cherish me forever. Now I knew it was not to be; nothing even close.

Momma had a fit when I entered our apartment. It was the first time she'd ever beat me into our place and she wasn't a happy camper. I must've had "freshly fucked" written all over my face because she knew it from the second she looked at me.

"You've been fucking!" she exclaimed, grabbing my arm and pulling me close to her so she could smell me.

"Momma, what are you doing?" I pulled away and headed for my cramped room down the hall. "I was at the movies."

"Rayne, it's three o'clock in the fuckin' morning. Ain't no movie theater open this time of night." I tried to shut my door in her face but she pressed hard against it. For a minute, I struggled with her but finally gave in so she could enter. "Who were you out with?"

"A friend," I quickly replied.

"What friend?"

"A friend from school," I lied.

Ruiz was in his third year of college and besides, Momma would've completely lost it if she knew I'd been out alone with him. She still was hung up on his father; at least it seemed that way. She never passed up an opportunity to trash him.

"Your ass better not be pregnant!" she screamed. "You better not be!"

"Momma, I'm not pregnant," I assured her, glad that Ruiz had been prepared with condoms. If there hadn't been any, I probably would've done it anyway. Having known him for so long and fantasizing daily about being with him, I could see how young girls could easily be trusting and give it up without protection.

I started undressing and that was a huge mistake. I didn't realize that my panties were spotted with blood.

"Damn," Momma said. "It really happened."

I paused in the middle of my bedroom floor before pulling my cotton nightgown over my head and down over my hips. I really wanted to take a shower but there was no way I was walking past Momma to get to the hallway. I could smell the sex on me—a new scent for me but an all too familiar one for her. There was no way she'd miss it and surely had already caught a whiff. With my clothes off and my panties airing out freely under my gown, it was unmistakable.

"Oh, my panties," I finally whispered. "I'm about to come on my period."

I climbed in my bed and turned off the lamp on my nightstand, hoping she'd take the hint and go to her own room so she could pass out from her regular alcohol poisoning.

Then I heard her sobs.

I cut the light back on. "Momma, what's wrong?"

She came over and sat down on the edge of my bed, patting my thigh under the comforter. "I really wanted something better for you, baby."

"What? What are you talking about?"

"I'd hoped that things would be different for you."

I was stunned. Somehow she knew that I'd lost my virginity that night; like she'd sensed it; like we were kindred spirits. I decided to come clean.

"Momma, I'll be honest. I did have sex for the first time tonight but it's okay. I don't regret it."

She ran her fingers through my hair. "Did he hurt you?"

"No, he didn't, Momma. It was . . ."

"It was what, baby?"

"It was special; it really was."

"Do you love him?" she asked.

"In a way." I lowered my eyes from her. "At least, I thought I did."

"So you gave it up for nothing," she stated with disdain. Her demeanor suddenly turned cold as she got up from my bed and walked into the hallway. "Welcome to the world of whoredom!" she yelled as she slammed my bedroom door.

As I sat there in my dorm room that Thanksgiving Day, surfing the Internet for information on upcoming activities on campus, that statement Momma had made that day flooded throughout my mind over and over. "Welcome to the world of whoredom!"

Since the loss of my virginity, I'd been with numerous men; each time believing that the current selection would be "the one." The one who'd love me; the one who'd cherish me; the one who'd stand in my corner. Each of them would enter my life, full of promises that quickly turned into lies and betrayal. I'd tried dating young men my age—the ones who appeared mature—but they were only after one thing; my sex. Once they got it, they moved on to their next victim. I'd tried dating slightly older men—the ones who wanted younger showpieces on their arms. They'd shower me with presents, take me to cultural events, and then expect me to give it up in return. I did most of the time. After all, they were at least spending some money on me; unlike the struggling college students who attempted to get some play.

I'd most recently been dating a man named Solomon. He was twenty-eight, nine years my senior, and a paralegal for a local law firm. We'd made it through three months of romance and sex and

I wondered how much longer it would last. There was no question that it would end. We weren't even halfway compatible. It was a shame. That night with Ruiz, I was simply something for him to do. Now Solomon was simply something for me to do; a way to kill some time until Mr. Right finally came along.

Solomon had gone to Texas to visit his grandparents for Thanksgiving; a family tradition of his. His parents and siblings were joining him there. Never once did he extend an invitation to me; even when he knew I would be on campus alone. That let me know that I wasn't special.

I went to a diner called the Jukebox for dinner. I ordered the blue plate special; obviously turkey, dressing, rice, and string beans because it was Thanksgiving. All the other booths were either occupied by families who'd burnt dinner or didn't feel like cooking in the first place, or individuals who had somehow ended up alone for the holiday—whether by their own volition or someone else's.

I spotted a young African-American male in a booth on the other side of the diner. I'd seen him before, on campus. He had a different major so we'd never had a reason to speak. He started eyeing me and I didn't break my stare. Why not flirt a little? Solomon wasn't thinking about my ass. He was down in Texas eating high on the hog—a real Thanksgiving dinner—and I was eating a blue plate special.

He was finishing up his meal and I saw his waitress give him a check. He got up, dropped a twenty on the table and walked toward me. Yes, he was definitely fine. About five-nine, chestnut skin, long, thick eyelashes over dark brown eyes, built nicely and bowlegged.

He stood over me while I took a sip of my sweetened iced tea. "There's something I've been wanting to say to you for a while now."

I glanced up at him. "Is that so?"

"Yes."

I pointed to the opposite side of the booth. "Then why not sit down and say it."

He sat and said, "You have the most beautiful gray eyes."

"Well, they say eyes are the portals to the soul," I replied.

"Then you must have a very special soul because you definitely have very special eyes."

I blushed. "I'm flattered. What's your name?"

"Bryant. Bryant Perrywood."

"I'm Rayne Waters," I told him.

"Oh, I know who you are, Rayne," he said, full of implications.

"Humph, and how do you know that?"

"Because I've been watching you."

I blushed harder. "Why have you been watching me?"

He shrugged. "We go to the same school, you're attractive, why not watch you?"

"There're a lot of women on campus; many of them attractive."

"Yeah," Bryant agreed. "But none of them turn me on the way you do."

"Oh, so I turn you on?"

He chuckled. "Oh yeah, you *definitely* turn me on. We work out at the same gym. Did you know that?"

"No, I didn't. I've seen you on campus, but not at the gym. I take a spinning class three times a week."

"Oh, trust me, I know." He grinned and his smile was great. "I love watching you spin."

Spinning was becoming popular back then and it was one hell of a workout. I was still struggling to get the weight off I'd gained from all the fast food in high school. The fat was falling off but I was still larger than I expected. Just meant to be, I supposed. When I was in class, I was in my own little world but I was still shocked I'd never seen Bryant there.

"You don't take the class with me?" I asked. "Surely, I would've noticed you."

"No, I usually live in the weight room, but I saw you there once, liked the vision, and have been checking you out ever since."

My mind flashed to Solomon for about five seconds and then I decided "fuck him!" He'd deserted me like I was a piece of trash.

"So, Bryant," I said, eyeing him seductively, "care to check out the rest of me back in my dorm room?"

"Better yet, why don't we go back to my apartment? I've got a *brass waterbed*." He said that mockingly, imitating Morris Day's line from *Purple Rain,* my all-time favorite movie. His as well.

As it turned out, Bryant and I had a lot in common. For the first time, I felt like I'd possibly found the one. My days of "whoredom" were over; at least temporarily. Bryant and I dated for the next two years. The sex was off the chain. He taught me a lot of things about sex and I'd imagine that I reciprocated his efforts. We had sex at least three times a week—mostly on his waterbed—and he had a crooked dick that hit my g-spot just right. Then we broke up over something stupid; something I can't even recall now. That's the funny thing about life. You go through so many ups and downs and years later, the actions seem so inconsequential. The one thing, the one memory that remained significant to me was the way Ruiz had taken my virginity and then simply acted like it had never happened. Good riddens to both him and his wife!

Four

Yardley Brown, Age 20
North Carolina Central University
October 1994

"Big Brother Smooth Operator!" His lip was trembling as he screamed it out. Yelling wasn't acceptable; they had to scream out our names to even be acknowledged.

"What, punk?" I asked my pledge as he stood in front of me, saluting me with his right hand. "What the hell do you want, punk?"

"I request your presence tonight at my honors banquet, Big Brother Smooth Operator!" he screamed.

Alicia Osborne was sitting beside me on the bench in front of the student union. She giggled while I glared up at him. "Why do you think I'd want to go to an honors banquet, punk?"

"Because I can't attend without your permission, Big Brother Smooth Operator."

"And?" I asked. It was true that he wasn't allowed to take a good shit without asking me first. Everything they did on line was our business. "You can go to your stinking banquet, punk, but again I ask you why I'd want to go?"

"Because I want to make you proud of me, Big Brother Smooth Operator!"

I had to give it to Belford. He managed to keep his calm on line, unlike most of the pledges. Hell, when I'd pledged the year before, I was scared out of my wits most of the time. Belford came from money; pure and simple. His father was a multimillionaire who had made his money with overseas investments. With only a fourth grade education, he'd managed to start out as a longshoreman in Maine, learn about life and money from the wealthy men he worked for, and make his own way in life. Belford Springfield, Sr. was a famous man and his son, Belford, Jr., my responsibility while he pledged my fraternity, was likely to follow in his footsteps. Belford was brilliant, polished from attending the best boarding schools in the country, and destined for greatness. Yet, he could get down and dirty like the rest of us.

Part of me wanted to tell Belford that I was proud of him, but that wouldn't have been considered "cool." The brothers of Psi Omega Chi didn't play niceness with pledges. Shit, all of us had been hazed and ridiculed to gain the honor for life. They had to do the same. It hurt me to come out my mouth with it but I said, "Belford, you can go to the banquet but I've got better shit to do." I took Alicia's hand. "I've got business to handle."

He seemed like he wanted to cry. All the late night degradation and stupid assignments were taking their toll on him. He had to be strong though. Once it was all over in two more weeks, I planned to make him my partner for life.

Felix, Mike, and Dwayne—my best friends from high school—had all decided to attend different schools. We'd decided that we could wreak four times the havoc by spreading out nationwide and meeting women from all over the country; possibly the world. They were more into being pussy bandits—seeing how many women they could get in the sack—while I was trying to find the real thing with someone special.

I'd never forgotten the expression on Roxie's face the night of my sixteenth birthday party, after I'd been sucked off by that hooker. I ended up sleeping with an older woman my first time. Her name was Joan and she worked as a nurse at the Washington Hospital Center. I'd taken a summer job there in the morgue. Dismal job but it was the only thing I could find at the time. My parents, both elementary educators, couldn't fathom why I'd choose to do that kind of work. They said I could do landscaping, painting, or work as a plumbing apprentice. None of that interested me and besides, no one was banging down my door to hire a seventeen-year-old.

Working at the morgue had given me a new appreciation of life. I remember my first day, seeing the dead bodies and thinking, *So this is how it all ends!* To think that one day I would be laid out on a slab, headed to a funeral home to be embalmed so I could push up daisies in a cemetery made me want to live each day to the fullest even more. I guess that's why I went for it when Joan, a thirty-three-year-old single mother of two, asked me out on a date. At first, she didn't realize I was still a minor; I definitely didn't look it. I lied and told her I was twenty-four. She bought it; hook, line and sinker.

Our first date was the circus, believe it or not. There I was surrounded by clowns, stinky elephants, and tigers, holding cotton candy in one hand and a stuffed giraffe in the other. Joan's two kids—a three-year-old boy named Adam and a five-year-old girl named Patti—were both products of a short-lived marriage. Joan's ex-husband wanted no part of sharing custody and had, in fact, moved away to California, which was as removed as he could get without leaving the country altogether.

The daddy thing wasn't fairing too well with me but I hung in there for two months. Joan was surprised that I didn't try to have sex with her right away. I was equally surprised that she didn't expect me to rock her world from time to time. She'd been married and had borne two kids so she was obviously experienced; something I definitely was not.

It all came to a head one night while Joan's kids were spending the night with her parents in Richmond, Virginia. We were sitting on the floor in front of her fireplace, watching the kindling merge into the flames, when she came right out and asked, "Yardley, don't you find me attractive?"

"Of course," I immediately answered.

"Then why haven't you tried to fuck me?"

Fuck? Not make love, have sex with me, but fuck!

"That's such a harsh statement," I told her. "I'd like to think that if we do anything, it would be making love, not fucking."

"What's the difference?" she inquired with a serious expression on her face.

At that point I was curious. Here was a woman with much familiarity with sex and she didn't know the difference between making love and fucking. I'd always thought there was a clearly defined line; even though I hadn't done either.

I attempted to answer anyway. "Making love is when two people genuinely care about each other and want to ensure pleasure for the other person. Fucking is when each person is out for themselves."

She giggled and took a sip of her Chardonnay. I was drinking a beer, even though I wasn't of age.

"Okay, whatever," she said. "That still doesn't tell me why you haven't made a move on me."

"You haven't made a move on me either; other than kissing." I teased her long auburn hair with my finger. "Besides, your kids are always here and I wouldn't feel comfortable doing something with them in the house."

That was a true statement. The few times I'd considered trying to get in her pants, the kids were in the apartment. Though they were asleep, I didn't want to run the risk of one or both of them waking up and catching us in the act. Joan had no local friends or family and barely associated with co-workers—other than me—so whenever we went out, the kids always tagged along.

Joan got on her knees and started unbuttoning her blouse. "The kids aren't here now. We're all alone and we can do whatever pleases us."

I stared at her. She was beautiful but I wasn't sure sleeping with her was the right thing to do. I hadn't been truthful about my age. She and I could never have a serious relationship because of the age difference and the fact that I wasn't ready to be anyone's daddy. I was going away to college soon and the thing between us would undoubtedly have to end. Yet, I yearned to experience sex and Joan was willing to experience it with me.

I'd been jacking off regularly since the Angel mishap, looking at pornos and dirty magazines, so I could build up my stamina and hold out longer when I did actually have sex. I'd come so quickly from that blow job that I was determined that sisters wouldn't crack on me throughout life for busting nuts within seconds. I felt like it was time. When Joan removed her shirt, then her bra, I realized it was definitely time.

We made love—not fucked—by the fire. Joan rode me first, nice and slow, and my dick caught the rhythm with her pussy muscles contracting up and down my shaft. I was swollen with pride when I lasted and lasted and lasted. The art of masturbation had paid off. It took me at least thirty minutes to achieve a full-blown orgasm. I got the feeling she had several.

After a brief rest, Joan rubbed me to stiffness again and I entered her from behind. The brothers had all been right; there was nothing like hitting it doggy-style. Not only did it allow for deeper penetration but the view of a woman's ass, so round and scrumptious, bouncing around in the air while she moans with delight, is incredible. One of the men's magazines I subscribed to had recently done a poll of the favorite sexual positions of men. Doggy-style had won out by a higher percentage and now it had my vote also.

I felt guilty later on that night when I had to leave Joan. She begged me to spend the night with her; especially since the kids were away. It had never come up before. I don't think she would've allowed me to stay the entire night while they were around. She'd mentioned that she didn't let men do that since her divorce because she didn't want them to get too attached or misconstrue the situation. She'd admittedly had lovers but nothing serious.

"I have to go, Joan," I told her, getting up from the living room floor and getting dressed.

"But we haven't done it in my bedroom yet," she stated suggestively. "We have free reign of the house. We can really get a workout."

"I don't know quite how to tell you this, but . . ."

She got up, still nude, and wrapped her arms around my neck. "But what, baby? . . ."

"You know I live with my parents, right?" I asked her.

"Yes, and that's cool. I lived with mine until I got married."

I let out a nervous chuckle. "Yeah, but I need to get home."

"Why?"

"It's eleven forty-five."

Then she threw her head back in laughter. "So?"

"So, I have a midnight curfew," I blurted out. She let go of me. "Think about it, Joan. Since we've been dating, have you ever seen me after midnight?"

Because the kids were always out with us, we never stayed out late and I would always stay only a few minutes once we came back. Long enough to make out on the couch, get hard, and then excuse myself.

She still didn't get it. "Why would you have a midnight curfew? At your age?"

I lowered my head in shame as I finished getting dressed. "That's the point, Joan. I'm only seventeen."

"Wha . . . Wha . . . Wha . . ." She was really struggling. Then I spotted it; a flicker of anger in her eyes. "What did you just say to me? You're only seventeen!"

"I'm sorry, Joan. I should've told you." She hauled off and slapped me across my chin. "Damn, not again!" I exclaimed, remembering Roxie doing the same thing a year earlier.

Joan stood there, in the middle of the floor, butt ass naked, gasping for air.

I kissed her on the cheek. "I really have to go. Can we discuss this later?"

She still wouldn't speak to me. I glanced at my watch and realized I'd be grounded if I wasn't back in Silver Spring in ten minutes and it was a twenty-minute drive. Not only did my parents impose a midnight curfew but so did the local police. On a provisional license, I couldn't be out on the road after midnight; for any reason.

I kissed Joan on the cheek and left. In the car on the way home, I was listening to the latest Tupac CD and thinking about the situation. I really should've come clean about my age up front, but what was done was done. I didn't mean to hurt her but I'd placed her in an uncomfortable position.

My mother gave me a fifteen-minute lecture when I arrived home late and then went upstairs to watch the late news. I got into bed and mulled over my first sexual experience. I was pleased but was Joan? Once again, I'd hurt a woman; something I'd never planned to do ever again.

The following Monday at work, Joan avoided me for the first seven hours of her shift. I cornered her in the nurses' lounge and made my best attempt at an apology. It didn't work. She sat there and glared at me while I explained how attracted I'd been to her, how friendly she'd been to me, and how the lie seemed to gestate itself into more lies as time went along.

In the end, all I got from Joan was, "Yardley, you've put me in an uncomfortable position. I had sex with a child last night and for that, I could go to jail. Do you realize that? You put me in jeopardy. I'm a mother and I'm a responsible adult and I'd appreciate it if you'd never speak to me again or even look in my direction, for that matter."

I respected Joan's wishes and left her alone for the remaining few weeks that I worked in the hospital morgue that summer. I started dating this girl named Lori when school started back up. She attended our rival school, Paint Branch, and she was cute and very sweet. We had sex about once a month during our senior year. Then she'd left to attend Hampton University and I'd headed to North Carolina Central.

Being a member of a frat, especially my frat, meant that all the women wanted to offer you their sex. They thought it would make them popular or land them a husband; mostly all they ended up with was disrespect. I'd faltered a time or two and participated in the numerous orgies that went on in the frat house. Part of my initiation into the frat was to run a train on this one chick who loved thinking she was the ultimate piece of ass. Thinking back now, I realize that she suffered from low self-esteem—like many of the women attending the school—and we were dead wrong for taking advantage of her. She ended up dropping out of school after getting pregnant and having no clue who fathered the child. It was more than a year after I'd been with her or else I would've done the right thing and demanded a paternity test; even if it was only to be relieved by the process of elimination. I couldn't live with myself if I thought a child was out there somewhere, fatherless because of my actions. That's why I'd always practiced safe sex but even that isn't foolproof.

Belford and the twelve other pledges went over during homecoming week at the end of October. We'd nicknamed the line the Tribe of Thirteen. Everything changed the night they went over. They went from being our objects of desecration to our brothers for eternity. I went all out for Belford, my protégé, and bought him a bottle of Johnny Walker Blue for several hundred bucks. He and I sat on the roof of the frat house and drank it shot by shot while people stormed the yard celebrating all the fraternities and sororities that had lines go over that night, and homecoming in general.

NCCU was known for partying, from full-blown parties in the cafeteria that were reminiscent of that lunchroom scene from the movie *Fame* to keg parties where everyone ended up completely smashed. Instead of getting laid like the rest of his line brothers that night, Belford chose to spend the time talking to me about life. I made sure he recognized that I was proud of him for being honored for his grades. He could've played the spoiled role and breezed through college simply because of his lineage. He had higher aspirations than that. In fact, he wanted to surpass his father and that was one hell of a goal to aspire to.

Belford became one of my best friends. He started coming home with me on holidays and I spent one summer with his family in Maine. Their compound—you couldn't even refer to it as a house—was on more than two hundred acres and had more than half a mile of oceanfront. Belford, Sr. had a seventy-foot yacht that was out of this world. We used to go out on it early in the morning and not come back until the next morning, chilling in the entertainment room or crashing in one of the five bedrooms lined with cherrywood.

They had both an indoor and outdoor pool. The tile surrounding the outdoor pool was imported from Jerusalem and never got hot. They had a pool house worth more than most people's houses and a showroom garage with a marble floor and more than two million dollars worth of automobiles housed inside.

Belford had an older sister who was hot and not remotely interested in me. That was a good thing because I'd never do anything to jeopardize our friendship. Contrary to what a lot of people assumed, I wasn't his friend because he was wealthy. I was Belford's friend because he was mine. We had a mutual respect for one another. When he came home with me to my parents' three-bedroom house, there was no comparison to his world, but he fit right in. Dwayne, Mike, and Felix thought he was mad cool and we used to go clubbing every weekend.

Most of the sisters ignored Belford, preferring to date "bad boys" and thugs. For the same reason, I found it hard to find women to date. If I wasn't doing something exciting like pushing smack or gun-running, they weren't into me. I decided to worry about women later and further my education after college. I'd always been fascinated with chiropractors; how they could actually realign bones and relieve the pain that millions of Americans suffer through because of injury, birth defects, degenerative arthritis, or even improper posture.

Belford did follow in his father's footsteps. He was in Hong Kong on business when he was murdered at the age of twenty-three for the money in his wallet and the gold chain his mother had presented to him on his eighteenth birthday with his initial on it.

I cried for three days when I heard the news directly from his father, who was so shaken up that he could barely get the words out over the phone. He told me, "All the money in the world can't buy happiness, Yardley. Remember that."

I said, "Yes, sir," and then heard the click on the other end of the phone. He was right. Happiness was a state of mind. All I wanted was someone special to share my life with. Ultimately, I was determined to find her.

True, we *love* life, not because we are used to living,
but because we are used to loving.
There is always some madness in *love*,
but there is also always some reason in madness.
—Friedrich Nietzsche

Five

Rayne, Age 28, Bank Administrator
Washington, DC
October 2003

I should have known. I should have known. I should have known. The second Boom—short for Boomquee-sha—opened her mouth exposing a mouthful of teeth with the remnants of Cheetos adhered to them, I should have known better.

"Rayne, girl, my brother wanna meet you sumptin' terrible." She blurted this out to me while she was ripping huge green rollers and bobby pins out of my hair faster than those chefs demonstrate Ginsu knives on infomercials.

I asked the obvious question, being that my only dealings with Boom were my weekly hair appointments. Every Thursday at 5:30 P.M. like clockwork. "How does he even know about me?"

"Girl, he saw you walkin' up out this joint a few weeks ago. Lookin' all good and shit 'cause I'd hooked your do up as usual. You know how I be handlin' thangs."

Boom scanned the salon right quick to make sure all eyes and ears were on her. Any time she so much as hinted about her styling skills, she wanted an audience. Most of the women were too busy watching the *Ricki Lake Show* on the fuzzy black and white television leaned forty-five degrees to the right so the picture would come in halfway clear. The show was about "metrosexual" men. I'd never heard of the term but apparently it was a recent label for men who spent large amounts of time primping in the mirror, making sure their clothes were wrinkle free, and even shaving their body hair. Three women on the show were pleading for assistance to determine whether or not their men were actually bisexual. It was off the chain. Ricki had some drag queens on as judges who were quite entertaining all by themselves. They showed videotapes of the questionable guys going about their daily routines and if they couldn't tell those men were sweet— even though they all proclaimed innocence to be strictly about punany—then something was seriously wrong with them. One of the guys even hung out in gay clubs and admitted to being flattered when homosexuals tried to flirt with him. He claimed that "a compliment is a compliment" and he was elated that both sexes found him attractive. I shook my head at the nonsense. Some women can't see the forest for the trees.

Boom was still waiting to make sure her comment had mad attention. A couple of the women sitting on the "pleather" chairs in the waiting area glanced up at her from the hairstyle magazines on their laps. One older woman, stranded in the hair dryer section even though her hair was already dry, stared at her. She let out a yawn, probably wondering when she would get into Boom's chair so she could get her hair combed out and head home. Like most beauty salons, From Naps to Baps was like participating in a game of musical chairs.

Satisfied that enough sisters had overheard her self-compliment, Boom continued. "Soon as you pulled off in your ride, Conquesto came runnin' in here, all up in my grill, sweatin' me for info on you like I'm four-one-one. Like I know what color panties you wear and shit. I told him I don't be sniffin' no hoochie's drawers. If I wanna sniff drawers, I'll sniff my own."

I had to give it to Boom. She sure had a way with words. "Conquesto? That's his name?"

"Yeah, girl. He's my baby brother."

I fought to suppress a laugh building up in my throat. What kind of narcotics were her parents introducing into their bloodstream when they named their kids Boomqueesha and Conquesto? Boomqueesha sounds straight-up ridiculous and Conquesto sounds like a brand of salsa.

"So what's up, Rayne, girl? Can I give him your digits or not?"

Normally, my answer would've been a resounding "no." Unfortunately, times had been tight and even the numerous middle-of-the-night booty calls I'd grown accustomed to receiving from my various exes had tapered off. I was sick of going to bed with only flannel pajamas and a pair of wool socks to keep me warm.

November was banging on October's back door and I shuddered at the thought of going through the kick ass winter weather alone. It's okay to be celibate in the summertime, but everyone needs a lover in the winter. That's why so many babies are born in August and September. You do the math.

"When you say baby brother, how old is he exactly?"

"He's five years younger than me."

That statement told me absolutely nothing, being that Boom had turned thirty-five on May 12th for the last five or six years in a row.

"Five years younger than you would make him what?"

"Girl, you know I'm thirty-five." I rolled my eyes. She couldn't see me because she was taking a sip of her orange Faygo soda. Out of all the vending machines in the world, From Naps to

Baps had a Faygo soda machine. "Conquesto turned thirty last month. You thirty, right?"

"No, I'm only twenty-eight." I threw that "only" in there on purpose. I wasn't thrilled at the prospect of turning thirty with no wedding bands, white picket fences, or crib mobiles in sight.

"Close enough." Boom broke out the hair spray and started laying it on thick. As usual, I had to hold my breath so I wouldn't choke. "He's really feelin' you. I think you had on some black booty pants that day 'cause he said you was a FAB."

"FAB? What's that?" I asked, knowing good and damn well she was exaggerating about my behind being anywhere near a pair of booty pants.

"Fine Ass Babe. Conquesto loves himself some thick women." Boom yanked the plastic smock from around my neck and handed me a mirror. "Look, I wasn't even gonna bring this up but I'm sick of his ass sweatin' me 'bout you."

I wasn't overjoyed with Boom's thick comment. I'd put on some weight over the previous two years and had gone from a size ten to a size sixteen. I still looked good though and my health was picture perfect. I was used to my weight going up and down; it was a battle to try to lose weight, only to find myself gaining it all back plus five pounds. I'd decided that God had blessed me with the extra weight and it was meant to be. A lot of bigger sisters had issues with their weight. I carried mine with pride because like Boom had stated, some men wanted a little meat on their bones. Still, I wasn't feeling the word "thick." Certainly, there had to be a better term.

I used the mirror to see the back of my hair. It was flawless and worth every dime of the fifty dollars I shelled out per week to have it done.

I got up to stretch, trying to get rid of the crook in my neck from sitting under the dryer for more than an hour, and retrieved my purse from underneath Boom's station. I should've paid my money and high-tailed it out of there, but something compelled me to make one of the stupidest mistakes of my life.

"Boom, is he cute?"

"Girl, hell yeah!" Boom squealed in my ear while I pulled out my wallet. She waved a comb toward the dryer. "Gloria, I'm ready for you now. Come on over here in my chair."

The older woman, now identified as Gloria, was obviously relieved to finally get in Boom's chair. When she got up from the low-seated dryer, she limped over toward us like a bout of arthritis had kicked in.

Boom took another sip of her Faygo and yelled across the salon to the rear. "Yo-Yo, girl, ain't Conquesto fine?"

Yo-Yo, the official shampoo girl at From Naps to Baps, took a break from sweeping up clipped hair off the floor with a straw broom and a handled dustpan long enough to leer at us and shrug her shoulders.

Boom moved closer to me. I could smell the sugary soda on her breath. "Don't even trip, girl," she whispered in my ear. "Yo-Yo mad 'cause he don't want her."

I wasn't so sure that was the case. I tried to read Yo-Yo's face, but she wasn't giving off any valuable hints.

I handed Boom two twenties and a ten. "Boom, I'm not too sure about this. Maybe you can hook him up with one of your other clients."

"Conquesto's a really cool dude, Rayne," Boom said, stuffing the money I'd given her down in her bra. "I wouldn't front on you like that. How long I been doin' your hair?"

I did a quick calculation. I'd moved to D.C. the day after my twenty-second birthday, the same year I'd graduated from college, seeking refuge from my drama queen mother.

"About six years," I replied.

"Exactly! We've been bonded longer than most marriages."

Boom did have a point. We'd outlasted a lot of marriages. Some women I know change hairdressers every other month.

"Think of me as his reference. I love my brother, but I ain't 'bout to lose a guaranteed fifty bucks a week over some nonsense."

"Not to mention the eighty you charge me during perm week," I stated jokingly.

Boom giggled. "If I didn't feel you two should hook up, I wouldn't even be talkin' 'bout this shit. For real!"

I'd always had a difficult time telling people "no." Boom wasn't playing fair. If I didn't at least take his number and call, she'd view it as a form of distrust. Not to mention a direct insult on her matchmaking skills.

"I'll tell you what. Why don't you give me his number and I'll give him a call?"

Then the hints came. Hints I should've paid close attention to. Like I said, I should've known.

I spotted Yo-Yo flailing her arms out the corner of my eyes. When I turned to face her, she put them down; probably because Boom was looking directly at her also.

Tamu, the manicurist, cleared her throat loudly. I glanced at her and she diverted her eyes down to the sister's nails she was steadily buffing.

Nia, one of the other stylists, was sitting at her station eating her dinner; a three-piece combo from Popeye's. She started choking. I rushed over and patted her on the back.

"You okay, Nia?" I asked.

She took a long sip of her Coke before responding, "Yeah, chicken's too greasy. I'm cool."

By the time I made it back over to Boom to get my purse and

leave, she'd written her brother's number down on the back of one of her business cards.

"Here's the number," she declared, handing it to me. "Don't call after ten, aiight? Momz will have a hissy fit."

Momz? He was thirty and still living at home with his mother. It wasn't so much a bad thing because rent was skyrocketing in D.C. Only about one percent of housing was even available during any given week. But I was accustomed to dating men with a certain degree of independence. Even if that meant he had three or four roommates, that was preferable to him still living with a parent.

"Okay, thanks." I started for the door. It was after nine and I wanted to get home to relax in a nice, hot tub. "I better run. I have to work tomorrow."

Tamu yelled after me from her manicuring station in the rear. "Hey, Rayne, you still work at that bank?"

"Yes."

"Can you hook a sister up with a checking account?"

"You don't already have a checking account?" I asked, taking a few toddler steps back in her direction.

"Naw, I had one over at Wachovia but they killed my account. Talkin' 'bout I wrote like fifty bounced checks. I still say they lyin', girl."

Yeah right, I thought. *That's what they all say.*

"Stop by one day and I'll see what I can do," I replied, forcing a smile. "More than likely, you'll have to clear up your issues with Wachovia first."

I prayed my statement would deter her from ever showing up at my job. It did.

"Dang! I guess I gotta keep goin' to that check-cashing place. They take twelve percent. Shit!"

I glanced at Boom, who was already working her magic on Gloria's hair, and then back at Tamu. "I thought you get paid in cash?"

"I do here, but I got another gig part-time over at Safeway. I work the express lane at night."

"Well, they should be able to cash your check for you. I've never heard of a grocery chain that doesn't cash employee checks."

"Really!" Tamu exclaimed. "Dang, I never even thought of that. Thanks, Rayne."

"You're welcome."

I made a mad dash for the door before someone else could ask me about finances.

I was almost to my car, a 2000 Toyota Camry that was nearly paid for, when Boom came out the salon to yell down the street at me. "Rayne, don't forget to call Conquesto!"

"I won't!" I yelled back at her.

"Cool! I'll tell him to expect your call tonight!"

Tonight? Did it have to be tonight? Calgon, aromatherapy candles, and a glass of White Zinfandel were all calling my name.

I did call Conquesto as soon as I got home since "Momz" didn't appreciate calls late at night. Much to my surprise, he possessed a greater command of the English language than his older sister. I told him I wouldn't be able to stay on the phone long. He said he was on the way out the door anyway. We made plans to check out a movie Saturday night and left it at that.

"Come on, Rayne, you've got to hang out tonight!"

Chance was riding me hard at nine the next morning about hanging out at Passion, a Latin club down on the waterfront that featured "the sexiest club atmosphere in Washington, D.C." according to them.

Chance had hopped on the bus with me when I broke camp out of Birmingham, Alabama. She said there was no way I was leaving her behind. We grew up together and went to the University of Alabama together. It was only natural that we should take that next giant step together and we did. Now we worked together at the First Community Bank. The only thing we didn't do was live together. That was where I drew the line.

I loved Chance to death, but she wasn't the greatest housekeeper. Therefore, I had a one-bedroom in Georgetown and Chance had an efficiency in Adams Morgan. Our salaries were comparable. But we had different priorities and I managed my money better. Chance was a jewelry fanatic. I told her all the time that she could build one hell of an investment portfolio with the money she threw away on earrings alone every month. How she could work at a bank and not take advantage of certificates of deposit and money market accounts was beyond me. I took advantage of everything. You'd never find me flipping burgers at Burger King when I was seventy.

"Rayne, you hanging with me tonight or not?" Chance asked from her desk, about five feet away from my own. The bank had recently opened and there was a long line at the teller booths. No one needed special assistance as of yet so we were engaged in our normal morning banter.

"Not," I replied, answering the same question for the fifth time in a row. "I have a date tomorrow so I want to rest up tonight."

"Date?" Chance's eyes lit up like moonbeams. "With who?"

"Boom's brother."

Chance broke out in laughter. "That hoochie momma hairdresser of yours?"

I was insulted. I'm not certain why, but I was. "Yes, Boom does my hair. What of it?"

"It's just that I've seen her and how ghetto she acts. If her brother's anything like her, I can't imagine you'd be feeling him."

"Actually, Conquesto was extremely nice on the phone. We only spoke briefly, but he seems interesting enough."

"Conquesto?" Chance folded her arms over her chest, cupping her elbows, and shaking her head. "This only gets better. Where are you going?"

"To a movie. We'll probably check out *The Fighting Temptations.*"

"Ricky and I saw that last weekend. It was hilarious."

Ricky was Chance's part-time boyfriend, part-time sparring partner. They hated each other one day and were madly in love the next. I personally thought the situation was unhealthy and never hesitated to express my opinion. Chance, of course, never wanted to hear it.

"Well, you and Ricky have fun at Passion tonight. I'm definitely passing."

"You'll never meet someone by staying to yourself, Rayne."

I felt another lecture coming on and started shuffling through some papers on my desk. I had this obsession with being organized and hated it when one thing was out of place, either on top of my desk or in my drawers.

Chance was still sitting there glaring at me, like my love life, or lack thereof, had a direct effect on hers. I said, "I told you I have a date tomorrow."

"So it's basically a blind date? You only talked over the phone, right?"

"Yes, so what of it?"

She shook her head. "I know absolutely nothing about the brother, but I seriously doubt he's your type." Chance got up, walked over, and sat on the edge of my desk. "Now he's your type," she whispered, pointing a finely manicured index finger toward the teller windows.

Sure enough, there he was. I'd seen him in the bank on several occasions, but didn't know his name. He was tall enough to be a professional basketball player and he obviously worked out. However, his tailored suits gave off a more professional air. I assumed he worked somewhere downtown near the bank. He had a strikingly handsome face, smooth chocolate skin, and wore his hair shaped close to his scalp. I couldn't imagine anything making him look sexier, with the exception of maybe going bald altogether. He looked about my age and he always walked like he was a man of power. Yes, he was the kind of man I needed in my life, but it was impossible for a man that fine to be single. Not in D.C. where women outnumber men by an eight to one ratio. Besides, I assumed he was probably one of those shallow brothers who preferred stick women to show off on their arms.

"When are you going to say something to him?" Chance inquired, prodding me with her elbow. "You're always staring at him."

It was hard, but I forced myself to return my gaze to the papers on my desk.

"I'm not about to make a fool out of myself, Chance. That man is surely married, shacking up or, at the very least, dating seriously."

"Maybe he is, maybe he isn't. There's only one way to find out."

I glanced over at the teller booths one more time. There was only one customer left in front of him. I dreaded the moment he'd walk out the door. He was so damn appealing to look at, if only from afar.

"You want me to go over there and get him for you? I can tell him you need to have a moment of his time?"

"Chance, you do that and I'll never forgive you," I stated vehe-mently. "I refuse to throw myself at the customers of this bank."

"Whatever, Rayne." Chance returned to her own desk. "You know you're interested. Life is short. You never know when it'll be the last time he walks in here. He could change jobs, move, anything, and you'll never know what could've been."

He finished up his banking a few minutes later. When he walked past me, even though he was a good ten feet away, I could smell his cologne. My heart almost jumped clear out of my chest. How could a man I knew absolutely nothing about have such an effect on me? Yes, a man like that was *definitely* taken!

Six

Yardley, Age 29, Chiropractor

I hadn't taken three steps out of the bank when my cell phone started chiming.

"This is Yardley Brown."

"Sup, man? It's Felix."

Why was I not surprised? Felix was always calling me while I was walking down the street somewhere or in the car.

"Sup, Felix? I'm coming out of the bank."

"Still stacking cash, I see."

I stood there by the picture window of the bank, pretending to be spellbound by the telephone conversation when I was really spellbound by her. Rayne Waters. I'd asked one of the tellers her name a couple of weeks before. I wanted to put a name to my fantasy but didn't dare venture close enough to her desk to read her name plate.

Rayne had on a black double-breasted suit and was sitting there talking to the Puerto Rican honie that occupied the desk next to her. I was dying to ask her out, but I was afraid I might not be able to show my face in the bank again if she turned me down.

In all actuality, I never needed to step foot in the bank. It was really my secretary's job to make the deposits every morning from the previous day's receipts. I'd made the deposit one day when Lisa was out sick, spotted Rayne, and then started making up excuses to make the deposits myself.

Rayne had the most beautiful gray eyes, a healthy physique, and legs for days. I loved all types of women but I was fond of having someone with enough meat on them to keep me warm in the winter. Rayne was ideal and tall, which I also appreciated. She had to be at least five-foot-nine. I'd never been one to pamper a woman, but I could envision myself running her baths, rubbing her feet, whatever and whenever.

I kept telling myself that one day I'd go for it. As far as I could tell, she wasn't sporting a wedding ring. On the other hand, I know a lot of sisters who don't wear their rings. Some of them lose their rings. Some of them gain too much weight and can't fit them. Some of them want to play around on their husbands. I'd lost count of the number of married female patients that came into my office offering me some midday sex. I'd always refused. I wasn't that type of man.

Nor was I the type of man to make a woman feel uncomfortable. I definitely didn't want to appear desperate. Those are the two reasons I'd never approached Rayne. Besides, as fine as she was, she had to have a man; married to him or not.

"Yardley, you still there?" Felix yelled into my ear.

"Yeah, what were you saying?" I started to walk away from the bank, embedding Rayne's image into my mind to help me through the rest of the day.

"I said, you're still stacking that money in the bank."

"Well, you know there's nothing wrong with a brother looking out for his future."

"True that." I knew that Felix was feeling me on that point. He'd gone all the way in his education, obtained his doctorate in philosophy, and was on a tenure track as a professor at Howard University. "I was calling to see what's up for tonight. I refuse to let you spend another Friday up in your crib listening to love song collections on your stereo."

"I'm not that bad. I'm not home every Friday."

I was offended. He was insinuating that I was a sap, a weak man, a wimp. I was still getting over my breakup with Sheila. It hurt because I truly cared. My friends could all get over a failed relationship in the span of an NBA game, but not me. Add to that the fact that Sheila's departure had taken me by total surprise and it was inevitable for me to harbor ill feelings. Looking at Rayne Waters was helping to soothe the pain.

"Man, ever since Sheila left you ass out with nothing but a mattress set and a toilet brush, you've been drowning in your own sorrow."

"Not hardly."

"Yes hardly, Yardley. Hey, that shit rhymes."

I couldn't help but chuckle as I waited for the walk signal so I could cross the street. It was a beautiful day for October; nippy but comfortable all the same. A dime of a sister pulled up to the light in a red Lexus and winked at me. I didn't bother to wink back. She was cool, but not my type. Women that were too forward and aggressive turned me off.

"On the real, though, I need your help tonight."

"With what?" I asked suspiciously.

The light changed, the sister took off in her car, and I crossed the street.

"Mona's cousin is here from out of town. I need you to double with me."

"Oh no, Felix! I don't think so."

I stopped on the opposite corner and searched my pockets for some change to buy a copy of *The Washington Post* from a vending machine.

"Come on, man. What do you have to lose? She's only here for the weekend."

Maybe getting out wouldn't hurt matters. I could show up, eat dinner, get my mind off things for a few hours, and then roll out. First, I needed to make sure she didn't look like Rin Tin Tin. I didn't consider myself shallow but I wasn't trying to have to look at Shrek all night either.

"You've seen her?" I asked Felix.

"Boy, have I! She's a hottie and peep this. She's from Hotlanta. The Dirty South. They don't call it dirty for nothing. Mona said cuz is a straight-up freak."

"Felix, you know I'm not into casual sex."

"Okay, how about casual dinner?" he asked sarcastically. "You into that?"

I sighed at his remark. "What's her name?"

"Get this." He chuckled. "Her name is Precious."

"Is she really fine, man? Don't lie to me."

"Yardley, you're my boy. We go way back. Would I lie to you?"

I reluctantly caved in. "Okay, okay. What time and where, Felix?"

"Eight o'clock. The Capital City Brewing Company."

I dropped two coins in the machine and retrieved a paper.

"Isn't that near the Convention Center?"

"Yeah. Right across the street."

"Cool. I'm going to do this Felix, but . . ."

"But what?"

"You know but what. Later, man."

"Peace. See you in a few hours."

The moment I stepped into the restaurant, I had no choice but to question Felix's sanity. The three of them were seated at a cozy booth in the rear. I could see the sister's gold front teeth from the doorway and her hair was standing up almost a foot off her scalp. I feigned a smile and walked over to the booth. It was going to be a long ass night.

We managed to make it through most of dinner without making any conversation. Mona and Felix had been feeling each other up underneath the table the entire time, whispering to each other, obviously about sex. I was past pissed off.

Precious was the epitome of a hood rat perpetrating Nubian royalty. She had four gold teeth in total, matching acrylic fingernails and toenails, and was dressed like a tramp. She had on sandals in October, a lime green skintight sheath, and enough gold chains to make Mr. T envious.

Her hair was fake. Her purple eyes were fake. Her nails were fake. I'd venture to say even her breasts were fake. However, I didn't know that for sure and I had no intention of finding out.

I was hoping the ladies—and I use that term loosely—would excuse themselves to the restroom so I could get in Felix's ass. The mere thought that he'd set me up with such a woman made me want to open a can of whup ass on him.

Mona was fine, past fine, but her cousin looked like she was a refugee from the sideshow at the circus. I could picture her sitting up on the stage right beside the elephant man, the shemale, and the bearded lady. They could call her the "Purple-Eyed Skank."

The silence was killing me so I decided to make the best of it until everyone else finished eating. I'd lost my appetite halfway through my baby back ribs. Besides, just because I wasn't attracted to her was no reason to be downright rude.

"So, Precious, are you originally from Atlanta?"

She flashed her gold teeth at me, looking relieved that I was finally talking to her. "Born and raised."

"That's nice. What do you do for a living? Are you on vacation from your job?"

Relief turned to anxiety. I could see it in her fake eyes. "Actually," she replied hesitantly. "I'm between jobs at the moment. There aren't that many openings around where I stay."

"Really? I heard the economy and employment market are both booming in Atlanta; especially for AA's."

"AA's?"

"African-Americans."

"Oh." She cut into the remaining half of her chicken breast, both elbows on the table. She had absolutely no manners. Twice she'd picked her teeth with one of her fake nails and she'd let out several belches; one that had people clear across the restaurant searching out the culprit. "You mind if I order another drink?" she asked.

Precious was already waving the waitress over before I could respond, "No, go right ahead."

She ordered another Seagrams Seven and Seven-Up.

"I'm thinking about moving up here. I might stay with Mona for a while."

Mona, who'd been sucking on Felix's earlobe like it was one of my baby back ribs, glared at Precious. "Humph, I . . . don't . . . even . . . think . . . so!" she yelled out, moving her head from side to side with each syllable.

"But, Mona . . . ," Precious whined.

"But Mona nothing. You're my fam and all, but there's no way you and your hard-headed ass kids are taking over my place."

I felt the vibration and audibly heard the kick Precious gave Mona underneath the table. Felix grinned at me and shrugged his shoulders, acting completely innocent of the charges of treason he knew I'd throw at him later on.

"How many kids do you have?" I asked, not that it really mattered. At first sight, I'd decided there was *zero* possibility of Precious and me hooking up. I just have a nosy streak and it reared its ugly head.

Precious yelled out, "Three!"

Mona yelled out, "Five!"

Felix cleared his throat.

I downed the rest of my draft beer.

Precious put her utensils down, took her elbows off the table, and started picking her fake nails to get rid of whatever she'd picked out of her teeth earlier. "I have five, but two of them stay with their daddies."

I was speechless. If two of them stayed with their daddies, that meant there were probably at least three babies' daddies involved.

Precious could tell I was turned off. Then again, she should've realized that from jump street.

She stroked my arm. Normally, if I was out on a date and a woman stroked my arm, I'd be aroused. But I didn't choose her as a date. In fact, I would never have chosen her for a date; even if I'd gone twenty years without a woman in my bed and had no other option than a blowup doll.

"Yardley, since we're done eating, you want to go sit over at the bar? That way we could talk in private."

We both had food remaining on our plates. Mine was definitely going back to the kitchen that way. Still, I had no intention of going over to the bar with her.

"Precious, I'm fine right here."

I glanced over at Felix and Mona. They were looking uneasy and whispering to each other.

"You guys don't need to move to the bar," Felix said, jumping up from the booth and tossing a fifty on the table. "That should cover our half of the bill. Mona and I are going to head back to my place."

That did it! I was going to cuss his ass out for sure. First, the set-up with a floozy and now he wasn't even paying the entire bill? It was going to be on when I caught up to him in private.

"Felix!" I lashed out at him.

Felix kept grinning at me nervously while Mona scooted over to the edge of the booth and got up, smoothing out the bottom of her tan dress. At least she had some clothes on, unlike her cousin.

Mona touched me on my shoulder. "You don't mind dropping Precious off, do you, Yardley? Of course not. You're always the gentleman. I already gave her a key."

Do I have a choice? "I guess not, Mona."

Felix reached out to shake my hand. I grabbed it tight, trying to cut off his circulation.

"I'll call you tomorrow, man," he said in agony, yanking hard until I finally loosened my grip.

They disappeared out the front door of the restaurant and into the night.

"You ready?" I asked Precious.

"You mind if I finish this drink first?"

"No, not at all." I searched for the waitress. I needed another beer myself.

"Isn't this one of those cars where you can put the top down?" Precious asked, settling into my black Porsche 911 convertible.

"Yes, it is. It's a *convertible*."

On top of everything else, I began to wonder if Precious had a frequent rider pass for the little yellow school bus. Who doesn't know the difference between a convertible and a hardtop?

"Cool. Maybe we can put the top down so my hair can blow in the wind."

I tried to suppress a laugh. As stiff as her hair was, we could've sped through a windstorm at ninety miles per hour and it wouldn't have budged.

"What year is it?"

"It's a ninety-eight."

I started my car and took off before I gave it a chance to warm up. I couldn't end the night fast enough. I still had a good thirty-minute drive to Mona's place out in Forestville, Maryland.

"Ninety-eight? I thought you'd have a newer model car with all the money you make."

"How much money do I make?" I asked, picturing Mona dishing out the dirt on me over a bowl of heavily buttered microwave popcorn.

"I don't know. Mona said you were getting paid."

I bet she did. "So when you were working, what did you do?"

"Promise you won't get mad."

I had to laugh at that one. I figured it must've been a doozy. "No, I won't get mad."

"I used to be a stripper, but I gave that up."

"Why'd you give it up?"

"Gary, he's my youngest son's daddy, he threatened to take Gary, Jr. away from me if I didn't quit. He has a lot of damn nerve, considering he met me at work. He paid me twenty dollars to let him lick whipped cream off my toes."

I instantly felt sick to my stomach. I wondered if she'd had fake toenails at the time.

"He told me quit, or I'm taking your ass to court. Out of all my kids, I love Gary, Jr. the most. I couldn't have that."

What type of woman would openly play favorites amongst her kids? Precious really had some issues.

"So what are you doing to support your kids?" I asked.

"I get child support from four of my exes. One's locked up so he doesn't have any damn money. I get a state check as well."

Great! Five babies' daddies and on welfare.

"I see."

"I had a gig for a while with Animal Control but I hated it. They had my ass out on the middle of highways picking up dead deer and chasing wild dogs all over the place. I was scared as shit sometimes."

Part of me wondered who was more scared; Precious or the animals.

Precious reached over and started rubbing my thigh. "Yardley, can I ask you something?"

I removed her hand. "Please don't do that. It messes with my driving."

"I'm sorry." She pushed her breasts up with her hands like she was adjusting them in her bra. Fake or not, I'd never lay a finger on them. "I was wondering if you'd ever kept a woman."

"Are you serious?" I asked incredulously. "No, I've *definitely* never kept a woman."

"Would you consider keeping one?"

"No, I wouldn't consider keeping one."

"Look, I'm going to cut the bullshit okay? I'm in a bind. I need to get away from Atlanta because I got mixed up with the wrong man and he got me involved in some illegal shit."

"Precious, I'm sorry to hear that." My nosy side wanted to inquire about details, but my wise side told me to leave well enough alone. "Sounds like you need a lawyer; not a man. Either way, I can't do a thing for you, my sister."

That was when she practically climbed over the gear shift, throwing a thigh over it to rub up against mine and clawing at my dick with her hand.

I pulled my car over on the side of Pennsylvania Avenue. We'd just crossed the Maryland State Line.

"Precious, I asked you not to grope all over me. I'm not trying to wreck my car."

"I can fuck you so hard, you'll cry," she told me, trying to sound seductive.

All I could do was laugh. *Me crying over some punta?* Never.

"Oh, you think that shit's funny?" she asked angrily.

"Actually, I think it's hilarious."

She put her leg back down on the passenger seat and rubbed her Elvira nails up and down her midriff. "I'm offering you all this and you see me as a fucking joke?"

"Precious, this may come as a shock to you, but we do have plenty of women here in D.C. I don't know who or what gave you the impression that I have to *keep* a woman in order to have one, but you've been seriously misinformed. I've bought women things but it wasn't in exchange for sex. That's for damn sure."

"Oh yeah, is that why your woman left you to bump coochies?"

That hurt. It hurt like shit. Not because Precious was speaking the words, but because it meant that Felix had betrayed me by telling my business to Mona.

I put my car back in drive and pulled off.

"You don't have shit to say now, huh? I guess not. Sorry motherfucker. You're such a lousy fuck that your woman would rather lick a pussy than be with you. I was going to do your ass a fucking favor and suffer through the two minutes every night in exchange for a place to stay."

Was she calling me a two-minute brother? Oh, hell naw!

"I can't imagine a man even giving you two minutes of sex, you skank."

"Skank?" She flipped me the finger. "I got your skank."

"If I were less of a man, I'd kick your ass out of my car right here. Luckily for you, I'm above that."

"Just take me back to Mona's and make tracks."

"No problem. I can't get your trashy ass out my car fast enough."

She waved me off and smacked her lips before crossing her arms in front of her chest and pouting.

We didn't say a word to each other the rest of the way out to Forestville. Fine by me. I turned on the radio and lost myself in thought. I analyzed the situation with Sheila for the hundredth time since she'd left.

I knew Sheila was bisexual when I'd met her. Like most men, I saw that as a definite plus as long as I could watch. And I did. I even joined in a couple of times with some of the sisters she'd picked up at lesbian clubs. I viewed it like this. Some women have a craving for chocolate chip cookie dough ice cream. My woman had a craving for pussy. No harm, no foul.

That is, until her former lover moved back from the West Coast and ruined a perfect situation. Raven wasn't having any part of sharing and neither was I; under the circumstances. I knew there had been real feelings involved between the two of them and I didn't like it. Matter of fact, I was jealous.

It turned out it was for good reason. Less than three months after Raven had hopped off the plane, Sheila had left my ass high and dry, leaving behind nothing but a five-sentence note.

Yardley,

What can I say? I love dick, but I love pussy more. I'm sure you'll find someone else. I'm in love with Raven and I need her in my life. I'm sorry.

Thanks for everything,

Sheila

Thanks for everything? I didn't invite her over for Thanksgiving dinner. I didn't loan her a cup of sugar. I'd given her my heart, two years of my life, and a Benz. She'd given me five sentences and a "thanks for everything."

I dropped Precious off fifteen minutes later. She got out and slammed the door. I pulled off before she even reached the stoop of Mona's townhouse. Forget about seeing her in safely. Even a blind crack addict wouldn't want to attack her funky ass.

On the way to my penthouse in Southwest, I passed the First Community Bank. Rayne Waters's bank. Now she was the total package. Beautiful, sexy, a good job. More than likely taken. I decided to go back into the bank on Monday to find out for sure.

Seven

Rayne

If I'd had the slightest suspicion that my mother would call me on a Friday night, I would've gone to Passion with Chance and Ricky with a quickness.

"Rayne, I'm glad I caught you in," she squealed into the phone. "I need to talk to you."

"What's going on, Momma?" I plopped down on my sofa, debating about fixing a cocktail to help me get through the conversation. "I thought you'd be down at the Eagle."

"The Eagle has played out."

"Humph, that's a surprise," I said sarcastically.

Truth be known, the Eagle was played out before it'd ever gotten started. For years, I'd been anxious to get in there to see what all the excitement was about. Once we were of age, Chance and I made a beeline for the place. The inside was barely bigger than my living room and the place smelled like funk. Instead of chanting that song "Ain't We Funkin' Now?" by the Brothers Johnson, they needed to be chanting, "Ain't we funky now? Ain't we funky like you like it?"

"Rayne, I need a favor," Momma whispered into the phone like she wasn't alone.

Not a big surprise either. Momma was still basking in all of her whoredom. That was the main reason I'd left Birmingham. Her reputation was rubbing off on me. Guilty by association and all that jazz.

"What's the favor, Momma?"

"I need to borrow a thousand dollars."

"A thousand dollars. Geesh, Momma, for what?"

"I'm two months behind on my rent."

I held in the expletives bouncing around on my tonsils. If nothing else, I still showed my mother respect; even when I didn't respect her actions.

"Why haven't you been paying your rent?"

"Truck won't give me any cash. He claims I've been cheating on him."

"Have you?" I asked as serious as a heart attack.

"No, I ain't been cheating!" She was raising her voice and I felt a migraine coming on. "I treat Truck like a king! He's just acting silly!"

I was anxious to get off the phone. "Momma, I'll wire you the money Monday morning. I have to go now."

"Thank you, baby." She giggled, her voice returning to normal. "I know I can always count on you."

I only wished I could say the same.

"Goodnight, Momma."

"Goodnight, baby."

A thousand dollars. One thing was sure; Momma had no apprehensions about asking me for money. I definitely needed a drink after that one. I went into my kitchen and hooked myself up with a rum and Coke.

I decided to do my laundry instead of waiting to do it on Saturday morning, as customary. By the time I finished up the second load, *The Wire* was coming on HBO. I'd barely sat down, prepared to get my drama on, when my phone rang again.

"Hello."

"Hey, Rayne. It's me."

"Me?" I asked sarcastically. The nerve of some men to think they're the only one calling.

"This is Conquesto."

"Oh, hey." Half of me hoped he was calling to break the date. After the comments Chance had made, it had gotten me to thinking. What if he wasn't my type? "What's going on?"

"I was calling to ask if we could head out a little later tomorrow than planned. I need to handle something about eight and I probably won't be able to scoop you up until about nine-thirty."

"Nine-thirty is fine."

"Okay, cool."

I heard him sighing through the phone and a noise like water running. *No this fool was not taking a leak while he was talking to me on the phone?* Five seconds later, the toilet flushed. Damn him!

"I'll see you tomorrow, Rayne."

I hung up the phone without saying goodbye. I was totally disgusted. I'd been on the dating scene for years and I'd never had a man take a leak while he was talking to me on the phone. Not even Will, and we were together for three years.

Will aka Mr. Know It All. Will was fine. Tall like I prefer, caramel, nice juicy ass. It might sound strange, but I'm an ass woman. I can't stand looking at a brother nude that has a flat ass. I need something to palm when a man's grinding in and out of me.

Physically, Will was a dream. Mentally, he left a lot to be desired. Will was from the old school. He held true to the player/pimp mentality. He thought expressing romantic feelings to a woman was taboo. A sign of "sweetness." On top of that, he never wanted to listen to me. I tried to tell him that a man can listen to a woman and still be hard; just like a woman can listen to a man and not be weak.

Looking back on it, I think there was probably never a time when Will wasn't cheating on me. I'd ignored all of the signs; until I caught him red-handed. I went by his office one night. He was in the garage banging some tramp inside his car, giving her all that good ass dick that belonged to me. Her greasy ass hair was smearing up against his back window.

I opened the door and she almost fell out the car, tits hanging upside down and all. I pulled the fire extinguisher from behind my back, the one I'd swiped from a nearby wall, and covered both their asses with the spray.

"Maybe that will put out the fire!" I screamed at both of them.

Will came home later that night, begging for forgiveness. I told him that my love life wasn't a game of Monopoly and I didn't pass out Get Out of Jail Free cards. I told him to pack his shit and leave.

Will messed up and was wrong for that, but the depth of my hurt was my own fault. I thought I was strong, but in love I was weak. I should've had the strength to see that all of his inconsistencies were enough, without hard evidence. I should've believed in myself enough to trust what I thought, what my intuition was saying, but I didn't. My intuition couldn't be wrong all of the time.

I needed a man who had reached the point where he realized

he was accountable for his actions; all of them. A man who realized he had to give what he expected to be rewarded in return. I
seriously doubted that Conquesto would be him, but I had to start
someplace. Pickings were slim in D.C.——for women——and competition was tight. A date was a date. I simply prayed I wouldn't
regret it.

Eight

Felix, Dwayne, and Mike were already on the basketball court when I pulled up on Saturday morning. We met every Saturday morning, without fail, to play hoops. It was a badge of manhood; right behind bragging on getting laid.

Dwayne threw me the ball when I was still about twenty feet away. I took it, palmed it, and threw it right into the small of Felix's back.

Felix yelped out in pain. He'd been down on one knee, tying his shoe, when I plummeted him without warning.

"Damn, man! What's that all about?" Mike asked.

"Ask Felix," I responded.

Felix stood up, reaching behind his back to rub it. "Yardley, that was totally uncalled for. You're being childish."

"I'm being childish? You set me up with that skank last night, left me hanging at the restaurant so you could go get some ass you get every night anyway, and I'm being childish? You were wrong for that shit, Felix, and you know it."

That was when Dwayne jumped all into the mix. "Dang, Felix, you told me you'd hooked our boy up with a fine ass honie."

"Fine?" I chuckled. "I'll put it this way, Dwayne. Those brothers you deal with down in the D.C. Jail wouldn't get with her."

Dwayne fell out laughing. "That's pretty bad then. Most of them would fuck anything; even each other."

Dwayne was a guard in the D.C. Jail. Being demanding and angry, it was the perfect job for him. Dwayne was one of those brothers that was angry about everything. He was an Internet junkie and got all these negative emails encouraging boycotts and phone marathons to lodge complaints against the injustices of the world. A person that went into a restaurant or bookstore and felt like they were treated unfairly because they were black. A security guard or policeman using excessive force on a black man. Every weekend, it's something new.

"Speaking of jail, I have to tell you something. This is deep."

Mike, Felix, and I stared at one another, thinking "here it comes."

"There's this brother in prison down in Texas on death row that's innocent, man."

"How do you know that?" Felix asked sarcastically.

"I read it in my email. Let me finish telling you about it."

"I've heard enough," Mike lashed out at him. "We came here to ball, so let's ball."

Dwayne got upset, militant even. "You fools don't care about anyone but yourselves. Don't you care that our people are being mistreated all over this country?"

"I care, Dwayne," I sincerely stated. "I just don't put much credence into all the stuff you get in your email. If it were up to you, we'd be spending every Saturday morning holding picket signs in front of some restaurant or typing letters to congressmen."

Dwayne rolled his eyes at me. "Just forget it. Forget about people dying in the streets, succumbing to fatal diseases, and those falsely incarcerated."

Mike fell out laughing. "Don't be so melodramatic, man. You need to go to some of these auditions with me. You're a natural born actor."

Felix and I had a good chuckle while Dwayne pouted.

Mike was an actor; a "thespian" as he put it. He wasn't very believable or fluent when it came to speaking roles, but he'd lucked up with a few commercials because of his rock-solid body. He did this underwear commercial and for more than a year after it aired, women were running up to him when we were out at clubs asking if he was "the one from the commercial." One sister even offered to surrender her panties on the spot if he'd go into the men's room, remove his, and relinquish them to her.

We played ball, got all hot and sweaty as usual, and stood around afterwards downing a few beers. Yes, we were all "men's men" and then some.

Felix followed me to my car. "Yardley, I heard what happened this morning when I dropped Mona off. I'm sorry I left you hanging, man."

"You know what, Felix? It's not so much you leaving me there with Precious so she could try to get me to take her to bed, work me over, and assume I'd take care of her for life in exchange for sexual favors. What really pissed me off was the fact that she knew all about Sheila."

Felix's mouth dropped open.

"Don't even try to play it off, Felix. You told Mona, she told Precious, and the damage is done. I'm not sure I can ever trust you again, man."

"Yardley, you're right. I fucked up big time." He stated this like he was telling me something I didn't already know. "I got drunk one night and it slipped out."

"You got drunk and started talking about my sex life with Mona? Is your own sex life that boring? That's ridiculous, if you have nothing better to talk about than me and who I'm dealing with on a personal level."

Felix punched me lightly on my arm and started walking away backwards, still facing me. "You're pissed and I know how you get. Rather than stand here and let this escalate, I'm going to jet and catch up to you tomorrow. Cool?"

I didn't reply. I got into my car and left. I stopped by Haines Point on my way home and took a quick run to relieve some stress. It wasn't so much mental stress but sexual stress. It had been a while since I'd been laid. However, I was nowhere near desperate enough to bed Precious or anyone who resembled her. Now Rayne, her I could make love to body and mind. I sighed as I finished my run and my daydream about her simultaneously. "Yardley, that woman isn't thinking about you," I told myself aloud.

Nine

Rayne

Nine-fifty. Conquesto was late. If ten came around and he wasn't there, I was planning to follow my golden rule. Thirty minutes after schedule was a certifiable stand-up, meaning I was free to get undressed, get in bed, and ignore the doorbell when it rang.

After that black booty pants comment Boom made, I'd selected a pair of sweat pants and a long sleeve Henley top to wear to the movies. I wasn't a hoochie and I wasn't trying to leave that impression either.

I decided to go out onto my balcony to get some fresh air. It faced M Street so I could always see the bustle of activity in Georgetown. That was why I loved my place so much. Inside, I could seal out the world, yet I could step outside and everything came to life.

I moved to Georgetown because it had character. I fell in love with it the first time I came down there to go window-shopping.

Georgetown was full of antique shops, hip clothing stores, and restaurants that boasted individuality, unlike all the customary chain stores.

I selected a building with underground parking. The extra two hundred a month tagged onto my rent was well worth it. Parking was scarce in Georgetown. People from the suburbs had to pay at least twelve dollars for parking to have dinner or take in a movie.

The air was nippy that night, but not cold. I was sitting on one of my Adirondack chairs when the doorbell rang. The moment of truth had arrived. Hopefully, Conquesto would be fine and ring more than my doorbell.

I took a restorative breath before I swung the door open. Good thing I'd braced myself. That was the only thing that prevented me from laughing.

Conquesto had a cute enough face. He was light-skinned and tall with a slender frame. His hair had to go. It was dyed platinum blonde and he was wearing a bright orange sweat suit with black dress loafers and no socks. He had a huge gold necklace adorning his chest that had his name spelled out in three-inch letters. I was too through.

"Hey, Rayne." He grinned at me, licking his lips in the process. Now, I could deal with the lips. He had some of those licking-me-downlow-and-lovely lips. "I'm sorry I'm late, but I had a hard time finding a space. I finally found one a couple blocks away."

"No problem," I lied. "I only finished getting ready a few minutes ago."

He barged by me before I even had a chance to invite him to step in. "Listen, you mind if I use your bathroom right quick?"

I pointed down the hall. "Not at all."

"Cool, I'll be right back." He paused in mid-step, turned around and grinned at me. "Damn, you're fine. I only got to see you from a distance before. I'm going to have to get Boom something special for hooking me up with you. Maybe I'll get her a phat outfit to rock when she goes clubbing."

I didn't know what to do other than blush. "Thanks for the compliment."

While he was in the bathroom, I psyched myself up for the rest of the evening. It was dark out so I didn't run the risk of really being seen until we got to the theater. It would be dark inside, but the lobby was still a problem. If any of my friends spotted me with a brother with platinum hair and a bama outfit on, I'd never hear the end of it.

I heard some strange noises coming from the bathroom and then I realized he was straining; letting out loud moans while he was trying to pass a turd. That was disgusting! Even if it meant him being another ten or fifteen minutes later than he was already, he should've found a public restroom and handled that business before he fell up in my place.

The toilet finally flushed a few moments later. I heard the door swing open but I didn't hear any damn water. *No his nasty ass did not come out without washing his hands?* That was the second time I'd witnessed his bathroom habits and we still hadn't been out on a date yet.

"You ready?" Conquesto asked, walking back out into my living room.

"Did you find the soap okay?" I wanted to see what his nasty ass would say. "I think I put a new bar out in the dish."

"Yeah, yeah, I found it okay," he lied.

I could put up with a lot of nonsense when it came to men, but poor hygiene was out of the question. I was going to endure the date, but Conquesto would never see me again. That was the bottom line.

• • •

On the way to the Loews Cineplex Dupont, the springs in Conquesto's jacked-up car, a big ass 1972 Ford, ripped a small hole in my sweat pants. It was a good thing I didn't get all fly for him. If I'd ripped a hole in something expensive or, worse yet, unique and irreplaceable, I would've gone into bitch mode for the rest of the night.

As it turned out, I had to wake my bitchy alter ego from her slumber anyway. Conquesto got into line at the box office while I stood over to the side to wait for him. He looked at me like I was crazy.

"You gonna get your ticket, or you want to give me the money so I can get it?"

I couldn't believe he'd said that to me. He actually thought he was going to play Mr. Cheap with me.

"Um, Conquesto." I scooted closer to him so other people wouldn't be privy to what I was about to say. "You might not know this, but it's customary for the person that initialized the date to pay. I'm not saying that the woman should never pay, but you asked me out tonight. Get what I'm saying?"

"Damn!" He got all loud on a sistah. People immediately started being nosy. "You mean you can afford to pay Boom a grip every week to get your hair done, but you can't buy your own movie ticket?"

"Oh, I can afford it," I replied vehemently, getting loud myself. "I can also afford a taxi to take my ass home. Later."

I headed for the exit onto Nineteenth Street. He must've thought he was taking a desperate hoochie out on a date. I'd show him.

"Rayne, hold up!" He came running up behind me and put his hands on my shoulders. "I got your back, woman!"

I yanked away from him and his nasty, shit-infested hands. "I don't need you to have my back. I have my own back. Thank you very much."

"Look, I'm sorry." *Oh boy, now he was going to start begging.* "I didn't mean to cause a scene. Let's go back inside and I'll happily pay for your ticket."

I didn't budge.

"It's just that money's kind of tight for me right now. You've seen my ride."

"I've seen and practically been cut up by your ride," I replied, referring to the hole in my pants.

"I got a J-O-B, but it's hard to get hooked up with something major when you've just got out."

"Got out?" Now that comment warranted my attention. "Got out of where? Prison?"

"Yes. I only got out a couple months ago. Didn't Boom tell you?"

"No, the hell she didn't. What were you in prison for?"

"My boyz and I got messed up in slanging dope, thinking we were the shit and untouchable. In fact, we called ourselves the Untouchables. We were running smack out a rowhouse in Southeast. That shit grew old quick and we all went down; one way or the other."

"What's that mean?"

"That means that three of us went to jail and five of us went to the cemetery." He shoved his hands in his pockets—*thank the Lawd*—and started looking down at the ground in an effort to avoid eye contact. "Much as I hated getting locked up, I'm one of the lucky ones. At least I still have breath in my body."

There I was faced with a dilemma; all because of my destructive habit of wearing my heart on my sleeve. I could've gone home, telling Conquesto thanks but no thanks for the date, or I could stay, grin, and bear it. My dumb ass stayed.

I ended up paying not only for my ticket, but his also. I even shelled out about twenty dollars on concessions. Everything had to be individual. Sharing popcorn and candy was out, for obvious reasons.

The movie was hilarious. I was all into it until Conquesto started trying to feel me up. I felt his hand on my thigh and knocked it off. Could he take a hint? Not if you drew "Don't fucking touch me!" with a marker on your forehead. He kept trying to get me to lean over the armrest enough for him to kiss me. I told him I didn't kiss on the first date; not ever. That's what those lying ass heifers always try to say on television dating shows about five minutes before the camera catches them locking tongues with the person they'd spoken that bullshit to. Yeah right! If they could say it with a straight face, so could I; except I wouldn't become a hypocrite and go back on my word.

When we arrived back at my building, I fully intended to have Conquesto drop me off out front. I was confident there wouldn't be any parking spaces at that time of night for blocks. Wrong! There was one right in front. He didn't waste a second grabbing it either.

"Can I come up and use your bathroom?" he asked, looking for justification to get in my crib.

"I thought you went before we left the Cineplex?"

"I did, but that large soda really did me in. How many ounces was it, anyway?"

"I haven't a clue, but the sodas at theaters are gigantic now. I guess that's why they can get away with the outrageous prices."

"I never thought about it like that."

"Do you ever think about washing your hands?" I couldn't help myself. I had to know.

"Huh? Excuse me?"

"I noticed you didn't wash your hands when you used my bathroom earlier. Frankly, I find that disgusting. So, if it's all the same to you, I'd prefer for you to find a restroom somewhere else."

"That's really fucked up!" he lashed out at me, his bottom lip quivering like he wanted to punch me dead in the face. "I take you out and you start dissin' me and shit!"

"You drove, yes. However, as far as I'm concerned, I took you out because I paid for everything. Comprende?"

"Fine, whatever, hoe!"

Oh, no he didn't go there!

"Hoe?" I was steamed, but tried to turn it around on him. After all, I was far from a hoe so his words were irrelevant. I snickered at him. "This evening has been interesting, but I've heard and seen enough. Goodnight."

I got out of his car and walked under the awning to the front door of the building. Before I could get my keys out, Conquesto had jumped out the car and lurked up behind me.

"I'm sorry, Rayne."

Umph, umph, umph! He actually thought that line was going to fly twice in one night! Not even!

"I was out of line for calling you a hoe. Rayne, I'm used to people hardballin' me so I hardball back. It's rough in the joint."

"I can imagine, but I hope to never find out," I replied honestly.

"Can I see you again?"

"No, I don't think so." I decided to be polite, turned around, and shook his hand. I planned to scrub the skin off my hand the second I got up to my place. "Thanks for the evening. Tell Boom I'll see her on Thursday."

I wanted to end the date on a pleasant note. After all, good hairdressers, ones that don't chop off half your head when you ask for a trim and ones that don't burn your scalp when they put in perms, are hard as hell to find.

Conquesto finally decided to give up. "Well, you take care, Rayne. I'm sorry if I offended you in some way."

"It's cool, Conquesto."

I got the door open, leaving it ajar long enough to watch him back to his car.

"Say, Rayne, you have any girlfriends that might be interested in a smooth ass brother like me?" He grabbed his dick through his trousers. "I'm hung like a motherfucker, too. Wanna see my schlong?"

"That's quite alright." I suppressed a laugh, wondering if the idiot would be stupid enough to really pull out his dick on M Street.

"Well, what about one of your fine friends?" He continued to pester me.

Then I ran a roster through my head of all the women I knew; wondering if there was someone I wanted to pay back for some dirt they had done to me. No one came to mind.

"Sorry, Conquesto, all the ones I know are already hooked up. Maybe Boom can hook you up with another one of her clients."

I disappeared into the building, ready to break dance. The night was finally over. Part of me wanted to call Boom at home and lay her out; even though it was after midnight. She was probably out clubbing anyway. Besides, I had some skin scrubbing to do.

"That's what you fucking get!" Chance squealed into the phone at me when I told her what had happened the next morning.

"Chance, it's Sunday. No swearing on the Lord's day."

"Get off the religious tip. You haven't been to church since we were fifteen."

I finished rolling up the cord to my vacuum and placed it inside the linen closet. I'd been cleaning up all morning, paying extra special attention to my toilet. I yawned into the phone. I was truly exhausted.

"You're right, Chance, and I've been thinking about that. We both need to start going back to church. This simply isn't right."

"You were never a steady in a pew. Why are you tripping now?"

"Quit! You know I used to go with you and your folks and your fifty-eleven siblings on a regular basis. Speaking of which, how is the Martinez clan?"

"Everything's kosher. Ruiz decided to tie the knot *again*."

"Damn, really?" I asked in dismay.

Ruiz had divorced his first wife, after he'd caught her cheating on him. I have to admit that I wasn't torn up about it—after all he'd taken my virginity and then patted me on the head—but part of me had kind of hoped we'd end up together someday since he was single again. Good thing he was safely tucked away in another state or I would've definitely embarrassed myself by running after him. Chance's parents and younger siblings came to visit her about twice a year but never stayed long because she had an efficiency and the decent hotels in D.C. were too pricey for them to swing more than a couple of nights.

"Now who's swearing?" Chance asked sarcastically. She'd asked me a few times why I seemed so bitter toward Ruiz but I'd never confessed our little "boning episode" and never would.

"You're right. My bad," I stated calmly. "I'm emotionally torn up over this. You know I have a thing for Ruiz."

"Yeah, me and the whole world." Chance folded her arms in front of her.

"I guess I've been rather obvious about it, huh?" I chuckled. "It's just that he's so, so, so—"

"Rayne!" Chance exclaimed. "I'd rather not hear any sexy talk about my brother. That's plain ole nasty. Besides, I know you. You're trying to change the subject. Not working this time, chica."

"You think you know me? I have more game than the Chicago Bulls."

"And you're full of more bullshit, too."

"Okay, so I don't want to discuss last night anymore." I sighed. "I told you all the lurid details already. I'm going to plop down on the sofa and catch the Redskins game."

"Who are they playing today?"

"Philly. Should be a hell of a game, too."

Chance giggled. "You and your football. Who ever heard of a female football fanatic?"

"There are tons of women into football. NFL.com even has a special section for women sports fans now."

"Why do I get the distinct impression you've been there a time or two?"

I rolled my eyes to the ceiling. "Let me run, girl. See you at the bank tomorrow."

"Later, Rayne."

I went into my bedroom, got a king-sized pillow off my bed, came back into the living room, and laid down on the sofa. I reached for my Dallas Cowboys fleece throw. I watched the Skins but I was a Cowboy all the way when it came to the playoffs and the two teams squaring off. All I needed was that NFL Total Ticket, but the tenants association of my building had placed a ban on satellite dishes. I loved my apartment, but the love of football had me on the brink of considering home ownership. Then I could do whatever the hell I wanted.

Ten

I never made it into the bank that Monday. My intentions were to head that way and find out all I could about Rayne Waters. However, before Lisa could get the deposits in order, I received a shocking telephone call. Roxie, the number one stunna, the woman I'd fantasized about throughout high school even after she'd caught me with Angel the hooker, called me out of the blue and asked me to lunch. There was no way I was rejecting *her*. Felix and Mike had both seen her recently and swore she was the finest thing walking.

I met her at B. Smith's in Union Station at noon. She was easy to spot. All I had to do is search for a little slice of heaven. She was still classy. She still had the wavy black hair and the sensuous brown eyes, but there was more. Roxie looked mature, as we all did, but there was still something more. Roxie looked like she could make a man have a seizure in bed. She had the look the brothers and I refer to as "DS." Yes, Roxie was definitely a DS.

Roxie had turned into a dick slayer. It was written all over her pretty ass face.

We stood there in the entryway, hugging and admiring each other's new look, until the hostess was ready to seat us at a cozy table by a window.

"Roxie, I can't get over how great you look," I said, continuing to shower her with compliments like I had been for the past ten minutes. "When I heard you were back in town, I was hoping we'd run into each other at some point. I never expected you to call, but I'm sure glad you did."

Roxie gave me the eye. The I-know-I-can-wrap-your-ass-around-my-little-finger-if-I-want-to eye. The one all women that are fine, who realize they are fine, dole out from time to time.

"How'd you know I was back from Minnesota, anyway?" she asked.

"Felix and Mike. They said they ran into you at a charity function."

"Yes, now I remember," she replied, a slight giggle escaping her sexy ass lips. I'm not sure what hue of lipstick she was wearing, but it was definitely doing her justice. I had to keep my mouth shut to prevent the drool from coming out. "They were at the benefit for the Washington Hospital Center. Why weren't you there? Aren't you a doctor?"

"Chiropractor. I didn't go because I was under the weather that night. I hooked Felix and Mike up with the tickets I'd planned to use. They're always interested in helping out the needy."

That was a straight-up lie. Felix and Mike swiped those tickets from me because they knew there would be a lot of fine, eligible sisters at the event.

"Well, I hope you weren't too ill. I'd hate to see you lose any stamina; especially now. You might need it later today."

I'd instructed my dick to stay down on the way over to the

restaurant. I had given him a lecture to that effect. "No matter how good she looks, Dick, stay the hell down." Once Roxie made that sexual innuendo, Dick said, "Fuck you, Yardley! Better yet, let's both fuck her! Let's get ready to rumble!"

We had a magnificent lunch, but the dessert was a hundred times better. I took Roxie to my penthouse and wore her ass out. I'd waited more than a decade to smoke her boots, and the wait was well worth it. Roxie did things to me they don't even show on the Playboy channel; things I'd only heard rumors about. Yes, she was a dick slayer and then some. The look is always a dead giveaway.

It all played out like something from a late-night movie on Cinemax—Skinamax as the fellas call it because of all the tits and ass they can see on any given night after midnight. Roxie slipped out of her red two-piece suit less than a minute after we'd walked into my penthouse. The only words preceding her quick exit from clothing were "nice place." Before I could thank her, her blazer was already off, exposing this red lace bra that could've only been described as "lovely." Her breasts were even lovelier as she slipped the bra straps down off her shoulders with one hand and unfastened the clasp behind her back with the other. I was gauging her to be about a C-cup, which meant she'd gotten a little top heavier since high school. The fellas and I used to always bet on bra cup sizes for certain girls back in our immature years. Once one of us had actually made out with a girl——normally that meant someone other than me because I did very little in high school, period—— they'd come back and report the actual cup size after examining the label in the girl's bra. No one had ever gotten the opportunity to see Roxie's bra but we could tell she was a B-cup. She was the same size as three other girls Felix had bedded down for sport.

I was admiring her breasts while she continued to provocatively undress. I licked my lips as she dropped her skirt, exposing a pair of red lace thongs that matched her bra. Damn, she was sexy as hell!

I stopped her there, picked her up and carried her to my bedroom. After I laid her on the bed, I said, "I want to take the rest off. I've waited years for this. Allow me to relish it."

She grinned. "Okay, but Yardley . . ."

"Yes?"

"I can't go on until I tell you that I've always wanted you. That night, at your birthday party, I was planning to go all the way with you. I'd spent hours getting ready, making sure my body was prepared for your taking. I'd even masturbated so my pussy juices would be marinated for you, for your touch."

Shit! I thought. *I missed out on all that and possibly more than a decade of good loving because of a hooker named Angel with musty feet!*

While she continued talking and playing with her nipples, my dick got even harder than it already was—something I didn't deem physically possible. I traced my fingertip down the side of her panties and slipped it under the lace. I dipped it inside her vagina, took it out and licked it. "Did you do that today, before we met for lunch? It damn sure tastes marinated to me."

Roxie giggled. "No, now it's seasoned pussy. All things get better with age; contrary to what some men believe who always want to trade their women in for younger models."

"I agree," I said. "It does get better with age."

"So does dick," she said, caressing my privates through my pants. "I bet you have a nice, sweet, juicy dick. Um, it feels like it's about what, nine inches?"

"Give or take a centimeter," I replied jokingly. "Want to see it?"

"Yes but only on one condition."

"What's that?"

"That we devour each other for a full hour before we fuck."

"An hour?" I asked in shock. I'd eaten my share of pussy in my day, but never for an hour. "An entire hour?"

"Yes, an *entire* hour." She sat up and started unbuckling my belt. "Now keep in mind that it means that I have to suck your dick for an hour; no matter how many times you come."

"Shit! I might need some Viagra for this!"

We both laughed.

"Stand up," Roxie said, climbing up on her knees as I obeyed and stood by my bed. She finished loosening my belt and began working on my zipper. She got my pants and boxers down and I stepped out of them as she began to stroke my shaft like a sister who knew what she desired. "Yardley . . ."

"Yes?"

"I have to warn you that I'm a woman with a strong sex drive. I'm not the same innocent, timid Roxie you knew in high school who was afraid to give it up. The one who was afraid to experiment. Now, I'm all about experimenting."

"Sounds good to me," I said as a wide ass grin spread across my face. Not only was the woman I'd always fantasized about in my bedroom, she was a straight-up freak. No man could possibly ask for more.

She fingered herself and placed her index finger up to my lips and slipped it inside so I could savor her flavor again.

"I'm serious, Yardley. I'm trying to have the real deal with you this time. I've been out there, in that meat market, dealing with trifling ass Negroes who only want to get themselves off. Women need to cum, too, and I'm not trying to play any more games. I need one man, a man who can fulfill my every desire, whenever and wherever. You feel me?" she asked.

"Oh, I'm definitely feeling you. Roxie, you don't have to worry about a thing. After what happened that night at my party, when you saw that hooker the guys had hired, I was devastated."

"So was I. Like I said, I was planning on making it a special night. Instead, all I got was a broken heart."

"Roxie, I'm so sorry about that but—"

"Shh . . ." She held her pussy-scented finger up to my lips and I drew it in, licking her essence off of it. "Don't worry about it. Everyone makes mistakes and after growing up, I can understand how a boy your age would go for it."

I felt horrible as the memory of the expression on her face flooded back into my mind. If not for the fact that she went back to stroking my dick, I might've lost my erection and that would've been a shame because I could've knocked a ball out the park with the one I was sporting at that moment.

"You're right," I whispered. "Let's not talk about it anymore."

"Let's not," she agreed. "It's time for some serious fucking."

Six hours later, after we were both spent, and I was in awe of myself for hanging that long, we drifted off to sleep. I was happy, Dick was exhilarated, Roxie appeared sated, and Rayne Waters was a distant memory. I had finally snagged my Mrs. Right.

Eleven

The praise service was off the hook. People were stomping their feet, falling down on their knees, and doing the jig in the aisles between the pews. I thought Southern churches were off the hook, but Great Mount Bethel Holiness Church was the ultimate religious experience.

They didn't simply have the traditional organist. They had an entire band: two electric guitarists, a horn section, a keyboardist, and a drummer. What a drummer he was, too.

The first Sunday Chance and I attended service, I was so busy looking at him that I couldn't even remember what the sermon was about. He was tall, about six-two, with blue-black skin and black eyes that looked like opals. He had on a neatly pressed white dress shirt that complemented the darkness of his skin and a pair of navy dress slacks. I'd heard that church was a good place to meet men. The sisters never lie.

After church, Chance and I introduced ourselves to the pastor, Reverend Tom Russell. He looked ancient, about eighty, but had more energy than the two of us put together when he shook our hands in the line of churchgoers exiting through the front door.

Chance and I spent the rest of the afternoon at my apartment, watching football of course. I was the main one watching it. Chance fell asleep on the floor after she'd stuffed herself with the leftover chicken fajitas I'd cooked the night before. I had no business fixing them. Onions, peppers, and mushrooms don't agree with me. In fact, you could say they hate my guts. They definitely put a hurting on them. However, like most people, the things I shouldn't succumb to are the ones I can't live without.

When we returned to church the next week, I had this tremendous sexual fantasy about the drummer. I know it was wrong, but I could envision him ripping my clothes off right there on the altar and wearing my coochie out. Sitting there in the pew, listening to the choir praise the Lord, I had an intense orgasm. My toes curled up in my suede pumps. My eyes started fluttering around in my head. I balled my hands up into fists. It was so much of a shock that I started weeping.

Chance leaned over to whisper in my ear. "What's wrong with you? Why are you crying?"

I grabbed onto her forearm and struggled for words.

"Rayne, you need me to get one of the ushers? You want a fan or something?"

"No, I'm okay," I finally managed to reply. "I'm just so moved."

I let go of Chance's arm, leaving my finger imprints on her honey-almond skin. I took a few moments to regain some composure, struggling to get my breathing pattern back into a steady rhythm. Then I panicked. What if I'd cum hard enough to wet the bottom of my dress?

• • •

My dress survived that day; probably because it was heavy suede. My dignity didn't survive. I set out on a campaign to get that man. I found out his name was Basil. Basil Richardson. That was easy enough to find out. I asked one of the older women sitting beside me the following Sunday. She seemed so comfortable in the pew that I figured she'd been sitting in the same spot for the past five thousand Sundays.

I complimented the choir and band, putting special emphasis on the musical talent of the drummer. That was when she spilled all of his business. His name. The fact that he'd grown up in the church, received his eagle badge from participating in the Boy Scouts, sang a ton of solos in the junior choir, went away to North Carolina State for college, and returned home to D.C. to take over the family landscaping business from his ailing father, one of the people on the sick and shut-in list on the back of the church bulletin.

"Does his wife also attend Great Mount Bethel?" I asked on the sly.

"No, Basil's not married. A lot of the women in the church would love to settle him down, but no luck so far."

"That's good."

She eyed me strangely.

"No, I meant that's bad. As far as the women not being able to get him to settle down."

She smirked at me and opened her Bible to the scripture selection.

Against her wishes, I convinced Chance to start attending singles night every Tuesday at the church. Basil never showed up, but a bunch of desperate other men did. Men I wouldn't date in a million years.

So, we tried Bible Study on Wednesday. No Basil.

I debated about joining the adult choir, which practiced on Thursday. For sure, he'd be there. He had to be. However, being that I sounded like a sick hyena on crack when I belted out a tune, I'd decided that wasn't the best course of action. I was planning to seduce him; not make him go invest in earplugs. Sooner or later, an opportunity would present itself. It didn't turn out quite as I'd planned.

When they made the announcement about the Annual Senior Citizens' Appreciation Dinner, I knew Basil would be there. The entire congregation would fall all over themselves to show gratitude to their elders; myself included. Anyone who could deal with life's bullshit for more than sixty-five years was A-OK in my book.

Chance and I volunteered for the YAMs, the Young Adult Missionaries, who were sponsoring the dinner. I signed up to bring deviled eggs and a sweet-potato pie; store-bought of course because I couldn't bake canned biscuits without burning them. Chance was supposed to be making enchiladas. I'd warned her that the people at the church wouldn't even know what they were, being that Chance was one of the three Puerto Ricans attending the church. She'd insisted on making them anyway. I'd decided it was better for her to show up with enchiladas than for her not to show up at all.

The night before the dinner, which was to take place on a Saturday, I heard the weatherman on the ten o'clock news predicting an ice storm. *Bull,* I thought. There hadn't been a cloud in the sky when I'd come in from the grocery store.

The next morning, the city was blanketed with snow and ice. I called Chance to see if she was ready.

"Chance, you got those enchiladas all wrapped up? I'll be there in thirty minutes."

"Rayne, the roads are covered with ice!" Chance yelled into my ear.

"I can see that. It's no big deal. I drive extremely well in bad weather."

"Snow, maybe, but no one drives *extremely well* on a sheet of ice. I'm staying home."

"Oh no, you're not," I said sarcastically. "You better get your ass dressed and meet me in front of your building in thirty minutes."

Chance set the phone down. I could hear her cursing in Spanish. Ricky asked her what was wrong. Like me, he didn't know what the hell she was saying when she starting speaking Spanish a hundred words per minute.

"Rayne?" Ricky inquired, picking up the phone. "What's going on?"

"Chance is supposed to be going to church with me today for the Senior Citizens' Dinner and now she's trying to back out."

"Rayne, damn right she's backing out! I'm sure they'll reschedule the dinner anyway. No one in their right mind is going out in this weather."

Maybe he had a point. What if the dinner was canceled and we were the only fools that showed up?

"Tell Chance I'll call her later."

"Rayne, you're not going out, are you?" Ricky demanded to know. "Don't be silly."

I placed the handset down on the cradle and started searching for my keys.

When I *finally* pulled into the church parking lot, some two hours later when it should've taken less than thirty minutes, it was practically deserted. There were a few cars scattered here and there;

at different angles since you couldn't see the white lines dividing the spaces.

"No! No! No!" I screamed to myself, cutting the engine of my car. I was lucky I even still had a car. On the way over there, I'd slid no less than ten times and had almost done a three-sixty trying to stop for a red light. There was no way I was about to turn right around and go through the same hell again.

"Get a hold of yourself, Rayne," I said, trying to seek comfort in my own words. "There are *some* cars here. Simply go inside, relax, and see what's going on."

Someone had to be there. As long as I could get in, I could warm up and maybe even scrounge up a pot of coffee. After all, when all else fails, you're supposed to seek sanctuary in a church anyway.

I retrieved the Tupperware containers with my eggs and pie from the back seat. Yes, I was frontin'. I'd taken the pie out of the Giant box and had placed it in something else.

I opened my door and stepped out with my purse hung over one shoulder and the containers in my opposite arm. I took two baby steps and then fell flat on my ass, hitting my head against the car door. My deviled eggs and pie tumbled to the ground and slid about ten feet away on the ice. I was too through.

"Miss, do you need some help?"

I heard the baritone voice, but I couldn't see anyone.

My stockings had ripped and I had a nasty cut on my left knee. There I was sprawled on the ground in my Sunday best, when Basil Richardson walked right up to me and extended his hand.

"Can I help you up?"

You can help yourself to any damn thing you want!

"That would be great! Thanks!"

His strong arms lifted me effortlessly off the ground. I was relieved for two reasons. My ass was no longer in danger of turning into an ice cube and I was able to stare him directly in the eyes.

"Oh, my!" I heard myself saying.

He blushed, exposing the cutest dimples.

"Do you want to get back into your car or go inside?" he asked.

"No way am I getting back in my car. I barely made it here."

"Then grab onto me."

I held onto his sleeve and fearfully took a couple of steps before I started slipping again. This time I was saved by the brotha in the gray suit. He caught me by my armpits from behind. How foolish we must've looked.

"I'll tell you what," Basil said. "Even though you don't know me, would it be all right if I carried you into the church?"

"I do know you. You're the drummer from the band. Basil Richardson."

He blushed again. "And you are?"

"Rayne Waters," I answered, looking up at him over my shoulder. "I'd shake your hand, but it would be kind of difficult from this angle."

We both laughed. He swept me into his arms and carried me into the church apse. He sat me down gently and returned to the parking lot to recover my purse and food, the spikes on the bottom of his boots cracking through the ice like it was butter.

There were less than two dozen people at the Senior Citizens' Dinner, including Basil and me. We had a great time, listening to the elders—who had dared to brave the elements to get there—reminisce about the early 1900's. That was worth the trauma I'd gone through to get there. Their wisdom and Basil's looks, that is.

The food selections were minimal, but everyone enjoyed my deviled eggs; even though they'd lost their visual appeal. As for my pie, I had two different women ask me for the recipe. One of them said it reminded her of her deceased aunt's sweet-potato pie. I told them I'd make sure to get it to them before I left. Thankfully, they both left before I did and forgot they asked.

Basil and I sat beside each other. I kept grabbing his kneecap whenever he told a funny joke. I was really trying to feel his muscles up. He got up to get another cup of coffee and that finally afforded me the opportunity to scope out his behind. *Sold to the lady in the torn stockings and blue dress!*

"So, Basil, are you seeing someone right now?" I inquired as he carried me back to my car.

"No, not right now." He was quite the blusher; almost shy. "I'm working most of the time. That is, when I'm not in church."

We'd been over all the vitals already. Employment, general vicinity of residences (apartment in Georgetown, rowhouse near Walter Reed), ages, education, etc. Now it was time for the kill.

"Would you like to come over for dinner sometime? Next Friday, maybe?"

"I'd love to!" he exclaimed, placing me into the driver's seat. I had my purse and containers on my lap and I put them on the passenger's seat. "Want to trade numbers?"

"Certainly." I reached into my glove compartment, where I always keep a pen and pad, and scribbled down my number. He recited his number to me and I wrote it on the next page.

Returning home from Great Mount Bethel was much easier. Shockingly, the D.C. Department of Public Works had actually done something for a change. The sand trucks had done an incredible job of powdering the streets. I did have to watch out for the infamous potholes, more like sinkholes, the city was renowned for.

I called Chance to tell her my wonderful news. She said I was out of my damn mind to risk going out in an ice storm for some dick. Then she congratulated me for finally making some progress.

"Now if you could only get up enough nerve to talk to the brotha that comes into the bank," she hissed into the phone.

"Chance, puleeze!" I snapped back at her. "Basil's fine and it's only by pure luck that's he's single. But, that man from the bank is taken. Mark my words. He's probably married."

"Well, you need to find out. You're not a fucking psychic."

"Find out for what? Are you loco? Basil's coming over here for dinner on Friday. I'm going to rock his world, too."

"You're going to give it up on the first date?" Chance asked, like she'd never freaked a man she'd met less than five hours earlier at a club; two hours even.

"You know how long I've been trying to hook up with Basil. If something happens, it happens. That's all I'm saying."

When Chance and I got off the phone, I rifled through my stack of mail-order catalogs for the Black Sex Goddess one and started looking at their skimpy lingerie. After all, there was nothing wrong with pushing things along a little.

Twelve

Yardley

"Roxie, hold up! I need to get a glass of water."

Roxie was pulling another rough rider act on me, about to
amputate my dick with her pelvic muscles.

"Yardley, who needs water?" she asked incredulously.

"I do. I've never sweated this much in my entire life. Not even
when I shoot hoops with the fellas."

"Well, this isn't shooting hoops. This is fucking."

"I'm quite aware of that, thanks," I said, pushing her off me
and getting up from the moisture-ridden sheets. "I'll be back."

I headed out to my kitchen, my dick bouncing up and down,
condom and all.

Roxie started yelling at me from the bedroom. "Yardley, get
your ass back in here and finish me off."

I ripped the condom off and tossed it in the wastebasket,
washed my hands in the sink, and fixed myself an ice-cold glass of

H_2O. Roxie was a freak. I was beginning to wonder if a freak was really what I needed.

We'd been seeing each other for about four months. Things were great at first. After years of "what-ifs," I had the sister in my life that had kicked me to the curb way back in high school.

Besides, Roxie was a decent catch. She was educated, witty, and had a great job as an event coordinator for one of the largest marketing firms in the nation. Unfortunately, that meant attending event after event, benefit after benefit, week after week. All the late nights were beginning to take their toll on me. Roxie accompanying me home nine times out of ten to slay my dick was not benefiting my sleep either.

Don't get me wrong. Roxie and I had a lot of fun; tons of it. I was at the point where I was even considering settling down permanently. Yet I couldn't be sure. I kept telling myself that it was all about Roxie and me, but subconsciously I knew better. Part of me was still wondering about Rayne Waters.

While I'd cut back on my visits to First Community Bank considerably, I still insisted on making the deposits from time to time so I could catch a glimpse of her. After finally putting one set of what-ifs out of their misery, I was faced with another set to take their place. What if Rayne Waters wasn't taken? What if she was open to having lunch or dinner with me? What if we got to know each other better? What if we had a lot in common? What if she was better for me than Roxie? What if? What if? What if?

Gina was Roxie's best friend. What covenant of witches she was raised in, I'm still unsure. Maybe the Witches of the I-Know-I'm-the-Shit-So-Back-Up-Off-Me Covenant based out of Minneapolis. That's where she was from. Roxie had met her when she was out there in college. Gina still lived there, but had stacked up a shitload of frequent flyer miles traveling back and forth to see Roxie.

Naturally—since she was borderline fine—I'd tried to hook her up with one of the fellas. She wasn't having it. She refused to even give Felix some play; a first for him.

Gina wanted to sit up underneath Roxie all the time; *literally*. I'd show up at Roxie's place and Gina would be walking around in a skimpy tank top with no bra and a pair of French-cut briefs in the dead of winter. Roxie didn't seem to mind her girl showing off her goods in front of me. That made me nervous.

"Roxie, why is Gina always walking around half-naked?" I asked one evening over pizza at Armand's in Chevy Chase.

Roxie took another bite of her spinach and cheese garlic bread before answering. "Gina's not always walking around half-naked."

"Yes, she is. She's always half-naked when I come over to your place."

"And? I mean, I could see if one of my male friends was sitting on my couch in his drawers when you come over. That's different."

I swallowed the rest of my draft. "Maybe, maybe not."

"Wait one damn minute!" Roxie lashed out at me. "Are you implying that Gina and I have something freaky going on?"

"You said it; not me."

"This is crazy!"

"Well, do you have something freaky going on?"

"As much as I love dick? I think not. You of all people should know better."

Our waitress returned with the check. I handed her my credit card, never taking my eyes off Roxie. She looked like she wanted to wring my neck.

When the waitress walked away, Roxie continued. "Yardley, let me tell you something. Gina's my girl. If you can't deal with her, then you can't deal with me. It's as simple as that."

Was she serious?

"You'd dump me because of Gina?"

"If I have to, yes," she replied, not missing a beat. "Men come and go, but female friends, *true* female friends, are hard to come by. If it weren't for Gina, who would I shop with?"

"Me. I go shopping."

"It's not the same thing and you know it. That's like me playing basketball with you every Saturday instead of Felix and them."

Okay, so maybe she had a halfway valid point.

"Let's drop this. You still want to take in a movie?" I asked her.

"No, Yardley. I don't want to take in a movie. I'm ready to head on home."

"I asked a simple question. There's no reason to get an attitude."

"An attitude?"

Damn, why did I go there? Any brother over the age of twenty should know not to ever accuse a sister of having an attitude. That was the kiss of death.

"You accuse me of doing freaky shit with my best friend and expect me not to have an attitude? Nigger, please!"

Now I was pissed. "Roxie, please don't address me with the *N* word. I'm not that."

"You're acting like one tonight."

I paid the check and we left. I drove Roxie home in silence. I was a lot of things, but I was nobody's nigger. I didn't call Roxie for two weeks. She was on my shit list and would've remained on there if not for one thing.

She'd shown up at my penthouse in a trenchcoat toting a bag of sex toys, determined to prove to me that she loved herself some dick and nothing but the dick. Some brothers might consider what I did punking out, but those brothers have probably never been with a dick slayer.

Thirteen

Rayne

Luckily, Black Sex Goddess offered rush delivery on orders over fifty dollars. I ended up spending almost triple that on an outfit that was guaranteed to make Basil salivate. I bought a black-lace demi bra and matching thongs, garter belt, lace-top thigh-high stockings, and a pair of whorish-looking spike heels.

I went to From Naps to Baps to get my hair done on Thursday, as usual. Boom and I had grown apart somewhat. She knew her ass was wrong for setting me up with her convict brother. The first time I'd shown up for my appointment after the hideous date, she'd been full of questions; like he hadn't already told her everything or at least something. I decided to play her ass big time.

"So girl, how'd things go with Conquesto?" she asked me, sipping her customary Faygo while she was waiting on a curling iron to heat up so she could work her magic.

"Thank you so much for hooking a sister up," I replied.

That got everyone's attention. Yo-Yo, who was shampooing

someone in the rear of the salon, ended up spraying water all over the woman's face. Tamu paused in the middle of touching up someone's nails. Nia, tossing the remains of yet another Popeye's dinner in the trash, wiped her mouth with a napkin; no doubt trying to hide her smile.

"Really!" Boom squealed. "See, I knew you two was gonna hit it off smoothly."

"Oh yeah, we hit it off alright," I managed to say with a straight face. "Conquesto sure is a sexy man. You weren't lying about that."

"Uh-huh." Boom giggled, bouncing back and forth on the heels of her feet like she wanted to break dance. She looked around at her co-workers. "I told you guys Conquesto is the shit. Ya'll always tryin' to playa hate on him when he comes up in here."

More eyes rolled at that moment than tires on the Beltway during rush hour.

I sat back and let Boom rant and rave about her brother while she finished up my hair. Every time she made a statement about him, I made it a point to agree with her. After I paid her, I got down to business.

"Boom." I struck my time-to-whup-some-ass pose.

"Yeah, girl?"

"You know good and damn well Conquesto's a loser. Why'd you do that to me?"

She genuinely looked stunned. Great actress. Wrong audience. "What you talkin' 'bout, Rayne? You said you had a great time."

"I was being sarcastic."

"Sarcastic?" Boom pretended like the definition of the word escaped her.

"I know he's your family and all, but he's not the dream lover you market him to be. You need to refrain from doing any further matchmaking." I didn't say the words. I hissed them.

"I was tryin' to help you out!" she lashed out at me. "You're always comin' up in here lookin' all sexually repressed and shit!"

"First of all, I'm not sexually repressed," I stated with confidence, lying through my teeth. "Secondly, that's none of your damn business. If you want to date convicted felons, cool, but don't set me up with any."

"You don't have to worry about me doin' your ass any more favors."

Tamu leapt up from her manicurist table. "Dang, ya'll not about to kick off the shoes, take off your earrings, and break out the Vaseline, are you?"

Boom and I both glared at Tamu, who looked like she was ready to microwave some popcorn and empty out the Faygo machine to watch the female version of the Tyson-Holyfield fight. I couldn't help but laugh. My laughter set off a chain reaction and before long, everyone was laughing; even Boom.

Boom walked me to my car so we could discuss things womano a womano without a bunch of instigators around. Conquesto had come back and told her some BS about me wanting to fuck him but him refusing me because I seemed too desperate and he didn't want to set off a fatal attraction scenario.

By the time I finished breaking the entire date down for her—the real date and not the imaginary version he'd made up—she was surprised I hadn't slapped Conquesto upside his head. She obviously didn't like cheap-ass men either. She was pissed off about him asking me to purchase my own movie ticket.

For me, forgiving Boom was a necessity. I couldn't afford to lose a hellified hairdresser over a man. No way, José! We've never talked like we used to since the Conquesto fiasco, but I still feel comfortable enough to let her work on my hair.

• • •

While I stood there in the mirror primping for Basil, I admired the fantastic job Boom had done. I glanced at my clock. Fifteen more minutes before Basil was due to arrive. Decision time. Was it better to take the subtle approach and put something on top of the lingerie that would keep my sexual readiness at bay, or was it better to answer the door damn near naked and get straight to the point?

By the time my doorbell rang, I'd come to the conclusion that a head-on attack was the best course of action. I swung the door open, greeting Basil in my Black Sex Goddess getup. His jaw almost hit the floor. He had a dozen roses tucked safely under his arm. They almost hit the floor also, but he managed to hold onto them. His lips started trembling and he turned around and placed his back to me. He looked down at his wristwatch.

"I'm sorry, Rayne," he whimpered. "I must be early. I haven't given you time to get properly dressed."

Was he kidding?

"Umm, Basil, I am dressed," I replied seductively, reaching out in the hallway, grabbing him by the back of his shoulders, and pulling him back into me. I slipped my tongue into his ear canal and relieved him of the roses. "Are these for me?"

"Ye . . . ye . . . yes," he stuttered. "I thought you might like them."

"Of course, I like them. I'm female." I used my free hand, lifted his coat jacket, and started palming his ass. "All female." Basil started making these gurgling sounds. Scared the shit out of me. "You okay?"

"I'm . . . I'm . . . I'm fine."

I let go of his ass. "Turn around and look at me. I spent a lot of time and hard-earned money to make sure I looked good for you tonight. Appetizing even."

"I can't turn around," he whispered.

"Why not?"

"I have to go, Rayne." Basil was halfway down the hallway to the elevator before my name left his lips.

"Why are you leaving?" I shouted after him, totally confused. I took a few steps out into the hallway.

He jumped into the elevator and peeked around the corner. His eyes were watering and his lips were still trembling. "I'll call you tomorrow, Rayne. I promise."

I was stunned. *What the hell was going on?*

"I'm sorry, Rayne!" I heard him yell as the elevator doors eased shut.

I suddenly realized that I was standing exposed in the hallway and made a beeline for my door. As I was about to close my door, I saw it. I almost missed it because of the dark green carpet. I squatted down and touched it with my fingertips, drawing it up to my nose. It wasn't urine. It was exactly what I thought it was. It was semen.

"Damn, a virgin!" I yelled out with delight.

I ended up eating the Mongolian beef and escalloped potatoes alone, but I was relishing the thought of discovering a bonafide male virgin in his late twenties. He had to be a virgin. There was no other explanation for him squirting his pants like that when I'd barely touched him. No wonder he hadn't hooked up with anyone. That was cool by me, though. I was determined to turn Basil's ass out.

Chance and I spent the following afternoon in Georgetown Park Mall doing Chance's favorite pastime: shopping. I'd always ponder over the same outfit for two or three walk-bys before I purchased it. Chance spotted an outfit she liked and whipped out her credit card at the speed of lightning.

During a lunch/foot rest break at the deli, Chance was once again afforded the opportunity to get her laugh on at my expense.

"Chica, what the fuck is wrong with you? You keep picking up these whack ass men!"

"Basil isn't whack," I stated defensively, taking a bite of my chicken breast on wheat. "I think he's sweet and has a ton of potential."

"Potential?" Chance guffawed. "A twenty-nine-year-old male virgin?"

"Yes, I see this as a good thing. I can mold him into what I need in a man."

"You've been messing with that ciggaweed again, haven't you?"

"Chance, you know good and well I haven't messed with that since freshman year in college."

"Humph, ain't a damn thing wrong with smoking weed," she said, referring to the regular chronic she and Ricky partook of. Chance took a sip of her lemonade. "You're acting like you've been smoking something. Getting all worked up over a virgin. You need a man that's already been schooled on lovemaking; not some fool that cums in his drawers the second you touch his ass."

I ignored Chance and concentrated on my food. Once I made my mind up about something, it was a done deal.

"And to think you were sitting up in church fantasizing about getting some," Chance continued on her rampage. "All that over a man that's probably never seen a coochie, rather less eaten one."

"Chance, please!" I smacked my lips. "I'm trying to eat here."

Chance moved her potato salad around on her plate. It looked three days old and the mayonnaise had started to darken. "Didn't you spend a grip on some lingerie from that slut catalog?"

"Black Sex Goddess," I corrected her.

"Yeah, the slut catalog."

"Chance, look." I could feel myself getting angry. "I like Basil. If I want to take it upon myself to transform the brother, that's my business."

Chance fell out laughing. I didn't see a damn thing funny.

"Now what, Chance?"

"I was thinking about the idiots you've gotten tied up with since Will."

"Don't bring Will's name up, please!"

"Okay, whatever, but you must admit you've met some fucked-up men."

She had a point, but I wasn't even trying to hear it.

"First there was Gideon, that fool you met over the telephone who turned out to be old enough to collect Social Security."

I cracked a smile. That had been a ridiculous situation. I'd called to bless out a credit collection agency over a threatening notice I'd received that didn't pertain to me. The man who answered had this Barry White thing going on with his voice. I was immediately turned on.

For two months, we chatted on the telephone about this and that. Casual conversation turned into phone boning and phone boning turned into the yearning to actually hook up and do the wild thing. Only thing was Gideon said he was thirty-four, tall, handsome, and sporting a Jag.

The night I met him outside of Giant in Calverton, Maryland, a spot right off the Beltway so I could hop right back on if need be, I sat in my car waiting for him. It got to the point where I knew he'd stood me up. Then I took a closer look at the older man that had been leaning up against the pillar in front of the one-hour cleaners since I'd arrived. *Naw, it couldn't be,* I told myself. I couldn't overlook the fact that he had on a gray suit, the same color Gideon said he'd be wearing that day.

I exited my car cautiously, figuring the lighting was playing tricks on my eyes and the man was really buff and only a few years older than me. When I got within a few yards of him and he called out my name, exposing a set of dentures, I wanted to scream.

I couldn't leave Gideon there looking pitiful. After all, one should always respect their elders. Even my proud-to-be-a-whore momma taught me that. I psyched myself up to go through with the date. The date didn't last long; only until Gideon got arrested.

First, he tried to insist that we take my car. I told him that I was low on gas and that we should take his Jag, my eyes searching the parking lot for the candy red dream. That was when he *claimed* that his Jag was in the shop and he'd borrowed the car of a *friend* so he could make it out to meet me.

Turned out he was driving a banged up ancient Yugo. *Didn't they stop making those about twenty years ago?* We went all of five miles when Gideon asked if I wanted to skip dinner and go straight to a motel. I glared at him under the streetlights on Route 29 as we sped past each one. Beady, wrinkle-ridden eyes glared back at me. I was about to curse his ass out with a vengeance when blue lights started flashing behind us and the siren almost shattered my eardrums.

Gideon hesitated, like he was debating about pulling over. I immediately grew frightened and had to get my anus muscles under control so I wouldn't shit in my pants. Was he one of those men you only read about in newspapers and see featured on *America's Most Wanted*?

Gideon finally pulled over in front of an all-night golf driving range. I was elated that he'd picked that spot. Dozens of avid golfers were digging balls out of buckets and knocking them out on the grass to join thousands of their friends. The more witnesses to what was about to go down, the better. If Gideon were some kind of serial rapist or killer, he'd be more reluctant to start some drama in front of a bunch of people.

I willed the police officer to walk right up to the car, rip the driver's side door off the hinges (an easy feat with such a cheap-ass car), and yank Gideon out by the collar. He didn't. The usual "can I see your driver's license and registration" speech started spilling from his lips.

Gideon had frozen in place and then the lies started rambling off his lips. I was in awe of how fast he was making them up. His name wasn't Gideon anymore; it was Samuel. He wasn't thirty-four anymore; he was fifty-eight. No, he didn't have the registration. No, he didn't have his license on him. No, he couldn't recall his Social Security number. *What kind of game was this man running?*

The police officer must've been wondering the same thing. He instructed Gideon to step out the car, frisked him, threw the cuffs on him, and called for backup. He escorted me out the car, at which point I quickly started delving out the facts. I'd only actually met him that night. He was someone I knew from the phone. He'd told me the car was a friend's. He was known to me as Gideon; not Samuel.

The officer told me to have a seat in his car while he and the other officer who'd arrived searched the Yugo for drugs, guns, or whatever. They said they had no choice but to take Gideon in. He tried to argue with them, but unless he could prove who he was, he was headed to lockup. And to lockup he went, with me trailing a safe distance behind in a second squad car. The police officer told me I should've considered myself extremely lucky that he pulled us over for a busted taillight because anything could've happened. I agreed.

When I arrived at the station house, they directed me to a pay phone where I called Chance and asked her and Ricky to come pick me up out in the middle of nowhere. I went to the 7-Eleven next door to get some coffee while I waited. They showed up an hour later.

Chance wasted no time going off on me in Spanish. Ricky tried to drown her out with his latest bootleg go-go tape, but Chance wasn't having it. After a volume-button battle, Chance finally turned the music completely off. I endured her rampage all the way back to Georgetown.

"You're lucky that Gideon bastard didn't rape your ass and leave you somewhere in a ditch," Chance said, reprimanding me. "Jaguar, my ass."

"Chance, I'd rather forget about that entire thing."

"Shit, even the Yugo wasn't his. That whore of his called you the next day and said it was hers."

"Chance, I don't need you to remind me of what happened."

Some sister named Wanda, the true owner of the lovely ride, discovered my number on a napkin the morning after when she retrieved her car from the impound lot where it had been towed. She went on and on about how Gideon was a con artist and how he had warrants out on him and that was why he didn't want to give his real name. I wanted to ask her if she knew all that already, why was she allowing him to use her car. I didn't want any more drama so I simply thanked her for the information and hung up.

Gideon tried calling me collect from jail several times. I was at the phone company to have my number changed when they opened Monday morning.

"You know who you need to be going after."

"Who?"

"That fine ass man from the bank."

I started blushing. *If only.* "Chance, I keep telling you that any man that damn fine is taken."

Chance shrugged her shoulders. "Maybe Yardley's taken. Maybe he's not."

"Yardley?" *Was that his name?*

"Yes, Yardley. I walked right up to him the other day while you were in the bathroom and asked his name."

"Girl, no!" I squealed, wondering what else was said.

"Yes, I did. His name's Yardley Brown and he's a chiropractor."

"Really?"

"Yes, really," Chance replied, smacking her gums. "I don't know if he's hooked up with someone, but he's definitely not married."

"You asked him?"

"Damn sure did."

"Did he think you were trying to pick him up?"

"I doubt it. He giggled and shit like he thought it was funny. He asked me if I needed anything else and I said no. That was it."

"I can't freakin' believe you, Chance."

"Believe it. Also, believe this. If you don't make a move on that man soon, I'm going to do it for you."

"I can't, Chance."

"You better. You've been forewarned."

I couldn't take another bite of my food. I was too excited. Yardley Brown. What a nice name.

Fourteen

Yardley

Super Bowl Sunday. All my boys were in the hizzzhouse! I had fools up in my penthouse I hadn't seen since we were all sporting hi-top fades like Kid and Play. Jackson, an old buddy from high school and deli manager at a local Giant, had hooked me up with some discounted platters of buffalo wings, vegetables, shrimp cocktail, and finger sandwiches shaped like little footballs.

Gina was in town, of course, sitting all up under Roxie as usual like she was feeding off her breasts. At least Gina did help cook. Roxie, who normally couldn't fry an egg—except possibly from the flames shooting out her pussy—actually broke out a recipe book and made some deviled eggs and potato salad. Damn shame she needed a book for that, but I wasn't complaining.

My Redskins were playing the Cowboys that day. I had more than five hundred bucks spread all over town in bets that they'd win by at least a dozen points. So what if the Cowboys had beaten the Skins twelve out of the last thirteen times they'd played. It was time for revenge and I didn't plan to miss a second of it.

Roxie had her Usher CD streaming through the sound system in the walls. It was annoying me—the CD itself was slamming but that day was all about football—but it was no more annoying than the loud ass chatter going on. There had to be at least forty people up in my place, but that was the way I'd envisioned it. Food, beer, football, a winning combination.

Some of my buddies had fine ass women with them, some of them had hood rats, and some showed up solo. It was all good. Felix shocked everyone by showing up alone. That was definitely a first. I teased him about it when I opened the door.

"Couldn't find a date?" I teased.

Felix pushed past me and into the foyer. "Man, please! I can get any woman I want. I want to kick back and enjoy the game today."

"Yeah right, man. Whatever!" I chuckled, following him into my living room.

Felix turned around and whispered in my ear so the others couldn't hear him. "You know I'm always trolling for pussy. I'm about to troll for some up in here so I have something to do after the game."

"Good luck. Every female in here is on lockdown except for Gina. Then again, since she's a troll she might be the one for you. Oh, I forgot, she did turn you down. There goes your 'I can get any woman I want' theory."

Felix fell out laughing. "Puddy is puddy, Yardley. Even troll pussy. One day you'll grow up, son, and recognize that. If I really wanted Gina, she'd be riding me like it's going out of style by the end of the night. She's not my type."

"Like I said, whatever, man!"

· · ·

By halftime, the Redskins were up by ten points and I was in heaven. I'd managed to drown everyone and everything out except for my sixty-inch high-definition television.

"Yardley, telephone." Gina tapped me on the shoulder and then handed me the cordless. If it wasn't halftime, I wouldn't have even taken the call.

"This is Yardley."

"Yardley, you throw one hell of a football party, man!" a voice screamed into my ear.

It was my boy, Kurt. A friend from undergrad at Howard.

"Hey, and you know this, man! Only thing we need here now is you. What's taking you so long?"

"I'm stuck in traffic, bro. I'm a few blocks away; enjoying the view at the moment."

"Forget a view. Come check out the game. We have a ton of food and all the beer you can drink." I wanted Kurt to hurry his ass up so I decided to embellish the truth somewhat. "Lots of fine honies up in here, too."

"I can see that." He chuckled into the phone. "Why didn't you tell me you were throwing a freakfest? I would've brought a little sumptin' sumptin' with a tight ass along with me."

He'd completely lost me. How could he possibly know what kind of women were lounging around my crib when he'd yet to step over the threshold?

"Kurt, what the hell are you talking about?"

"I'm talking about the serious sex action taking place on your balcony, bro." Kurt started panting in the phone. If I didn't know better, he sounded like he was whacking off in his car. "Damnnnnnnnnnnnnnn, he's tearing that pussy up! Is that Felix?"

I scanned my place and didn't see Felix anywhere. He'd been profiling on my leather sectional less than ten minutes earlier. I got up and started for the balcony, throwing the phone on the ottoman and leaving Kurt hanging on the other end.

"Yardley, you got any more chips?" Mike asked as I walked past him.

"Yeah, there's some in the kitchen."

I did a head count of the women on my way to the sliding glass doors. All ladies were present and accounted for except for one; my own.

I stepped out on the balcony and braced myself before I looked to the right. I gave a sigh of relief when no one was there. Kurt was trying to fuck with my mind. I was about to break out in laughter and then I heard the moans. I turned around.

"What the fuck is this?" I roared, seeing nothing but Felix's ass muscles flexing as he worked his dick in and out of Roxie. "Roxie?"

Felix had been holding Roxie up spread eagle against the adobe brick but let her fall. She managed to prevent herself from toppling and pulled the bottom of her dress down. Her panties were flung over the railing. I was sick to my stomach.

"Yardley, I can explain, man." Felix walked over to me and tried to lay his hand on my shoulder. I stepped back away from him. "We didn't mean for this to happen. Not at all."

"You say that shit now, Felix," Roxie hissed, looking like the cat that swallowed the canary. She was actually enjoying being caught. *What a tramp!* "You've been after me for months. For that matter, you've been trying to fuck me since high school. Don't front."

Jackson poked his head around the corner. "Shit, Felix and Roxie out here fucking! You gotta come peep this!"

"Oh, shit!" I heard someone exclaim.

"Let me see!" someone else hollered out.

"Move so I can look!" yet another voice blurted out.

Within seconds, my balcony was packed like a school parking lot during a fire drill.

"Felix, you low-down piece of shit!" Mike yelled.

I didn't have shit to say. I wanted to be alone.

"Excuse me." I pushed my way through the crowd, seeking refuge in my bedroom. "Can I get through please? This is my fucking place."

"Yardley, come here, baby!" Roxie called out after me. She caught up to me and tugged at the back of my shirt.

"Stay the hell away from me, Roxie," I said, pulling myself free from her grasp. "I can't deal with this now!"

I went into my bedroom, slammed and locked the door.

"Yardley! Yardley, open the door, bro!" Felix demanded, banging on the cedar.

I punched the door and then sat on the bed, my hands still balled into tight fists. "Everyone get the fuck out!" I screamed out.

"You heard the man!" The militant side of Dwayne came out. He bellowed at people like he was playing the lieutenant in a military flick. "Everyone get to stepping! Roxie, that means your skank ass, too! Make some fuckin' tracks and don't fuckin' look back!"

"Dwayne, you can't talk to me like that!" I heard Roxie complain.

"I just did! Party's over! Grab a sandwich and a beer and take them with you!"

I could hear people being shuffled away from my bedroom door and over the next few minutes, the noise and chatter tapered off. I stuck my head out the door and didn't see anyone but Mike and Dwayne. Both Felix and Roxie were gone. Then Kurt showed up, a day late and a dollar short.

"Hey, Kurt! Bye, Kurt!" Mike said.

"Damn, what happened? Was that Felix and Yardley's girl out there?" Kurt asked in wonderment.

"Hell yeah, it was!" Dwayne exclaimed.

"Shit!"

"Party's over, Kurt." Mike pushed Kurt gently toward the door.

"What about the game?" Kurt asked, still expecting to chill out and get his eat and drink on.

"Fuck the game! Go watch it at a bar or something!" Mike slammed the door in Kurt's face.

I remained in my room for the rest of the game. Mike and Dwayne were *so-called* whispering, but I only missed about two words. An expensive penthouse and thin ass walls.

"Yardley, you want me to stay? I could spend the night," Mike finally offered through the door.

"No, I want to be alone."

"You sure?"

"Positive."

"Aiight, man. Peace out."

"Peace out."

They let themselves out and I stared up at the ceiling. I was pissed at Roxie. No damn doubt about that. Felix had genuinely hurt me, though, and it wasn't the first time. First he'd spread my business in the streets about Sheila and now this. *What the fuck was up with him?*

My mind drifted to her again. Rayne Waters. Her friend, Chance, had approached me in the bank the week before and played twenty questions. I was overwhelmed because I could tell she was on a fact-finding mission for her fine ass friend. I didn't pursue the possibilities. I had Roxie to think about and I'd already betrayed Roxie once in high school with a hooker named Angel. No way was I going to intentionally hurt her again. Instead, she'd hurt me. She'd fucked my best friend during a social gathering at my home. No, Roxie had to go. Her ass was grass.

I called information and got Rayne's number. Since she worked downtown, I took a chance that she lived in D.C. and not in the suburbs. The commute would've been insane, even though hundreds of thousands of people did it daily. There was only one Rayne Waters listed, which came as no surprise since her name was so unusual.

I picked up the phone no less than five times before I finally worked up the nerve to punch in her number. Just my luck, I got her machine.

"Hello. You've reached Rayne. I'm not in right now. I'm at the ESPN Zone watching America's Team kick some Redskin *be-hind*. If you're a Cowboys fan, you're welcome to leave a message. If you're not, then I guess this simply isn't your day. Later."

I had no idea what to say. Her voice was so damn sexy. The first time I'd actually heard it. I hung up a few seconds after the beat. That was all wrong. Leaving a message on her home phone when we'd never held any form of conversation at the bank was inappropriate. I didn't want her to think I was a stalker. I didn't know a damn thing about the sister except she was fine, but I knew I wanted her to be a part of my life. I'd wanted that for a long time and now that it appeared she was available also, nothing and no one was going to stand in my way. However, if she and I were going to become an item, she'd have to give up the damn Cowboys and convert to a Redskin.

Fifteen

Basil and I had a ball at the ESPN Zone. The plush leather seats and walls full of televisions provided the ultimate viewing experience. The Cowboys won the game 35–14 and I was floating on air as we walked around the corner of my building. I was damn near skipping down the street.

After much discussion, Basil and I had mutually decided that it was in our best interest to remain friends. We'd hung out a few more times since his *accident* and he was a really cool individual. His only drawback being that he wanted to remain a virgin until he was married. I truly admired that and I told him as much. However, I was blunt with him. I needed sexual stimulation on a regular basis and I wasn't willing to get married sight or, in this case, dick unseen.

Once Basil realized I wasn't going to jump his bones, he relaxed and enjoyed our little escapades. We'd go out, he'd bring me home, stay about ten or fifteen minutes, and then break out.

Since Chance was Ricky-whipped, it was good to have someone else to hop around the District with. I had a few other local girl-friends but most of them were always on a date, going away for the weekend, or busy trying to climb up the corporate ladder.

Basil had barely left when my phone rang.

"Hello, this is the Washington, D.C., Dallas Cowboys fan club," I yelled into the phone. "Can I help you?"

"Rayne? Is that you?"

I recognized the voice immediately. Sexy, sexy.

"Hey, Kahlil," I said seductively, lowering my voice.

Kahlil Peterson was my version of Mr. All That. When Chance and I had first started working at the bank, Kahlil was the head teller and our direct supervisor. A little over six feet tall, hazelnut skin, and slanted charcoal eyes. Too damn fine.

Of course, trying to get with him was out of the question. You never shit where you eat. That didn't stop me from fantasizing about him day and night. He was one of the funniest people I'd ever met; always greeting Chance and me in the morning with the joke of the day. Kahlil was one of those people that everyone, male and female alike, got along with.

When he left to take a job with a competitor, I couldn't blame him since it meant a promotion and raise; something First Community Bank had been slow to come up off of. I'd missed him terribly. To have him call me after the game of the decade only added to my great mood.

"Rayne, I'm sorry to call you up out of the blue."

"Don't mention it, Kahlil. It's good to hear your voice." *Damn, was it!* "What's new?"

"Not much. What about yourself? You still at First Community?"

"Yes," I answered. "Chance and I are both still there."

"Chance. How's she doing?"

"Great."

"She still hanging with Ricky?"

"Uh-huh, they're still together."

"Cool."

I unlaced my FUBU sneakers and slid out of them, kicking them off in the hallway on the way to my bedroom.

"So . . ." Kahlil said hesitantly. "What about you? Are you seeing someone?"

I froze in time with one arm pulled out of my sweater and the zipper on my jeans halfway down. Kahlil was inquiring about my status. *Go Rayne! It's your birthday! It's your birthday! It's your birthday!*

I cleared my throat to prevent myself from sounding too anxious. "No, I'm not seeing anyone," I replied casually. "I was seeing someone a while ago, but things didn't pan out."

"His name was Will, right?"

I almost bit my tongue. "Yes, that was his name all right."

"Well, his loss, my gain."

"Is that right?" I giggled.

"Rayne, I know this is going to sound insane but I wanted to ask you to attend a dinner at my parents' house next weekend."

I was stunned. "Kahlil, can you hold on a second?"

"Sure?"

I tossed the cordless on my bedspread and finished taking off my sweater and jeans. I pulled down the covers and climbed onto the cold sheets, hoping they'd warm up with a quickness.

"I'm back," I said.

"Good. I was beginning to think I'd scared you off."

I laughed. "I was getting undressed and into bed. I just got in from the game."

"Oh, you went to a bar?"

"The ESPN Zone. Been there?"

"No, but I've been wanting to check it out."

"You definitely should." There was a brief silence. "If you want, we could check it out together."

"Sounds good." I could hear a door slamming somewhere in the background. "What about dinner?"

"Don't get me wrong, Kahlil. I'd love to spend some time with you and get to know you better. I was craving to do that the entire time we worked together. I think you knew that, didn't you?"

He chuckled and I could imagine him blushing. "Kind of."

"I'm not sure dinner at your parents' is the right atmosphere for us to get intimate."

Kahlil sighed into the phone. "Can I be honest?"

"Certainly."

"I took the liberty of telling my parents that I've been seeing this great woman for several months and I've really played the whole thing up."

"Ah, let me guess." It was becoming clear. "There's no woman and now that there's a family dinner in the works for you to pre-sent her to the world, you need someone to present?"

"I'm totally embarrassed by this but, yes, that's it exactly."

I couldn't help but be amused. On top of that, I was flattered. Out of all the women I was sure Kahlil knew casually, he'd chosen me to be the type to take home to his momma.

"Sure, I'll do dinner."

"Really?" Kahlil yelled in the phone. I could hear the relief in his voice. "That's great, Rayne."

"What day and time would you like for me to be ready?"

"Saturday at six."

"I'll be waiting."

"Thanks, Rayne."

"No biggie."

"Goodnight."

"Goodnight."

I was about to call Chance to spill the news, but a sporadic dial tone alerted me to messages waiting. I dialed into my voice mail service and there were two calls from Momma wanting more cash and one strange one. Someone was only breathing on the line for a few seconds and then hung up. I assumed it must've been Kahlil since my Caller ID registered my last two calls as "Blocked ID." He'd probably called one time earlier and didn't want to leave a strange message. No matter. I was simply happy as hell that he'd called back.

Boom hooked my do up once again. When Kahlil showed up Saturday evening, I was ready to make my official debut as his woman. I went out and purchased a three-hundred-dollar suit, which was totally absurd behavior for me. If it meant winning Kahlil over and, better yet, his parents so they'd sweat him about getting serious with me, then it was well worth it.

I was waiting out front when Kahlil pulled up in his Volvo; another first. I never wanted to seem pressed about a date, but I was standing there anxiously with a grin on my face when he pulled up. When I spotted another brother in the passenger seat, I was shocked. Granted his friend was fine. I couldn't help but notice when he got out of the front and hopped in the back. Kahlil got out the car also, walked around, and held the door for me. I reached out my arms to hug him, but didn't even get so much as a kiss on the cheek in return.

He introduced his friend as Oliver. Oliver was golden honey with brown dewdrop eyes and an aquiline nose. I could see Chance hooking up with him right off the bat, if Ricky weren't in the picture.

The ride out to Kahlil's parents' house in Alexandria, Virginia, was a pleasant one. Oliver did most of the talking. He'd moved to the D.C. area less than a year before from San Diego and was struggling to get his PhD from American University. Kahlil seemed kind of preoccupied. I wondered what all that was about.

"You okay, Kahlil?" I asked him.

He took his eyes off the road long enough to flash me a cinematic smile. "I'm fine. Just wondering if we need to go over a few things before we get there."

Oliver started chuckling in the back seat. Obviously, he knew Kahlil planned on passing me off as his longtime girlfriend; even though we hadn't seen each other in ages.

"What types of things?"

"How long we've been together, where we met, those sorts of things," Kahlil replied.

"You think your parents are going to ask me all that?" I felt a sharp pang in my stomach. I hadn't thought of the possibility when I'd accepted his invitation.

"I'll try to keep them away from you."

Oliver was still laughing. "Kahlil, you're going to scare Rayne. With hundreds of people at the party, your mother won't have time to go for the jugular."

Jugular? Was Kahlil's momma a queen bitch or something?

Kahlil turned the radio up and Nina Simone cranked through the speakers the rest of the way there. We pulled into a long, circular driveway and pulled up to a palatial home. There were dozens of cars parked on the spacious lawn and three valets standing out front to do the honors.

I was glad I'd parted with the cash to buy an expensive outfit. It made me feel better when I met "the folks." Rich and phony; an interesting combination. Luckily, they barely said ten words to me between the two of them. His mother simply looked me over and made no effort to mask her actions. His father zeroed in on my bustline, licked his lips, kissed my hand, and then headed into another direction.

Oliver seemed to be having more fun than anybody. He danced with practically every available woman in the place; from twenty to eighty-five. I was checking him out big time for myself. I was crazy about Kahlil, always had been, but Oliver looked like he could show a woman a good time.

I was lost in the buffet for most of the night. I hadn't seen a spread like that since a Christmas party I'd attended a few years ago at a bonafide billionaire's home. Rack of lamb, crab meat parmesan canapés, roast duck, braised veal with green olives and capers, vegetables in spicy cream sauce, parisienne apples with calvados butter. It went on and on as far as my eyes could see. Throughout the night I tried a little of everything, vowing that I'd utilize my lifetime membership at Bally's the next morning and endure at least two step classes.

I was nursing a pink pony, beginning to feel the effects of the tequila, when the live band finally played a song I was feeling. I surveyed the room, searching for Kahlil so we could take a spin around the dance floor but he was nowhere in sight. Neither was Oliver.

I ventured out of the ballroom and explored the mansion. The farther I got away from the center of the party, the quieter it became. I was about to forget about looking for them and head back to the party when I heard a noise coming from the end of the hall.

After pushing open a set of French doors, I saw them. Oliver and Kahlil were tonguing the shit out of each other in front of this painting of a woman that was larger than both of them. They didn't see me, thank goodness. I wouldn't have known what to say. I'd seen a lot of things in my life up until that point, but I'd never seen two men slobbering each other down. I watched for a few minutes in silence, my feet glued to the floor. Then I high-tailed it out to the parking area where I begged one of the valets for a ride. He said he didn't have a car. I convinced him that it would be all right to *borrow* a car from one of the guests since the party was still in full swing. All he saw was pussy potential, but I didn't care as long as I made it home.

I had him drop me off on the corner of Wisconsin and M, gave him a fake number, and then walked the rest of the way home. Kahlil had left three messages on my voice mail, wanting to know why I'd left the party. I was so disappointed, I cried. I was sick of men. I didn't really fault Kahlil. He was what he was and felt obligated to put up a pretense in front of his parents. He could've been open with me and I probably still would've gone with him. After all, it was hard as hell for me to tell anyone "no" about anything. But he shouldn't have let me get my hopes up about the two of us. *Why did men always insist on playing games with me?*

That was it. I was done with all the foolishness. All the good men were taken, scooped up by sisters who had determined what they wanted and needed early enough in life to still grab a decent one while the grabbing was good. I wondered what lucky sister had snagged Yardley Brown. Now he was definitely a keeper.

He came into the bank on Monday, looking like he'd stepped out of *GQ* magazine. Chance cleared her throat and pointed in his direction, as if I could miss his fine ass. He had on a perfectly tailored black suit and a wool overcoat. His hair had been freshly cut. I noticed he was growing a goatee. Sexy as sin.

He did the usual. Waited in line at the teller window for next available and then made a deposit. He was on his way out the door when he stopped dead in his tracks, turned in our direction, and walked straight over to my desk.

I started shuffling some papers around, trying to look busy. I was a nervous wreck.

"Excuse me, Miss. I was wondering if you could assist me with something."

I looked up into his eyes and almost creamed in my panties. He was ten times, a hundred times, finer up close.

"Yes . . . yes . . . yes . . . ," I stammered. "What can I do for you, Mr.? . . ."

I already knew his name, but didn't want him to know that Chance had reported back to me after her inquisition.

"Brown. Yardley Brown." He extended his hand and I took it. It was strong, but he had very soft skin.

"Rayne Waters." I motioned to the chair across my desk. "Please have a seat."

"Thanks."

He sat down and his cologne invaded my nostrils. All I could think about was licking him. I told myself to gain some control. While not married, according to Chance, he was definitely involved.

We stared each other down for about thirty seconds. It was the longest thirty seconds of my life. I broke the gaze, straightening up my desk and folding my hands on top of my desk pad.

"Mr. Brown, how can I help you today?"

"I'd like to reorder some checks."

"Oh, well, you could've done that at the teller window. It's a really simple process, if you're getting the same type and number sequence. However, I'd be more than happy to take care of it for you. It won't take but a moment."

"Actually, I'd like to look at the others you have available. I feel like I need a change in my life."

For the next fifteen minutes, I showed him the binders full of designs for checks; everything from angels to athletic teams. He finally decided on a modern design and I helped him complete the paperwork. He was indeed a chiropractor, which explained the soft hands. Who wants ashy hands all over them?

"Well, that should take care of it," I informed him.

"Can I ask you a question, Rayne?"

"Certainly, Mr. Brown."

"Please call me Yardley."

"Okay."

I glanced over at Chance and she was hanging on every word.

"Are you seeing anyone right now, Rayne?"

I almost fell out. He was coming on to me.

"Uh, no, not really." I didn't want to seem desperate so I added, "I do have friends but I'm not seriously involved."

"Me either."

Was he for real? How could a man that fine be unshackled?

"Rayne, I was wondering if you'd like to take in dinner or a movie sometime. Maybe a play. There's a new one down at the Warner Theater. The latest one from the Destiny Wood National Theater Group."

Chance was about to pop her eyeballs out to get my attention, mouthing the words "go for it."

"I'm sorry, Mr. Brown, but I don't engage in flirting with customers of the bank. It appears unprofessional."

Chance yanked her index finger across her throat, putting me on alert for the beatdown she planned to dole out later.

"I see," Yardley responded, looking like someone had already slashed his throat. "And here I thought I'd found the lady of my dreams."

I started shuffling some papers around on my desk again, adding his check reorder form to my outbox so it could go to the correct department for processing. I looked up at him and his sexy ass eyes and melted.

"I do wish you the best in finding the young lady of your dreams. You're very attractive and you seem to have it together, so finding a mate should be a breeze."

Damn, why did I say that? Here was the man of my own dreams, asking me out, and I was turning him down because of work ethics. Or was it simply old-fashioned fear?

"No, it's definitely not a breeze," he corrected me, standing up and putting on his wool overcoat.

"Under different circumstances, I'd consider getting to know you better myself. I do know a good thing when I see it." To this day, I still don't know where those words came from but I was definitely flirting with him.

"Different circumstances?" he asked excitedly. "So, if we were to run into each other someplace else, say the grocery store or out on the street, you'd talk to me?"

"Rayne, shut the hell up!" my insecure side screamed up my ear canal.

"Yes, I'd say that's a safe bet," I replied.

"Well, I better get back to my office. Thanks for assisting me with my checks."

I stood up to shake his hand. "It was a pleasure."

Yardley started for the door and Chance wasted no time jumping up to come over to my desk. I was hoping she didn't plan to lay me out in Spanish.

Before she could open her mouth, Yardley turned around and came back.

"After work today, around five, I think I'll check out that new bagel place a couple of blocks away. Bagels by the Bag. Ever been there?"

"No, can't say that I have."

"I hear they have the most delicious coffee," he said, eyeing me seductively. "Maybe you should try it out sometime. Maybe even today."

Chance elbowed me in the side and pinched my arm. I yanked my arm free.

"Maybe I will."

Yardley started backing away from us. "Have a nice afternoon."

"You, too."

He walked out and paused outside of the window long enough to wave. Chance and I both waved back.

"Rayne, if you don't go to that bagel place tonight, I'm going to kick your fucking ass!" Chance warned me.

I plopped down in my desk chair. I'd been through so much shit lately with Will, Basil, and Kahlil; even Conquesto. I'd always told myself that I'd judge each man individually, but saying it and doing it were two entirely different things. The bottom line was that an opportunity had presented itself. I didn't embarrass myself by going after Yardley. He'd taken the leap of faith and come after me. The only question was would I leave him hanging.

Love is life. And if you miss love, you miss life.

—Leo Buscaglia

Sixteen

Yardley

I couldn't believe I'd done that. Then again, I couldn't believe I hadn't done it sooner. Rayne Waters had invaded my thoughts for a long time. It was time to see where her head was.

I went back to my office and saw my afternoon patients, glancing at the wall clock or my watch every thirty seconds. Five o'clock couldn't get there fast enough for me. If Rayne showed, that meant we could at least explore the possibilities. If she stood me up, then I'd know she simply wasn't interested and I'd have Lisa make all the deposits from that moment on.

I got to Bagels by the Bag at four-thirty. I couldn't wait until five. I was worried she might show up early, see I wasn't there, and leave before I even arrived. I peered inside and the place was deserted; except for a teenager with freckles behind the counter.

I paced the sidewalk out front for ten minutes before deciding I looked ridiculous. I went down to the newsstand on the corner and browsed the latest sports magazines. There were a ton of them I hadn't heard of before. It seemed like every sport from golf to cycling had its own monthly. The days of *Sports Illustrated* cornering the market were over.

I spotted Rayne in the crosswalk at three minutes to five. I started to dash for the door of Bagels by the Bag so I could beat her inside. I didn't want to seem hard up so I let her go in first, but I was right on her tail.

When I came in she was standing in front of the long glass case inspecting the different varieties available. I walked up close enough behind her to smell her vanilla-scented shampoo. I could see her reflection in the glass and she was eyeing me.

"Excuse me, this is my first time here and I was wondering if you could suggest a flavor," she said. It was music to my ears. "I always have such a difficult time making up my mind when there's so much to choose from."

I tried not to laugh at her little game. She actually intended to pretend like we'd never met.

"This is my first time here also. However, the cinnamon raisin ones look delicious."

"I hate raisins," she replied, glancing over her shoulder at me.

I locked that into my memory so I could fantasize about her later that night, glancing over her shoulder at me while I was riding her from behind. I had no grand illusions about taking her home with me from the shop. She definitely wasn't the type, nor was that the type I was looking for.

"The sesame look good, too."

"Yes, they do. Sometimes sesame seeds get stuck in my throat though. I wouldn't want to choke."

"No, we definitely don't want that." I moved to her side and tapped my index finger on the case. "Ever tried garlic parmesan bagels?"

"No, I try to stay away from garlic." She giggled. "They say it's healthy but it causes bad breath."

"True, and you never know when some stranger might kiss you out of the blue. You always want to make a good first impression."

She blushed. She was so damn gorgeous. "I think I'll have a plain bagel with vegetable cream cheese."

"Plain? All of these choices and you're going with a plain?" I chided her.

She grinned and batted her long eyelashes at me. "I always like to proceed on the side of caution."

"Can I help you, sir?" the teenage employee asked.

"Yes, I'd like two plain bagels with vegetable cream cheese," I told him, not wanting to risk bad breath either.

"For here or to go?"

"For here." I turned to Rayne. "You don't mind if I buy yours, do you? I haven't done my good deed yet for today and I can't go to sleep at night knowing that I missed an opportunity."

Rayne rubbed her shoulder up against my arm teasingly. "I wouldn't want to be the cause of you losing any sleep, so buy away."

"Would you like some coffee to go with that?"

"Actually, I'll take a cup of hot chocolate."

I held up a peace sign to the teen. "Two hot chocolates."

After he'd put our bagels and hot chocolates on a tray, Rayne said, "Thanks."

"Don't mention it. Listen, since it's so crowded in here, do you mind if I share a table with you?"

We were the only customers in the place. The teen looked at me foolishly.

"No, I don't mind. I'm surprised to see so many people in here at this time of day. Besides, it's vitally important to share. That's one of the first things we're taught as children."

"By the way, my name is Yardley. Yardley Brown."

We shook hands.

"Rayne Waters."

The game continued after we sat down by the window.

"So Rayne, what do you do for a living?"

"I work at the First Community Bank. Customer Relations Specialist."

"Aw, I happen to have an account there."

"Really?" Rayne giggled. "Small world."

"Very, very small world."

"How do you pay your bills?"

"I'm a chiropractor."

"Wow, I've never met a chiropractor before. You help people improve their posture and straighten their spines?"

"Among other things. Maybe I can show you my office one day. You might find it interesting."

"I'm sure I would."

Both of us picked at our bagels. I don't think it was bad nerves, but excitement. At least that's what it was on my part.

"Can I be frank?" I asked her.

"I wouldn't want it any other way."

"You're the most beautiful sister I've seen this year."

She leered at me like she thought I was full of shit.

"Hmm, I guess it's a good thing you saw me this year."

"Why's that?"

"If I'm the most beautiful for only *this* year, then last year's competition must've been fierce."

"Well, I didn't want to use the 'in my entire life' line because I figured you wouldn't believe me."

"But I'd believe a year is more reasonable?" she asked sarcastically. "Besides, we're barely into this one so you'll probably still find someone more beautiful."

"You're a clever girl!" I couldn't withhold my laughter. "I can see I'm going to have to watch what I say around you."

"Only for the next fifteen minutes. Then, I'll walk out that door and I guess we'll never see each other again."

The mere thought of her walking away sent a chill through me. The only plus was that I knew exactly where to find her if she did.

"I don't think that's wise."

"You don't think what's wise?"

"For us to never see each other again."

"How come?"

"I really want to ask you out, but . . ."

"But?"

"But, I've been through so much pain and anguish lately over women that I'm a bit apprehensive."

She removed the top from her hot chocolate and blew the surface lightly. I imagined those same lips blowing into my ear.

"And I could say the same about men putting me through drama," she retorted.

"I don't know. It's risky. We've barely met. I don't really know anything about you, other than you're fine. You could be a psychopath or something."

"So could you."

"Plus, I'm not used to picking people up like this. Do you do this often?"

"Hardly ever."

"I tell you what, here's my card. I'm writing my home number and cell phone number on the back. My pager number is on the front. Why don't you give me a call sometime?"

She stared at my business card like I'd written a novella. Four phone numbers was a bit much. I hoped I wasn't coming off as desperate.

"I'm very bad at calling," Rayne said, sliding the card back across the table to me. "If you really want to see me again, you'd better make plans right now."

I couldn't believe she gave my card back. "Is that so?"

"Yes, I'm an extremely busy independent African-American woman and my social calendar tends to stay full."

"In that case, how's tomorrow night?"

"Hmm, let me think. I do have plans tomorrow night. Sorry."

"Just my luck."

"I'm supposed to be going to the Playground Arena for their monthly adults' night out."

"Adults' night out?"

"Yes, you know how a lot of places have kids' night out?"

"So their parents can get a break?"

"Yes, and the kids can feel like they're grown by hanging out late."

"Intriguing."

"Well, the Playground Arena has an adults' night out once a month where adults can act like children."

That seemed like an interesting concept to me. I'd never ventured off into something like that. Besides, if Rayne was going to be there, that's where I needed to be. If she was going to a floral show, I would've wanted to go.

"Are you going with someone, Rayne?"

"No, all the people I know think they're too special to get down like that. Like it's beneath them. I don't care because I have a ball."

"Can I join you?"

"You mean, like a date?"

"Yes, a date."

She grinned at me and took another sip of her hot chocolate.

"No, I don't think so. If we were on an official date, I'd have to act respectable and let you win at everything."

"But, if we were on an unofficial date? If I just happened to be there and you just happened to be there?"

"Then, I'd be a competitive opponent and wear you out in every event."

We both laughed.

"I seriously doubt that."

"Talk is cheap."

I could tell that she was serious about being competitive, but I liked the idea of it.

"So what time does adults' night out start?"

"Nine on the dot."

"I'll be there at eight-thirty to warm up," I told her.

Rayne got up from the table and put her gloves back on. I hated to see her go so soon but I was thrilled that she'd even shown in the first place. I was even more excited about seeing her again the next night.

"I'll be there at eight-fifteen doing some stretches," Rayne boasted.

"See you there, tiger," I said and then growled at her.

Rayne leaned over and whispered in my ear. "You better wear a jock strap. I wouldn't want to cause you any permanent damage."

I watched her walk out the door and couldn't help but wonder what kind of damage she could do to me in the bedroom.

Seventeen

Rayne

I decided to save Chance the trouble of ringing my phone off the hook and called her as soon as I got home to tell her what had happened at Bagels by the Bag.

"Girl, why are you home so early?" was the first question out of her mouth.

"What? Did you expect me to spend the night with Yardley or something?"

"As fine as he is and as long as it took your ass to hook up with him, you need to be over his place or yours boning right this second."

"Chance, I'm not giving it up to him that fast."

"Puleeze, you were planning on giving it up to Basil the first night; until he came simply on a coochie sighting."

"He never saw my coochie, only lingerie," I said, correcting her.

I had to admit she had a point. I was planning on jumping

Basil's bones. But, it was different with Yardley. I wanted our first time, and I already knew that there would be a first time, to be extra special. Something neither one of us would ever forget.

"Coochie sighting. Lingerie sighting. Whichever. The point is that you were willing to give it up."

"Okay, Chance, I get your point. Do you want to know what happened or not?"

She giggled. "Hell yeah, I want to know. Spill it."

I told Chance all about how Yardley and I had pretended to be strangers that had bumped into each other, how I'd asked him about bagel selections, and how we'd shared a table on the pretense that the empty place was overcrowded.

"All that's cute and shit," Chance hissed into the phone after I was finished describing it. "However, you two need to stop playing games. On that note, when are you getting the dick?"

"Chance, this isn't about getting a dick," I said, totally offended but not surprised at Chance's bluntness. "I can get a dick anywhere. I want Yardley to be my man."

"You can get a dick anywhere except over at Basil's crib."

I banged the handset of my phone on my end table so it would irritate Chance's eardrum. Then I stated sarcastically, "Hello! This isn't about Basil! Basil has left the damn building! Can we talk about Yardley, please!"

"Damn, you didn't have to go there, Rayne." Chance got back at me by squealing like a pig into the phone.

"You're going to mess around and get you and Ricky kicked out your apartment," I said jokingly.

"Humph, I seriously doubt that. The way I scream out in bed, if someone was going to complain, they would've done that a long ass time ago. Then again, there was that one time last year—"

"You scream out in bed?" I asked, interrupting her.

"All the time, chica."

There was a pregnant pause while I wondered why I never had. Chance must've been reading my mind. "You've never had a man make you scream out in bed, Rayne?"

"No, never."

"Not even Will?"

"Will was a good lover but he never laid it on me like that. I really don't think it's possible for a man to make me scream out in bed anyway. I'm a quiet lover in general."

"But you do have orgasms, right?"

"Absolutely!" I exclaimed. Hell, I'd even had one in church that time while I was daydreaming about Basil.

"Well, maybe Yardley will lay it on you."

"I sure as hell hope so."

"When are you seeing him again?"

"Tomorrow night. We're going to adults' night out."

"At the Playground Arena?"

"Yes."

"Why go there on a first date? You need to go to a movie or something," Chance suggested.

"No, in a movie you can't really talk and get to know each other. Those kinds of dates are okay if you only want to get out the house; like when I endured that disastrous date with Conquesto. Besides, I'd already planned to go and Yardley seemed halfway excited about it."

Chance giggled. "I bet you said something silly like 'I'm gonna beat you in every game' or 'Be prepared for battle,' didn't you?"

"Who me?" I said innocently; even though she was right on point.

"Yes, you. Don't forget that I know your ass, chica."

"Okay, so maybe I voiced something along those lines."

"You're so silly, Rayne." I heard some Marc Anthony start

playing through the phone. "I do have to run, Sis. Ricky's waiting for me in the bedroom."

"Aw, leaving me in my time of need for some sex. You're not right."

Chance knew I was joking with her. "Like you wouldn't do it to me."

After I got off the phone with Chance, I decided to take a long, steamy bath and listen to *Teena Marie's Greatest Hits*. I thought about Yardley as I reminisced to "If I Were a Bell," "Dear Lover," and "Casanova Brown." Damn, that woman can blow. I'd been meaning to pick up a new CD she'd recently put out after a long hiatus. I was glad she was finally coming back to reclaim her throne.

Once I got out of the tub, I broke open a new jar of cocoa butter and rubbed it all over my body. The miraculous effect of cocoa butter on skin is one of the few valuable things my mother had taught me. Most of the time she'd schooled me on the power of the pussy and how to use it to get the finer things in life.

I lit an orange cream scented candle and crawled into bed. I thought about Yardley's smile and his sexy ass bedroom eyes and wished I'd handled things differently. I craved to have his warm arms around me at that very moment. Then again, good things happen to those who wait.

Eighteen

Yardley

I wanted to call Rayne so badly that night and tell her what a good time I'd had sharing bagels and hot chocolate with her. However, she didn't realize that I not only had her number but that I'd also used it before without leaving a message. I was glad the ice had been broken and I couldn't wait to see her the next night.

I was hoping she'd called me to say something, anything—since I was listed also—but the only messages on my machine were from Felix and Roxie, both whining for forgiveness. I'd arrived at the conclusion that they could both kiss my ass; especially Roxie. That might seem foul to place one evil over another, but I knew Felix was a dog all along. I just failed to realize how much of a dog he truly was. He'd always bragged about trolling for pussy but I'd never expected him to troll for my woman's pussy; and in my own home at that.

Roxie, on the other hand, had really damaged me. She'd come

back into my life like a rainbow and had left it like a hurricane. For her to not only betray me, but to fuck Felix on my balcony while there were dozens of people over visiting, was downright skank. I had no intention of taking her back. I'd made that clear when I'd packed up the things she'd left over my place into two boxes and had a courier deliver them to her apartment.

Roxie had left a ton of messages. One, in particular, had taken the cake. She'd said, "Yardley, I know I fucked up, baby. Please search deep into your soul and ask yourself one thing. Can you really see yourself existing without me? Don't I take good care of you? Don't I satisfy your every want and desire? If you let me back into your life, I promise to make all of this up to you. It was a simple misunderstanding. I had a little too much to drink and my hormones got the best of me. Besides, this is all Felix's fault. He was after me; even way back in high school. Please let me come back to you, baby. I want you and I need you and if you truly think this entire thing through, you'll realize that you want and need me, too."

For about two seconds after I'd listened to the message, I'd honestly thought it was sincere but then I'd started having flashbacks of the action on my balcony. I'd never get those images out of my head. It was definitely time to move on. That's why I'd made the decision to go to the bank and talk to Rayne; no matter what. Making a move on her had been long overdue. To think I'd missed out on such a special woman because of a loyalty to Roxie. Dick slayer or not, her ass was history.

I showed up to play basketball with the fellas the next morning for two reasons. First, I wanted to get a jump start on getting my adrenaline rushing so I could hang with Rayne at adults' night out later that day. She seemed extremely serious about having an all-out competition and I wasn't about to get my ego bruised by a woman in any shape or form. Secondly, I hadn't played in a couple of weeks and I didn't want Felix to think that he had enough power over me to make me stay away indefinitely.

As soon as I got out of the car, Dwayne bum-rushed me; probably thinking I was showing up to kick Felix's ass. Felix stayed over on the court; practically hiding behind Mike.

"Yardley, you all right, man?" Dwayne asked me, grasping my shoulder like Steve, the head of security on *The Jerry Springer Show,* does to people he anticipates might pounce at any second.

"I'm fine, Dwayne." I pulled away from him and started toward the court. "I came to shoot hoops, as usual."

"What about Felix?"

I shrugged. "What about him?"

"Aren't you still mad at him?"

"About what?"

"Roxie."

"Oh that," I stated casually. "That's over and done with. Let's get busy."

Mike and I slapped each other our customary high-five when I reached him and Felix. Felix smirked at me and didn't utter a word.

"Sup, Felix?" I asked coolly.

"Did you get my messages?"

"Yeah, I got *all* of them."

"I really am truly sorry about what happened with Roxie, man."

"Forget about it. In fact, you did me a favor."

"A favor?"

"Yeah, a big one."

Mike and Dwayne worked their heads from side to side like they were watching a tennis match; trying not to miss a word that Felix and I exchanged.

"How could you possibly view what happened as a favor?" Felix asked me.

"It's simple really. Roxie wasn't the one for me and you helped me see the light. I mean, any woman that would do such a thing doesn't deserve to be the mother of my children. That's where it was headed, too. I'm glad she revealed her nastiness before I went out and plunked down a grip on a ring."

Felix looked dumbfounded. "Are you serious? You were planning on marrying her?"

"I'd considered it. After all, I did have the hots for Roxie for years." I looked him up and down and then brushed past him. "Then again, I guess I wasn't the only one."

Felix came after me. I picked up a ball and started practicing my dribbling.

"I had too much to drink, man. If you decide to make up with Roxie, I promise it won't happen again."

I laughed. "I will definitely not be making up with Roxie. You're welcome to her. In fact, I'd appreciate it if you'd hook up with Roxie so she'd stop ringing my phone off the damn hook."

Dwayne slapped me on the back. "That's my boy!" I slapped him a high-five. "Tell that hoe to move on."

Mike guffawed. "Ya'll Negroes are crazy. Let's play some ball already."

"Yeah, let's do this," I responded, slamming the ball into Felix's chest.

He leered at me and slammed the ball back at me. "I don't want Roxie."

"Why not?" I slammed it back at him. "Because she's no longer my woman? Not a scandalous enough scenario for you?"

"It's not even like that, Yardley. I've tried to explain but enough is enough. I'm not gonna kiss your ass or anything."

"That's because you're too busy kissing Roxie's," Mike stated jokingly.

All of us shared a good laugh; except Felix.

The tension was thick throughout the entire game. And it was one hell of a game. I couldn't recall a time when the four of us had played so hard. Not to mention so roughly. I knocked Felix on his ass numerous times and he elbowed my ribs continuously, knocking the wind out of me a couple times.

"That's it for me," I finally said, taking a seat on a bench to catch my breath.

"Good game!" Mike exclaimed. "I'm gonna be sore for days though."

Dwayne came over and sat down beside me. "Say, what do you have planned for tonight? Want to check out that new Morgan Freeman flick?"

"No, I can't," I told him. "I have a date."

"Date!" they all yelled out in unison.

Felix, the last one that needed to say shit, was the first one to ask for details. "Who do you have a date with? I guess you really are over Roxie."

I snarled at him. "Felix, if you want to stay stuck on the Roxie topic, be my guest. I've moved on to better things."

"Like?"

"Like a real woman that's not into playing games."

"And you've figured all that out about the sister already?"

I sighed and got up off the bench. "I'll catch you fellas later. Enjoy the rest of your weekend."

I was halfway to my car when Felix tapped me on the shoulder. "Yardley, hold up! I was wondering if you want to get together for drinks this week. Maybe we can hit the happy hour over at the Zanzibar."

"I'm not ready to start hanging out with you again, man. Basketball's one thing, but I'm not trying to chitchat over buffalo wings and tortillas."

Felix shook his head. "That's cold."

"That's not cold. That's the way it is. Maybe, in time, I can begin to view you as a close friend again, but that remains to be seen. You have to earn my respect all over again."

He dropped his eyes to the ground. "I understand."

I realized that Felix genuinely felt regret, but it was time for him to grow up. If I'd forgiven him like it was nothing, he would've assumed that he could get away with scandalous behavior at will.

"Do me one favor, Yardley?" He stood tall and stared directly into my eyes. "Think about taking Roxie back. I take full responsibility for what happened. All I'm saying is consider it. Please consider it."

"I appreciate you trying to be the fall guy but Roxie's a grown woman and she knew what she was doing. After she embarrassed me in front of my friends like that, I could never be with her again. Besides, like I said, I have a date tonight and I'm really looking forward to it. The young lady's very special and she's someone that had me feenin' long before Roxie ever came back into the picture."

Felix chuckled. "Damn, it's like that?"

I grinned. "Yeah, it's like that."

"So who is she? You've got to tell me. You've never mentioned having the woody for anyone."

"Woody?" I laughed. That was a term I hadn't heard in ages. "You're sick, man. I didn't tell you about Rayne because I'd assumed she was taken."

"Rayne?"

I have no idea why I decided to tell Felix my business. Maybe I felt like bragging to someone, anyone. After all, I was excited as hell at the prospect of seeing her again.

"You know how you used to always call me and I'd be coming out of the bank?"

"Yeah?"

"Well, I was doing a little bit more than making deposits. I was checking her out."

"So she works at the bank?"

"Yes, and after I went in there one day I was hooked."

Felix laughed and punched me lightly in the arm. "Damn, she must be fine as shit!"

"Yes, she is. That's why I'd assumed she was taken all this time."

"So how did you find out she wasn't?"

I sighed uncomfortably. "After what went down, I decided to take a chance and find out. I'd planned to do it before but, ironically, that was the day Roxie called me up out the blue and asked me to have lunch. I got hooked up with her and tried to do the right thing by not going after another woman. It's a shame I did that, too, because Rayne and I could've been getting to know each other all this time. Then again, that wouldn't have been the appropriate way to start things off, so it's all good."

Mike and Dwayne were still over on the court shooting layups, obviously trying to give Felix and me the space and opportunity to make amends. While that didn't happen, I did feel a little better since I'd managed to somewhat clear the air.

"I have to jet, Felix, but you take care of yourself."

"You, too, and call me."

I didn't reply to that either way. I wouldn't be calling but I did plan on seeing him on the court the following weekend.

As I was driving away, my thoughts turned to Rayne. I couldn't wait to see her.

Nineteen

Rayne

The Playground Arena was packed, as usual. Adults love the chance to act like children without the risk of being scrutinized. If everyone is acting immature, who can cast a stone?

I got there at eight-fifteen and ran straight toward the ball pit, kicking off my shoes on the way. I jumped in and immediately started a ball fight with two stringy-haired white girls that appeared to be college age. That was the most fun.

We plummeted each other for a good twenty minutes and, other than getting sideswiped by a red one right in the eye, I was all into it. I wanted to get my adrenaline going so I'd be hyped up before Yardley got there. Then again, I was already hyped up. I had been all day, wondering if he was still coming. I'd finally convinced myself to relax. Either he showed or he didn't but after the way he'd flattered my ass the day before, I told myself that he'd be there.

Just as I told myself that for the hundredth time, I heard a slice of heaven.

"Having fun, Rayne?"

I was about to launch an all-out war with an armful of balls when I looked up and saw him standing there in a pair of black sweats and a white tee. Damn shame how the simplest of clothes can make a fine man look even finer.

I cleared my throat and stared at my playmates. "I have to run, ladies. My date's here."

I climbed out of the ball pit. Yardley was standing there with his arms crossed and a gigantic grin on his face.

"Oops, did I say date?" I asked bashfully.

He started laughing. "Yes, I believe you did."

"Well, you know what I meant."

"Hey!" Yardley threw his arms up and slapped his chest. "Calling it a date was my preference in the first place."

I poked him gently in the arm. "Then let's call it a date."

Yardley blushed and I started searching for my shoes amongst a pile of them on the floor. I found the first one and then paused. "Before I put these back on, did you want to play in the ball pit?"

Yardley shook his head. "No, no thanks. I don't like playing with little balls."

"What about big balls?"

He chuckled. "Sure, basketballs."

I located my other shoe and put them both on while Yardley allowed me to lean on him for balance. After I was done, I told him, "For the record, I enjoy playing with all kinds of balls."

I winked at him. I was sure he got my drift.

"So, Rayne, what would you like for me to whip you in first?"

"Very funny!" *He had to be kidding.* "How about laser tag?"

"I've always wanted to play laser tag."

"So why haven't you?"

"My buddies think they're too grown to do something like that, I suppose."

"Have you ever asked them to play?"

"Good point," he replied. "I never have."

"Well, after I give you a beatdown, you probably won't ever want to play again anyway."

We both laughed.

Yardley said, "Let's get it on!"

I wanted to get it on all right, but not the way he had in mind.

Yardley beat my ass in laser tag. I was highly disappointed but I realized that if he was the typical man, he probably had at least three video game systems at home that had much wear and tear and was about to wet himself waiting for the next one to come out. After laser tag, we moved on to virtual golf. He whipped my ass again. That was when I started getting frustrated. I hated to lose at anything. I did beat him in the water shoot. I knocked down more than a dozen ducks that floated by and he only got two.

"Aha, I beat you," I boasted, blowing imaginary smoke off the tip of the pistol before pointing it at him and squirting him in the face.

He chuckled. "Lucky shot. If we play it again, I'm sure I'll beat you."

I wasn't willing to take any chances. "Naw, that's perfectly all right. I think we should move on to something else."

"Fine, what do you want to try next?"

I picked up a diagram of the amusement center off a nearby table and scanned over the choices. That was a stall. I already knew the place like the back of my hand but I needed a moment to gain some composure. There was something about the way that Yardley asked me the question that had aroused me to the point where my heart had started pounding in my chest. I knew what I wanted to try next, but I wanted to take things slowly. Even so, I imagined pulling him into a quiet corner of the place and feeling him up at the very least.

"So have you decided?" Yardley asked.

"Hmm, how about wall climbing?"

"Oh, I don't know about that, Rayne. I wouldn't want you to get hurt."

Surely, he was joking. "Me? Get hurt?"

"Yes, you."

I started walking toward the room where the wall climbing section was located. "You need to be more worried about your-self."

"Why don't you give it up?" I yelled across the wall at Yardley, who was struggling to hang on and maintain his footing.

"Not in this lifetime," he responded, out of breath. The look of frustration on his face was priceless.

I wanted to laugh but was too afraid that I might fall, trying to be cute. I said, "Fine. I'm going to have to make you look like a fool in front of all those people down there watching."

He glanced down at the onlookers who were laughing and pointing at him. He looked like a puppet dangling from a string.

"This might be a strange time to ask this but Valentine's Day is coming up," he said after managing to place his right hand on the next mount.

I waited for him to continue his comment, assuming he wanted to ask me something. When he didn't, I commented, "That didn't sound like a question to me. That was more of a statement."

Yardley lifted another foot and slid it on top of a mount, try-ing to catch up to me. I was at least three feet ahead of him and still moving swiftly.

"I was wondering if you had any plans," he said.

I grinned. "Hmm, you're getting closer to a question, but that was more of a spoken thought."

"You're silly, Rayne." He paused and stopped trying to climb the wall. It was obviously a lost cause. "Would you like to spend Valentine's Day with me?"

"Now that sounds like a question."

"Good. This is the point where it's customary for you to say something that sounds like an answer."

"Is that right?"

"That's the general idea."

We both giggled.

I said, "Well, it depends."

"Depends on what?" Yardley asked.

I looked up and then back down at him, deciding to give him an out instead of being totally embarrassed about losing to a female. I answered by saying, "Depends on whether or not I get to the top of this wall first."

Yardley quickly jumped on the opportunity to give up, let go of the mounts, and slid down the rope to the cushioned mat. "Oops, I must've slipped."

We stayed at the place for another hour or so, opting to get something to drink instead of continuing our male-female competition. Yardley was much fun to be around—playful and lighthearted. We discussed our childhoods—*briefly*. I wasn't trying to scare him away by revealing TMI—too much information—about my mother. Yardley had grown up locally in Silver Spring, Maryland, and his parents still resided there.

I was hoping that I'd get to meet them one day, but only time would determine that. He did tell me that he rarely took women over to his parents' house because they'd always expect him to marry and settle down. He said that he hadn't found the one yet.

Then, he backtracked and started reminiscing about some chick named Roxie. I didn't like him talking about her because she had a name. It was cool for men to discuss their past but when they started talking about particular women and addressing them by name, it usually meant that there was still some baggage loaded on their hearts. This Roxie chick sounded like she had major issues. He'd caught her screwing one of his best friends on his balcony during the recent Super Bowl. That meant that he was merely days out of a relationship, which worried me even more. Men on the rebound can be high-risk and I wasn't trying to have my heart broken again anytime soon.

I asked him, "Are you sure that you're over this Roxie lady?"

Yardley nodded. "Oh, I'm positive about that. I'll admit that Roxie and I go way back, to high school. I wanted to date her then but I did something to mess things up before they even got off the ground. Now, years later, I guess it all came back to me. Karma is something else."

I laughed uneasily. "Yes, it is."

Yardley asked about my past relationships and I didn't elaborate. I told him that there are no accidents, I had no regrets, and everything happens in its own time. True love would find me when it was supposed to, and not a second before.

He wanted to know who I'd been recently dating. I told him that I wouldn't classify any of them as real dates. I described the entire Conquesto fiasco—without mentioning his name—and briefly went into the Basil the Virgin story; also without mentioning his name. I left out the part about my date tonguing down another date at his parents' party, though. Yardley didn't need to be privy to all that and I didn't want him to think that I could turn straight men gay. I knew a sister like that once. My mother's best friend, Phyllis, would turn men off so much with her shenanigans that I could name at least five men that went from pussy lovers to booty bandits. I had no intention of remotely making that my claim to fame.

Since we'd driven separately, we decided to call it a night. Yardley walked me to my car and the nervousness hung in the air. He wanted to kiss me; that much I was sure of. However, I debated about whether he'd find me easy if I allowed it to happen or, worse yet, made the first move.

"Well, Rayne," Yardley said, gazing deeply in my eyes after I had my door unlocked and was standing in the doorway of the driver's side.

"Well, Yardley," I said back to him after he hesitated.

We smiled at each other.

He took my hand and kissed my palm. "I had a ball this evening. I'm so glad that we finally met—*officially.*"

"Me, too, Yardley."

"You have no idea how long I've wanted to say something to you. Every single time I came into the bank, I wanted to approach you but never had the nerve. I bet that sounds ridiculous, doesn't it?"

I shook my head. "Not at all. Ironically, I've always wanted to say something to you also. I had no nerve at all and I'm glad you finally made the effort. Otherwise, I'd still be wondering about your situation and what could've been."

"Like you said earlier, everything happens when it is supposed to."

I giggled. "Exactly. Besides, you weren't technically available a few days ago, so that wouldn't have been cool."

"Want to hear something funny?" he asked.

"What?"

"The day that Roxie came back into my life, I was planning on coming into the bank to ask you out. Then she showed up out of the blue and basically sidetracked me for a while. I'm not the type of man to divide my time between women. Never have been and never will be. I only need one woman and I need that one woman to only need me."

I couldn't help but blush. "Wow, that was deep!"

Yardley laughed. "Yeah, I can be pretty profound late at night."

I glanced at my watch. "It's not that late."

"Is that a hint?"

"No, it's not," I replied. "I don't want you to think that I'm sweating you by trying to monopolize your time."

He shrugged. "I'm only going to head home, watch some late-night TV and fall off to sleep."

"I'll probably do the same."

"So why don't we fall off to sleep together?" Yardley asked suggestively.

I took a deep breath and then exhaled. "That sounds enticing but I better pass. At least for tonight."

Yardley seemed disappointed when he said, "Well, with that said, I bid you goodnight, Miss Rayne."

"Goodnight, Mr. Yardley."

He kissed me on the cheek, made sure that I got into my car okay, and stood there as I drove off into the night.

Twenty

Yardley

Roxie wouldn't give up. She was still sweating me and trying to get me to commit to seeing her on Valentine's Day. She'd even come by my office and copped an attitude with my receptionist, demanding to speak to me. I'd allowed her into my office. I didn't want the patients in the waiting room to overhear her ranting and raving.

"Yardley, we need to talk," she said after she was seated across from me at my desk.

"Roxie, for the last time, there's nothing to talk about."

"Yardley, you and I belong together. We've got that fire and desire Rick James and Teena Marie were singing about."

I laughed. "You seem to have the fire and desire with several people, *like Felix,*" I stated nastily. "Why don't you call him up and beg him for some more of that dick action he was giving you on my balcony."

"I don't want Felix. That was a mistake." She got up, walked around the desk, positioned herself behind me and started massaging my shoulders. "Come on, baby, let me make it up to you."

I pushed her hands off my shoulders and stood to face her. "Roxie, you don't get it. We're through. In fact, I have my mind on someone else."

Roxie pouted. "Oh, I get it. You've already replaced me. You're such a bastard. This is the second time you've hurt my feelings over another woman."

I was stunned. "Come again?"

"Back in high school? At your sixteenth birthday party? You dogged me out for that hooker."

I shook my head and chuckled. "This isn't hardly the same thing. The woman I'm seeing now is definitely not a hooker."

"Seeing? You're already seeing her?"

"Yeah, you could say that," I responded.

"Damn, you didn't waste five seconds. Did you?"

"Why would I?" I went to the door and opened it; hoping Roxie would take the hint and leave. "Roxie, for what it's worth, I really did care about you. However, those feelings are all gone. I'm determined to see where things can go with the new woman in my life."

"So, who is she?" Roxie asked, being nosy.

"She's someone I've been interested in for a very long time. The opportunity to feel things out has come about and I'm jumping on it. She's beautiful, sweet, fun-loving, and everything else I crave in a companion."

Roxie smacked her lips. "I bet she can't fuck you until your toes curl like I can."

"I bet she can," I replied sarcastically.

Roxie smirked. "Aw, I get it. You haven't even taken the coochie for a test drive and you're already whipped. I hope she's a dud in bed. That'll be what you fucking get."

"Roxie, this is my place of business. You can't be in here cursing. I have to ask you to leave. I have patients with appointments who've been waiting while we deal with this nonsense." I waved her out the office. "Have a nice life."

Roxie paused as she passed me and ran her tongue across my lips. I didn't reciprocate. "You're going to miss me. Let's hope you come to your senses before I do find someone else." She grabbed my dick through my pants, then let it go. "This is far from over."

After she walked out, I slammed my office door. I was pissed. How dare she think that I would still want to have *anything* to do with her?

I called the bank and asked for Rayne. She sounded lovely on the phone and I asked her, "So, what are you doing tonight?"

"Nothing," she replied.

"How about dinner and a movie?"

"What time?"

"You name it?"

"How about eight o'clock? Is that too late?" she asked.

"No, that's perfect. See you then." I was about to hang up when it dawned on me. "Hold up, I need your address so I can pick you up."

Rayne gave me her address and then we said our goodbyes. The rest of my day went smoothly. I had nothing but pleasant thoughts about seeing Rayne on my mind.

Twenty-one

Rayne
Valentine's Day

Yardley and I had been seeing each other for a couple of weeks. Even though we were taking things slowly—meaning we weren't sexing each other down—I felt myself getting emotionally attached to him. I'd never dated a man who could stimulate me on so many different levels. I felt so comfortable with him and found myself opening up to him with ease.

No matter what topic I brought up, he was knowledgeable on the subject; even makeup, which had completely shocked me. Actually, I was a bit panicky when we'd gone to Nordstrom's together and Yardley seemed to know more about the MAC cosmetics line than me. For a brief moment, I wondered if he might've been one of those metrosexual men that Ricki Lake had been discussing; one of those "iffy" men. After what had happened on my date with Kahlil, I was much edgier about men being sweet, acting sweet, and talking sweet. This book had also just hit the market about men being on the downlow—black men in particular—and sisters were starting to scrutinize brothers closely.

I'd actually sat at home one evening making a list of all the men I'd ever dated and any behavior patterns they'd had that could've been signs of loving to intake dick as much as I did. I'd come up with a list of five possibles; men I'd crossed paths with that might've been slapping dicks with friends. I was disgusted. As far as Yardley, I'd decided that he was definitely all man and probably simply knew a lot about makeup so he could purchase it for women he was feeling. Since he was feeling me, I was hoping he'd hit the MAC counter *hard* on my behalf before it was all said and done.

Don't get me wrong. I could afford my own stuff but it was always nice to receive gifts as well. For years, I'd never wanted birthday gifts or Christmas presents. I wasn't used to receiving them. Momma never felt the need to buy me things. She was too worried about buying things for herself. She wasn't like traditional mothers—single mothers especially—who'd save up money to layaway toys and clothing to make sure their children were happy. I'd never believed in Santa Claus. The first time I'd come home from prekindergarten excited because the teacher had read a book to us about Santa Claus, Momma told me, "His ass don't exist! Don't be expecting nothing special for Christmas 'cause I'm flat broke!"

I was the opposite of Momma. I had a very giving heart. I was always the giver and generally, my mother had become the main receiver. I did a lot for Chance as well and she appreciated it; unlike Momma. In fact, one time Chance decided to treat me to a day at the Red Door Spa and I was in torment when it came to allowing it. Chance finally convinced me by stating that "a person who always gives must also learn to receive because otherwise, they'll never know how special they make others feel." Chance could get deep like that sometimes. She was also an excellent poet with a collection of poems to rival many of the greats. I used to try to encourage her to do spoken word at some of the local clubs but she wasn't even having it. Crazy as she was and as much as she loved to run her mouth, she was shy in front of crowds.

Speaking of running mouths, she and I were sitting at our desks on Valentine's Day doing just that.

"So what are you and Ricky doing tonight?" I asked as I watched a pair of lovers walking down the street through the picture window of the bank.

It was amazing. People who fought like cats and dogs on other days would be filled with adoration on Valentine's Day—if only for one day.

Chance had spotted them also and commented, "Aw, aren't they cute?"

"Yeah, they are," I replied and sighed. I couldn't wait to see Yardley later on. "Again, so what are you and Ricky doing?"

"Probably the same thing we did last year."

"Which was?"

"Don't you remember?"

"No." I smacked my lips. "Why would I keep tabs on what you and Ricky do?"

Chance giggled. "We're going to do some role-playing?"

"Role-playing?"

"Yes. This year we're going to try something we saw on cable."

I had a feeling she was about to give me a visual I wouldn't care for and decided to avoid it. "Never mind. Don't tell me."

Chance got up and came over to my desk. "But I want to."

I shook my head. "But I don't want to know. The fact that you came over here to whisper tells me all I need to know. For the record, I didn't know you did role-playing last year."

"Oh yeah, girl. It was the shit. We pretended to be panthers."

"Panthers?" I couldn't help but ask.

"Yeah, panthers."

"And the point of that was?"

"They had this special on the Discovery Channel about the mating rituals of animals and the panther segment turned us both on, so we acted the shit out. The neighbors down the hall actually called the police. They thought some wild cats were loose in the building or right outside."

"You're joking," I said, laughing. "You two were making the noises and everything?"

"Yes, and it was so hot. I came about ten times in an hour."

"Humph, yeah right. Now I know you're making the shit up."

Chance eyeballed me and slapped me on the arm. "Rayne, have I ever lied to you?"

I slapped her back. "You're not seriously asking me that, are you?"

We both giggled.

"Okay, so maybe I've lied to you once or twice," Chance said. "But, hell, everyone fibs about something from time to time."

"Like the time you told me that Shea could throw her tits over her shoulder."

Chance stood up and started jumping up and down, smacking her thighs. Then she decided to get loud on a sister. "I swear, Rayne, she really did it!"

"Okay, calm down already," I said, searching the bank for our boss. Sure, we spent a large part of our work day goofing off but we didn't need to make it obvious. There were busy periods when a lot of people would come in all of a sudden but for the most part, the teller windows were the only ones with a constant flow. I didn't see him around so I continued, "I found that shit hard to believe. That's all, Chance."

"We have to look ole girl up so she can do it for you."

"That's quite all right," I said with disdain.

We were referring to an incident with one of our college classmates, Shea. She had these huge tits and wore something like a 40-I bra. I'd never heard of anything above a D until I'd seen Shea's tits. Anyway, Chance swore up and down that one night, when Shea was drunk, she'd taken off her bra in front of a group of them and had literally thrown one tit over each shoulder. I'd been elated that I'd been out on a date that night.

Chance came to her senses and went to sit back down at her own desk. About thirty seconds later, she said, "I guess you're hooking up with Yardley."

"What gives you that impression?"

She grinned. "Well, for starters, he just walked into the door with a big ass bunch of balloons and a dozen roses."

I was so busy trying to kill this fruit fly that was annoying me, I hadn't even seen him come in the door. "Oh my!" I exclaimed as his sexy ass approached us. He was wearing a navy Ralph Lauren double-breasted suit with a crisp white shirt and an incredible solid red tie; the color of love.

"Excuse me. I have a delivery for a Ms. Rayne Waters," Yardley said, once he was beside us.

I blushed and decided to play games. "I'm sorry, sir, but there's no one employed at the First Community Bank by that name."

He arched an eyebrow. "Really?"

I stood up and reached for the flowers and balloons. "However, since you've obviously put a lot of time and effort into making Valentine's Day special for her, I'd be happy to accept those gifts on her behalf."

Yardley and I stood there, eyeing each other seductively, oblivious to everyone else in the bank.

Chance broke us out of our reverie with her cynicism. "Speaking of role-playing."

I rolled my eyes at her, then concentrated on Yardley again. He assisted me with setting the flowers on my desk and attaching the balloon strings to my desk chair. Then he took my right hand. "Has anyone told you that you're loved and deeply appreciated today?"

I shook my head. "No, not a soul."

He lifted my hand to meet his lowering head and kissed it. "Now they have."

"Awwwwwww," Chance cooed. "Rayne, you better hang onto him, girlfriend."

"I think I might do that." I gave Yardley a big hug and kiss on the cheek. "Thank you for making today special."

He ran his fingers through my hair. "Imagine, today's not over yet."

"This is true and I have something special to give you also." I reached up, caressed his hand and then kissed the inside of his palm. "I'll have to give you mine tonight. It wouldn't be appropriate to give it to you in public."

He licked his lips and started to back away from me. "In that case, I'll see you tonight."

I winked at him. "Oh yes, you'll see a lot of me tonight."

Yardley and I kept staring at each other while he exited the bank. Once he was outside, he blew me a kiss through the window. I blew one back at him.

"The two of you sound like you're on one of those late-night soft porno flicks," Chance commented. "It's mad cute, though."

"He's mad cute," I said, looking forward to seeing him again in a few hours.

"He's mad fine. You don't call a man that looks like that cute. He surpassed that a long time ago." Once again, Chance had invaded my space and started whispering. "Since you're talking all dirty and thangs, I guess you two are doing the nasty."

I pushed her away from me gently. "Yardley and I have only been dating a couple of weeks."

"So? You were ready to give it up to Basil on the first date, ordering that raunchy outfit to wear and all that. Poor man couldn't handle it."

Chance was riding my last nerve; bringing the Basil fiasco up on the regular. He was cool as a friend but his balls had to be cobalt blue, being a virgin at his age.

"Don't remind me *again*. Basil's a sweetheart but most women in this day and age want to sample the goodies before they settle down."

"True. It's wild how times have changed. Men used to be the only ones talking such stuff but now the chicas are demanding to window shop before they buy, too."

"Honestly, I think women have always felt that way. It's only more acceptable now, thank goodness. We still have a long way to go because some women are automatically branded a whore if they don't have any inhibitions."

"Yeah, men do seem awfully intimidated by aggressive women."

I swept my fingertips across the rose buds. "Let's hope Yardley isn't because I plan to get aggressive on him tonight."

"Aw, sookie sookie now." Chance laughed.

I bit my bottom lip. It was time to see if Yardley could live up to the imaginary sex I'd been having with him in my mind. While we'd only been dating for a couple of weeks, the time we'd wasted not speaking also counted, as far as I was concerned.

"Then again," Chance added. "Some of the married women in that church you've been dragging me to seem to think sisters need to be celibate before marriage."

"Chance, ignore them. Every woman has to live their own life and it's easy for married women to say that nonsense because they have someone to lie next to every damn night."

"This much is true, chica. This much is true."

"Marriage may or may not ever come. So what? We're supposed to do without? Please, not in this lifetime. I'm not one of those women who have to fornicate every day, but I do need some action every now and then."

"Fornicate?" Chance giggled. "Girl, you're beginning to sound like your old self again. I was getting concerned. It's been a while since you've had some. I was afraid you were either going to listen to those chicas at church or start switch-hitting."

"Switch-hitting! Not as long as they sell vibrators because those jimmies never fail." I threw a pen at Chance. "It's been a while but everything happens for a reason. If I'd really turned Basil out or Kahlil had really been about me instead of Oliver, I probably wouldn't have talked to Yardley when he approached me. God closes some doors so we're forced to walk through other ones."

Chance threw the same pen back at me. "Damn, now you're getting spiritual about getting the dick."

I picked up my entire pen cup and threatened to throw it at her. "You worry about your role-playing, panther ass."

Life is just one damned thing after another.

—Elbert Hubbard

Twenty-two

Rayne

There are times in life when you wish you could crawl into a hole and drown everything out. Times when you wish you were someplace else, anyplace else, than where you currently are. That's exactly how I felt when I left work an hour early to go home and get sexy for my Valentine's date with Yardley. Not because I didn't want to see him. I wanted to see him, every inch of him, in every sense of the word. However, I didn't want, or plan, to see my mother sitting in the hallway in front of my apartment door when I arrived home.

"Momma, what are you doing here?" I asked the second I stepped off the elevator and spotted her.

"Baby!" she exclaimed, jumping up and exposing her black satin panties underneath the skimpy lime green dress she was wearing in the cold February weather. "Surprise!"

She spread out her arms to embrace me and a chill ran up my spine. I gave her a slight hug and then pushed her away from me.

"Momma, again, what are you doing here?"

She smirked and put her hands on her hips. "Check your attitude, missy. I came all this way to see my one and only kid and this
is the treatment I get? The older you get, the meaner you get."

I wanted to tell her that I'd inherited the mean streak from her
but didn't feel like getting into a fight. "I'm sorry for coming off
like that," I lied as I unlocked my door. "I had no idea you were
coming; especially not today. After all, it's Valentine's Day and I
assumed you'd have plans with . . . Um, what's his name again?"

"Very cute, Rayne. You know good and damn well that I'm
dating Truck."

"Humph, oh yeah, Truck." I held the door open while I placed
my briefcase on the table in my foyer. "Come on in."

Truck and my mother had this on-again, off-again thing going
that was sickening at best. They'd be together for a few months
and then she'd go out on a "whore binge" as she called it. They
called him Truck because of his massive size. He had to be at least
six-eight and weighed at least four hundred pounds, which made
him about three of Momma. Personally, I couldn't understand
how she could have sex with him. The thought of him laying on top
of her, pounding his dick into her, was mind-boggling, and her riding on top of him wasn't a pretty picture either. Yet, they'd found
something special in one another. Who was I to judge them? I was
simply glad to be the hell away from them, in another state.

"So where's Truck tonight, Momma?"

She smacked her lips at me. "In his skin." She pointed to the
hallway. "Aren't you going to bring my bags in?"

I went back out in the hall and froze. I'd been so shocked to see
her that I hadn't even noticed the *three* suitcases sitting beside her.
"Momma, what's with all the luggage?" I asked as I struggled to
bring the heaviest one in first.

"Don't have a baby. I'm not staying long. A woman like me can never decide what to wear so I have to bring a lot of shit, so I can look good at all times. You know how I roll."

"Whatever you say," I replied as I carried the last one in and tossed it in the corner with the other two. "How long are you going to be here?"

"Oh, who knows? A week or two, or maybe three."

"I see," I said, beginning to feel heated. "Will Truck be able to live without you for that long?"

"Shit, he's had to do it before." She plopped down on my sofa. "Besides, I haven't seen my baby in a while. I decided that I needed to come check on you."

I sat down in the armchair and glared on her. "Check on me? Since when has that been a priority for you?"

"I call you all the time, baby."

"Only when you want money," I stated with disdain. "When you call, you rarely even ask me about my life. You talk about yours, and yours only, and then ask for money."

You could've cut the tension in the room with a knife. For a few moments, we stared at each other. I could tell that she wanted to curse me out, but realized doing that would defeat her ultimate purpose. It had to be about finances; it always was.

"It suddenly dawned on me," I said, breaking the silence. "How can you take off work for three weeks? You do still have a job, don't you?"

"Yes, I have a damn job!" She shifted in her seat. "A shitty ass job but I have one."

"Are you still working at the drugstore?"

"Yes, night shift. Sick fuckers."

"What sick fuckers?" I asked in curiosity.

"Rayne, you wouldn't believe the sadistic shit that goes on in there all night. Can you believe that we had to start keeping the Preparation H behind the counter?"

"That's ridiculous! Why would you have to do that?"

"Thieves! Druggies!"

"Okay, I'll bite, Momma." What she was saying made no sense. I'd heard of people stealing cigarettes but Preparation H? "Why do people steal it?"

"Drug addicts use it to rub inside their noses so they can continue to snort shit. Then they steal a ton of lotion also, to rub on the tracks on their arms."

"Okay, I guess that I understand."

"And check this out," Momma said, moving up to the edge of the sofa in excitement. "Some of the bastards are bold as shit. They'll come in, head for the paper goods aisle, open up boxes of aluminum foil, use some to smoke crack and then leave their trash back there. Nasty asses."

"Hmm, I'm not too sure about you working there," I said with genuine concern. "That doesn't sound too safe; for you to be in there at night. Can you at least switch to the day shift?"

"I'm not trying to work there *period*. I hope they do fire my ass before I get back. Let someone else deal with those addicts. I'm above all that."

While I knew it was going to be a low blow—a very low blow—I couldn't resist. "But aren't you still addicted to alcohol?"

I saw her ball her left hand into a fist and figured she didn't even have the nerve to come at me with it. She'd punched me quite a few times when I was a child but once I'd turned into a woman and headed off to college, I'd set her straight. The night that I was packing for school, she came into my room in a drunken stupor and started going off about how I was deserting her. I attempted to explain to her that it wasn't a matter of desertion but simply me trying to move on with my life. Although, truth be told, I couldn't wait to escape the nonsense.

The argument had escalated until she'd tried to punch me in

my face. I grabbed her fist and flung her backwards, halfway across the room. "Momma," I'd said. "The days of you laying your hands on me are over. Don't ever try to hit me again, or I *will* hit you back."

Those words must've been resonating through her head at the same time they were echoing through mine because she relaxed her hand.

"Rayne, why must you insist on hurting my feelings?" she asked in her most pitiful sounding voice. "I know that I like the liquor, dammit! But that's a far cry from doing crack and heroin."

On one hand, I agreed with her. On the other hand, an addiction was an addiction. I decided not to comment further. I knew that before her visit was done, she'd prove my point for me without me having to utter another word.

Sure enough, before I knew it, she was pulling a bottle of vodka out of her suitcase and getting the ball rolling.

Twenty-three

Yardley

I got to Rayne's apartment at nine o'clock on the dot that night. I was feeling good about the activities that I'd planned for us and couldn't wait to see what she was wearing.

When she answered the door, the first thing I noticed her wearing was a gigantic frown. "What's the matter?" I instinctively asked.

She shook her head and folded her arms in front of her. "I'm so sorry about this, Yardley."

I was completely puzzled. "Sorry about what? Are you okay?"

Suddenly, a hand appeared over her right shoulder and pushed her to the side. A woman who had to be Rayne's mother stood there, eyeing me up and down like she was deciding whether or not she wanted to be in my presence.

"This." Rayne nodded toward her mother. "I'm sorry about this."

I cleared my throat and said, "Hello. How are you?"

Her mother wriggled her mouth around like she was trying to find her tongue and bellowed out, "How the fuck are you?"

"I'm fine, thank you." I held out my hand. "I'm Yardley Brown. You must be Rayne's mother."

"Fuckin'-A, I am." She glared at my hand and refused to reach for it. Instead, she turned around and headed deeper into Rayne's place. "So you're the latest panty sniffer, huh?"

Rayne had told me very little about her mother; like she was ashamed of her. Now it was obvious that her mother had a drinking problem; evidenced by the bottle of vodka she picked up from the coffee table and started guzzling down.

"Excuse me?" I asked, not quite believing that she'd actually asked me if I was a panty sniffer.

"Panty sniffer!" she repeated, shouting it louder this time. "Pussy hound! Cat chaser!"

Rayne took a deep sigh, livid from her mother's comment. "Momma, go sit down!"

"Who the fuck do you think you're talking to? I'm Arjay Waters, the heifer that birthed you! You go sit your ass down!"

Rayne took my hand and guided me over to her dining room area. "Yardley, I'm so sorry. I'm not going to be able to keep our date tonight." Rayne looked like she was close to tears. "I wasn't expecting Momma. She simply popped up." She moved closer to me and whispered, "More like touched ground like a tornado."

I embraced her tightly. "It's no problem. I understand."

"Do you really?" She leaned back from me so she could see my eyes.

While I didn't really understand, being that Rayne was a grown woman and her mother had decided to barge in without notice, I still lied. "Sure, I'm disappointed. But I understand, Rayne."

She kissed me on the cheek and I craved her to do more than

that; not a possibility at the moment. I did take her face in my hands and plant one long, soft kiss on her lips and then let her go.

She blushed. "Thanks. You're so sweet."

We stood there, captured by one another. I could tell that she wanted me as much as I wanted her. *Damn, why did her mother have to show up!*

"Hey! Hey!" her mother yelled out at us from the sofa, where she'd decided to take a seat despite Rayne ordering her to do so.

Rayne broke our gaze and turned to her mother. "Yes, Momma?" she asked, disgust permeating her voice.

Her mother crossed her legs and took another sip of her vodka. "Ya'll don't have to cancel your plans. We can still hang out."

"We?" Rayne asked in dismay. I was sure that Rayne wasn't about to have either one of us sitting in a cozy restaurant on Valentine's Day with her mother in between us, ranting and raving loudly.

"Yeah, we." Her mother pointed at us and then back at herself. "Rayne, Harley, and Arjay. The three musketeers." When neither one of us responded, she added, "I know your ass doesn't expect me to sit up in this shithole by myself."

Rayne started for her and I managed to grab her by the elbow and pull her back. "Momma, first of all, my apartment isn't a shit-hole. You need to take a look at your own home before——"

"There you go again, smart ass!" Arjay catapulted up off the sofa and came for Rayne, since I'd stopped her. She got within a foot of us and asked me, "Do you see the way my baby talks to me, Harley?"

"His name is *Yardley,* Momma. *Yardley!*" Rayne screamed out in anger.

"Harley! Yardley! What the fuck ever!" She still stared at me with bloodshot pupils. "Do you see the way she treats me?"

I wasn't about to get into the middle of the mess between Rayne and her mother. The embarrassment Rayne was feeling was obvious by her facial expression.

"Mrs. Waters. That is your correct name, right?" I asked, knowing she had already stated it earlier. I was trying to change the subject anyway I could.

"Yes, and I like being addressed that way. It makes me feel like a lady," Arjay replied, smoothing her dress down over her hips. Then she looked at Rayne and added, "Now that's what I'm talking about. A brother who acts like a gentleman. He might have some potential after all."

"Ma'am, my parents raised me that way. In fact, it would be an honor to escort both you and your lovely daughter out to dinner this evening."

"Yardley, you don't have to do that!" Rayne exclaimed. "We can do it another time."

I smiled at Rayne. "I beg to differ. I made reservations for us at the Iron Gate Inn and it's a dining experience that we all must have tonight."

Her mother whistled, reached behind me, and grabbed one of my ass cheeks. "My, my, my! This might be your lucky night, Harley. I mean, *Yardley.* You ever had a mother and daughter in your bed before?" She came closer to me and licked my earlobe. *"At the same damn time!"*

"Momma, get off him!" Rayne yelled out, pulling her away from me. "That does it! I'm going out on my date tonight, with Yardley, by myself."

"What about me?" Arjay asked. "You can't leave me here by myself."

"That's exactly what I'm going to do. And to think, I almost let you sucker me into canceling my date to stay here with you. I'm keeping my plans." Rayne headed toward her bedroom.

"Yardley, give me about ten minutes to get ready and we can roll."

"Not a problem," I said, feeling like a mouse in the middle of a brawl between two pitbulls. "Whatever you wish."

Rayne's mother hissed under her breath and headed to the kitchen. Before I could get situated on the sofa properly, she was headed back with a new bottle of vodka in one hand and two shot glasses in the other. She slammed everything down on the coffee table and sat down beside me.

"Do you drink?" she asked me.

"From time to time. Mostly beer," I responded.

She placed her hand on my knee. "Care to take a walk on the wild side?"

I politely removed her hand and placed it on her lap. "I appreciate the offer, Mrs. Waters, but I'm trying to get to know your daughter. One day, I hope she and I can have a serious relationship, so I can't . . ."

She started giggling and slapped her hand across her chest. "I'm not talking about fucking," she said. "I'm a whore and a proud one at that, but I was teasing with you earlier. I'd never fuck the same man as my daughter. Even whores like me have limitations."

I couldn't think of a thing to say so I finally uttered, "Well, that's certainly good to know."

"When I said wild side, I meant vodka. Beer's nothing but a chaser for me. Vodka's the real shit."

"Oh, I see." I held my palm up. "No thanks on the vodka. I have to drive and I'd never jeopardize your daughter, or myself, by driving drunk."

She glared at me for a moment. "You really do seem like a good man. Are you?"

"I like to think that I am. I try my best to be a good man."

"Well, Rayne's a good woman," Arjay said. "She'd never believe that I'd tell you as much. She thinks I hate her, but I don't. I love my baby. She doesn't love me back."

"I'm sure Rayne loves you, Mrs. Waters."

"Really?" She scooted over closer to me as she poured a shot of vodka for herself and downed it in one gulp. "Does she talk about me a lot?"

"Well," I started, reluctant to tell an all-out lie, "Rayne and I have only been dating a little while but she's definitely mentioned you."

"That's good. That's good," she said, seemingly content with my response. "Yardley, let me say this and then I'm going to take my two cents and zip them in my mouth."

"Go ahead and say it."

"Rayne has problems when it comes to men."

"What kind of problems?" I asked curiously.

"She has some trust issues and I'll admit that a lot of it is my fault."

"How so?"

"When Rayne was younger, back when the panty sniffers first started zeroing in on her, I broke it down for her and she couldn't handle the truth."

"What truth is that?"

"The fact that men only care about money and pussy."

I suppressed a laugh. "Not all men think that way, Mrs. Waters."

"Bullshit! Yardley, can you honestly tell me that, on any given day, you're not concentrating on money and pussy the majority of the time?"

"There may be some men out there like that." I thought about Felix. "In fact, I'm positive there are men out there like that, but I'm not one of them. I'll be honest by saying that I enjoy sex, but I won't sleep with just anyone. A woman has to stimulate me on various levels for me to enjoy her company."

She poked me in the chest. "Make sure you don't hurt my baby or you'll have to deal with me. I'll chop that dick and those little ass balls clear off your body."

I chose to ignore that statement.

"Arjay, I can honestly say that my mind is not zoned in on sex. I concentrate on my patients while I'm at my medical office and I concentrate on many other things in the evenings."

"Medical office? Aw shit! You mean to tell me you're a damn doctor?"

"A chiropractor."

"Ain't those the doctors that crack backs and shit?"

"Sometimes but there's a lot more to it than that. We can do everything from help people recovering from car accidents to preventing menstrual cramps."

She giggled and slapped me on the thigh. "Damn, you can cure cramps?"

I laughed right along with her. "I've been known to cure quite a few cramps."

That must've really excited her because she inched her way even closer to me. "So you must have some magical hands in the bedroom, huh?" she asked teasingly.

Thank goodness Rayne returned right on time. In fact, I jumped up and said, "Right on time! We don't want to lose our reservation."

Rayne was gorgeous in a black skintight dress and three-inch pumps; simple yet elegant. She had on moon drop pearl earrings and a small strand of pearls adorned her neck.

"You look fantastic!" I exclaimed.

She blushed at me. "Thanks and so do you. I didn't get a chance to mention that earlier." She eyed her mother, who was sitting on the sofa—acting like she wasn't trying to feel me up a second ago—hanging on our every word. "Well, goodnight, Momma."

We'd almost made it to the door when her mother jumped up and strutted toward us. "So I'm supposed to sit here and starve tonight?" she asked Rayne.

Rayne reached into her purse and pulled out two twenties. "There's a stack of delivery menus in the top right-hand drawer in the kitchen; beside the sink. I have every type of food you can imagine in there, so order whatever you like." Rayne opened the door, then paused, reaching back into her purse. "Here's another twenty. The liquor store is two blocks down to the right, on the corner; in case you decide you want some more vodka for dinner."

Her mother grabbed the money out of her hand. "Very cute, missy! This is truly fucked up, but you seem dead set on treating me like a stranger. So be it," Arjay said.

"I'll see you later, Momma." Rayne leaned in and made a smacking noise with her lips. "Give me a kiss. M'wah!"

"Get the hell out of here already," Arjay stated vehemently. "But if I've jumped out the window by the time you get back, it's all your fault."

Rayne grabbed my arm and led me out of her place. "Let's make a run for it," she whispered.

I heard her front door slam behind her and Arjay yell out, "Bitch!"

"I can't believe your mother called you that," I said in shock.

"Believe it." Rayne pushed the button for the elevator. "I didn't plan on you finding out this way, but I eventually planned to tell you."

"Tell me what?" I asked.

"Yardley, my mother's an alcoholic; always has been since I

was a child. On top of that, she's extremely promiscuous. I hope that doesn't cause a bad reflection on me in your eyes. I'm someone totally separate from her. She did give me life, but I'm so ashamed of her."

I reached out and placed my hand on Rayne's lower back, near her waist. She was trembling. "It's okay, Rayne. I understand about your mother. Maybe I can help you get her into a rehabilitation center."

"She has to want to take that step, or there's no point. I used to go to all the family support groups my senior year in high school and I realize it's an illness, but she still pisses me off sometimes with her behavior."

"I'm sure there have been good times, though."

Rayne smirked as the elevator doors opened. Once we were on and headed for the lobby, she said, "I love her, I do, but it's so difficult to deal with her. That's why I moved so far away from Birmingham. I had to get away before I went crazy."

"She's not serious about the suicide comment, is she?" I asked with genuine concern.

"Huh? Oh, you mean the window thing. Momma's a drunk but she loves herself way too much to ever do that. Trust me on that one."

"If you say so," I said. I drew her close to me and gave her a gigantic hug. "In that case, let's go out and have a good time tonight. Okay?"

She gave me a peck on the lips, which turned into a deeper kiss; one I'd come to enjoy over the previous two weeks. She was quite the passionate kisser.

The elevator doors opened while we were still engaged in an embrace. There was an older man waiting to get on. He chuckled. "All this Valentine's Day smooching is making me jealous. I might have to go find me a new babe."

"Hey, Mr. Silverton," Rayne said, blushing. "Sorry for the display."

The old man chuckled. "It's okay. I've been seeing action all day in Georgetown. People act like Valentine's Day is Sex Day."

"It's all about being romantic," I told him.

"Young man, I've been around the block many a times and we both know romance ultimately leads to sex."

Rayne giggled. "He got you on that one, Yardley."

He got on the elevator while we got off. When the doors closed on him, Rayne said, "I should've sent him up to my place to romance Momma."

We both laughed. I said, "From the looks of him and the looks of your Momma, she might kill him in bed."

Rayne replied, "I wouldn't be surprised if she's already left a trail of bodies in her path."

I was kind of disappointed that she hadn't introduced me to her neighbor. It made me feel insignificant in her life. Then again, we'd only started dating and if I had my way, soon she'd be introducing me to all her friends and family.

Twenty-four

Rayne

We arrived at the Iron Gate Inn Restaurant on N Street in the Dupont Circle area and it was mesmerizing. I had heard people speak about it but had never been. It was almost impossible to get reservations on a normal night so I knew Yardley must have made ours the second I'd agreed to spend Valentine's Day with him.

The entryway was cobblestone and they had a cloistered stone terrace courtyard. The Baroque wood booths inside were cozy and I could see why people voted it one of the most romantic restaurants in Washington, D.C. They had a Mediterranean menu, which I wasn't familiar with except for a takeout I had ordered from once or twice. I asked Yardley to order for me and we both had wild mushroom salad, braised lamb shank with orzo, and chocolate truffle pie for dessert.

The food was delectable but I had trouble concentrating on the ambiance because I was still pissed off at Momma. I couldn't believe the way she'd acted in front of Yardley, offering to have a threesome with him. She was getting even sicker as she grew older. Heaven knows what she'd said to him while I was getting dressed. I'd started to ask him to go wait in his car but that would've seemed rude so I'd taken the chance of leaving him alone with her for a few minutes.

"What's the matter, Rayne?" Yardley asked as he poured the last of a bottle of Chardonnay into my glass.

"I'm sorry that I'm not better company tonight." I toyed with the last of my pie with a fork. "I'm so ashamed about my mother."

He reached across the table and took my free hand. "It's okay, baby. I realize that your mother and you are two completely different people. Although I must imagine that there was never a dull moment growing up in your house."

I managed a smile. "That's true, but she gets out of control and I don't know what to say to her to calm her down. Now you see why I moved so far away from home."

He and I had briefly discussed my childhood, my lack of a father figure and my mother's drinking problem, but at the time, I was more like skirting the issue. Now it had shown up on my doorstep.

"How long will she be here? A couple of days?" he asked.

"From your lips to God's ears." I sighed. "She said she might stay for three weeks but I might be an alcoholic by then," I stated jokingly. "I don't think I can deal with her that long."

He eyed me seductively. "Well, if you need a place to get away, you can stay with me."

My pussy got wet as I gazed into his eyes. "If you keep staring at me like that, I might take you up on your offer."

"I wouldn't mind. Not one bit."

We sat there, eyeing each other down for a lingering moment and then Yardley grinned and said, "I thought that we could go hear some jazz music after dinner but if you'd prefer, we can head straight for the destination I had planned after that."

"And what destination might that be?" I asked, hoping he meant his place. I was ready to give myself to him, even though I feared he might get the wrong impression of me after meeting Momma.

"Actually, I got us a suite at the O Street Mansion."

"Really?" I was so excited. I had toured the place once and it was off the chain.

"Yes, really. If that's cool with you."

He seemed kind of nervous. We both knew he was basically asking me to fuck him.

The O Street Mansion was ultraprivate, offering guests a variety of unique rooms and suites. They had everything from insomniac suites and suites for people who love television with as many as eight televisions to suites full of antiques and a two-level log cabin suite. The Mansion was designed in 1892 to be inhabited by three brothers with the last name of Clark. In the 1930s, it was converted into three separate rooming houses for FBI G-men.

Ironically, on Valentine's Day in 1980 a new owner purchased it and converted it into a hundred-room mansion by reconnecting the three and making it one of the most unique and intimate environments in the world, full of secret doors and numerous fireplaces.

Yardley had reserved the Art Deco Penthouse Suite, no doubt the most expensive suite in the place. It was fantastic. It had a private elevator and kitchen, two stereo systems and a secluded outdoor balcony.

Yardley put on the Kem *Kemistry* CD, one of my all-time favorites, and followed me outside on the balcony, where I was admiring the courtyard below.

"Aren't you cold?" he asked me, wrapping his arms around my waist.

"No, I'm not cold," I replied, "but I have this pain."

He released me and turned me around to face him. "What kind of pain?"

I pouted. "It's really starting to irritate me. It aches all the time."

He grinned at me, obviously onto my game. "Oh, you poor baby. Where does it hurt?"

"You promise not to laugh?"

His grin widened as I continued to pout like I was in serious agony. "I promise. Let the doctor fix you up."

"Let's go inside so I can show you." I took him by the hand and led him back into the living room area of the suite. Then I got on the sofa on my knees, reached behind me and pointed to the base of my spine. "Okay. It always starts here, in my lower back."

Yardley climbed on the sofa beside me and started pressing into my spine with his thumb. "Right here?"

"Yes, and then it moves down lower."

He lowered his hand to the top of my ass and then started rubbing it. "Right here?"

"No, lower," I said teasingly, slowly hiking up the back of my dress, allowing him to see my black lace thongs.

He let out a deep sigh and I could feel his breath on my ear as he moved his head closer to me, whispered in my ear, rubbed the middle of my ass and asked, "Right here?"

"No, still lower." He took the hint and let his fingers explore between my legs. He started rubbing my clit through my thongs and I moaned. "Um, yeah, that's it."

He kept rubbing and whispered, "Hmm, well, I think I can remedy that."

"Really?"

"Indeed. You know chiropractors specialize in taking aches away."

I started grinding my pussy on his finger. "That's what I've heard but I've never had a chiropractor work me over before."

"What a shame."

"Yes, it is quite a shame. But wait, there's more," I said excitedly.

He grinned at me. "Oh, you poor thing. Where else does it hurt?"

"Let me see your hand." He took his finger out my pussy and I lifted it to my mouth. "It hurts right here," I said, taking his finger fully into my mouth and suckling on it.

"Really?"

I could tell he was turned on by me sucking my pussy juice off his finger. "Oh, yeah."

"How often?" he asked, taking the same finger and brushing my hair away from my cheek.

"It started out periodically but now it's quite frequent."

"How frequent?"

I gazed into his sexy eyes. "Almost every day; especially at night."

"That's common. Most pain gets worse at night, in cold weather, that sort of thing."

I stood up and started getting undressed. There were no inhibitions left with me. I wanted him and I was going to have him that night. "Hmm, that could be it. My bed is awfully cold at night."

"Is it? Have you tried turning up the heat?"

He sat there, watching everything come off me. We continued to carry on the conversation like it was casual. Like I was a new patient in his office seeking a consultation.

"Yes, but it doesn't work. Adjusting my thermostat in my hallway isn't the problem," I said nonchalantly as my last piece of clothing hit the floor.

"I see."

I pulled him up off the couch and undid his tie, removing it swiftly and then starting in on the buttons on his shirt. "No matter what I set the temperature on, no matter how many blankets I put on my bed, it's still cold. Freezing even."

"Aw, well, I see what your problem is."

Yardley grabbed my hands and kissed the knuckles on each one, refraining me from taking the rest of his shirt off.

"You do?" I asked him, breathing heavily with our mouths mere inches apart. "Explain it to me."

He released my hands, took his open palms and ran them down over my breasts and my nipples that were as hard as black pearls. "All of these aches you're feeling are caused by a misaligned spine. You need me to straighten it out."

I lowered my hands and started undoing his belt buckle. "And how would you go about that? It sounds painful."

Yardley closed his palms around my breasts and squeezed, exerting just enough pressure to make me wince with pleasure. He knew I liked it.

He whispered, "Actually, I think you'll get a significant amount of pleasure from it."

"Oh, yeah?" I asked as he started sucking on my neck.

"Oh, yeah."

He sat down on the couch and pulled me on top of him, my knees straddling his thighs. He drew my left nipple into his mouth and devoured it like it was a peach.

I moaned. "So explain it to me. How you would go about it, I mean."

I braced my hands on his shoulders as he pushed my breasts together and licked and sucked back and forth between the two. He worked them over for a good five minutes before responding, "I can straighten out your spine in one of two ways."

"What are the two ways?"

Before he could answer, I slid my tongue into his mouth. I'd never wanted to feel as one with another soul as much as I did at that moment. The intensity of our passion grew as he embraced me tightly around the waist. We played a concerto with our tongues and Yardley started fingering my pussy again. It was so exhilarating that I had to break the kiss so I could catch my breath.

He hadn't forgotten my question. "Option A would mean me taking you to my office, putting you on an examination table, taking some X-rays and then using a professional technique to make you feel better."

I grinned. "Hmm, sounds interesting but let me hear Option B."

"Option B is a good one; a better one even."

"I'm listening."

Yardley scooted to the edge of the sofa and stood up with me in his arms. I locked my legs behind his back as he carried me to the bed.

"I could tell you but I think at this point, I better show you. This seems like a medical emergency to me, Rayne."

"Oh, yes, Doctor, it's definitely a medical emergency."

After placing me on the bed, Yardley whipped out a jar of maraschino cherries from somewhere, placed a folded towel on the bed underneath me so as not to ruin the sheets, and then spread my legs open. He dug a cherry out the jar with his finger and placed it right inside the cusp of my vagina. He lobbed the cherry around with his tongue and then slipped it as deep inside of me as he could get it. The cherry felt cool against my insides and I giggled as Yardley proceeded to dine on me for the next fifteen minutes or so. Then it was my turn to reciprocate. I pulled his shoes off, finished unbuckling the belt I'd started working on earlier, undid his zipper, and pulled his pants off while he was on his back. I took off his black cotton briefs next and there it was; his dick; my new best friend.

"It's a pleasure to make your acquaintance, Yardley's dick," I stated teasingly. "Do you have a nickname or should I simply call you Mr. Dick, Dick, or The Dick?"

We both laughed.

Yardley responded, "I guess I can answer that. Why don't you call him "My Dick" because he belongs to you now."

"Does he really?"

"Yes."

I ran my fingertips over the veins that were pulsating throughout his dick. "Are you asking me for exclusivity, Yardley?"

He reached out for my left nipple and started rubbing it between his thumb and forefinger. "Absolutely. I've wanted you for a long time, Rayne. I'm not about to screw this up by doing something stupid. I'm also not about to put on pretenses. I want you," he said to me in the sexiest voice I'd ever heard. "I want all of you; not only the part I'll get to enjoy here tonight. This is the real deal for me, and I hope it's the real deal for you."

There was an air of seriousness in the room, and I felt a jolt go down my spine. I'd wanted him for a long time too, but I was so used to disappointments. Things often started out seemingly perfect with a man, only to turn into disaster later; even if it was years later.

He raised an eyebrow. I was still getting to know "My Dick" and he was still rubbing my nipple. "No response, Rayne? I pour my heart out to you and no comment?"

"Yardley, I'm glad we've decided to take this to the next step," I said softly. "Can we just let it be what it's going to be though?"

"Meaning?"

"Meaning who's to say that I won't give you my heart, and months, weeks, or even days from now, you might change your mind?"

He seemed sincere when he said, "I'm not going to change my mind, Rayne."

"How can you be so sure?"

"Because I've waited my entire life for you. I have. I didn't know your name in the beginning but your face went to bed with me every night. When I came into the bank, it was because I wanted to see you. My secretary could've made the deposits and handled banking matters for me, but I'd come in there hoping to catch even a glimpse of your lovely face." He took his free hand and caressed my ass cheek. "This lovely body."

"You really like my body?" I asked.

"Who wouldn't?"

"Lots of men would consider me too 'thick' or 'big-boned' for them."

"That's their stupidity and their loss." He pulled my face down to his by my neck and kissed me tenderly. "You're perfect, Rayne Waters."

I was on the brink of tears. "No man's ever talked to me like that before."

"Like I said, their stupidity and their loss."

"Well, I wouldn't want you to lose out on the cherry action," I said, trying to lighten the mood. "Let me taste *my dick.*"

I had him sit on the same towel and I poured the sweet cherry juice all over his dick, which was sticking straight up in the air. I placed one cherry on top of it and then pretended that I was enjoying an ice cream cone. It was ten times better than the death by chocolate flavor I was addicted to. This was a new kind of chocolate and I was addicted to it already.

Yardley moaned loudly as some precum squirted out the head of his dick. I took him deep inside my mouth and devoured it. "Um, I think the pain in my mouth is gone."

He laughed and propped himself on his elbows so he could watch me enjoy him. I stared at him. There's something about watching the expression on a man's face while you suck his dick. Some of them squeeze their eyes shut like they can hardly take it, some of them give you this evil glare like they really want to strangle you but can't because they're frozen in ecstasy, and some of them look at you the way Yardley was looking at me; with eyes that let a sister know how much they appreciate you going down on them.

Yardley started running his fingers gently through my hair and that turned me on even more. "What about that other pain?" he asked, referring to my pussy. "Did I help that out?"

I paused for a second, let his dick exit my mouth and gave him a hand job, letting my grip replace the pressure my cheeks had been putting on it.

"You prepped it for surgery."

"Is that right?"

"Uh-huh, now I think it's time for you to operate, Doctor." I licked a trail from his belly button up the center of his chest as I moved my hips into position over his dick, which was still holding steady. I marinated my pussy lips with the head and the cherry juice that remained. "One thing, though," I added.

He knew what I was talking about. "In my right pants pocket."

I lifted his pants off the floor and got the small box of three condoms out his pocket. I took one of them out, ripped the packet open, and propped it on my lips. Then I did something I'd seen on television once and put the condom on his dick with my mouth.

I was about to climb on him when he said, "Wait."

"We don't want to wait too long." I slid my wrist up and down the rubber. "I want to take full advantage of the situation."

"I need to know one thing, Rayne."

"What's that?" I asked.

"Tonight means something to you, right? I mean, you're not going to sleep with me and then disappear out of my life. Are you?"

"No, I have no intention of doing that, Yardley. This is happening fast, you know? We've only been dating a few weeks."

"But it seems like much longer to me."

I had to be honest. "It seems that way to me, too. Let's see what happens. Tomorrow's not promised to anyone so let's take it day by day."

"Tomorrow's not promised; this much is true. That doesn't mean you shouldn't look into the future; our future."

"Yardley, you're the most special man I've ever met. I agree that we've been placed together, in this space, in this time, for a reason. I won't run away before we figure out what that reason is." I picked up the jar of cherries and poured all of them, the remaining juice and all, over the rubber on his dick. "Right now, let's make some cherry smash."

We both laughed as I mounted him. The sensation of the cherries mixing between us was tickling me. We both came numerous times throughout the night. When Yardley took me from behind, it was so intense—or maybe my feelings were—that I screamed out in bed for the very first time.

It started raining and we opened the windows to let the fresh air in. We laid there, for what seemed like an eternity, with me on my back and his dick inside me. There were no words spoken between us; we spoke only with our eyes. Tears started streaking down Yardley's left cheek and he shuddered. There it was, in those mesmerizing eyes; *love.*

Twenty-five

Yardley

She'd actually made me do it. Rayne Waters had made me cry during sex. It wasn't because she'd pussy-whipped me or anything like that. Most brothers swear that's the only thing that could make them lose it. Up until then, I'd felt the same way. But it wasn't a pussy-whipping that made me cry. It was love. I was in love with her. I wasn't sure what the other women had been to me anymore. Some of them I'd thought I was in love with. Obviously it was something beneath that; powerful lust maybe.

I couldn't believe that I'd opened up so much to her that night; even though I was expecting Valentine's Day to be special. It was almost as if I was begging her to be with me. Rayne had some serious issues she needed to overcome; I could see that. I was going to help her work through them. After all, a person's thoughts and emotional tendencies are a culmination of everything they've ever seen or experienced. No one knew that better than me.

Rayne didn't trust men but I was determined that she would trust me.

Saturday morning the fellas and I were all present and accounted for on the court. It was getting colder and soon we'd have to give it up until the spring. Indoor basketball wasn't an option for us. We liked being out in the open, doing our thing. So for a few months a year, we'd hibernate. We'd still hang out from time to time but not every Saturday. We'd bullshit around playing poker for phony money because I didn't believe in gambling. I'd been to Atlantic City a few times and to Las Vegas once on business and it amazed me how people would sit glued to the same slot machine or blackjack table for hours at a time; steadily losing money. What really tripped me out is that as loud as casinos are because of the machines and hustle and bustle, the one thing you rarely heard in there was laughter. People would sit there with these deadpan expressions on their faces, stressing over something they clearly chose to engage in.

Felix used to take women to Atlantic City for the weekend to impress them. Then he figured out he was silly for taking sand to the beach. With all the cocktail waitresses and showgirls prancing around in skimpy outfits, a playa like him was better off traveling alone.

"So, you guys," Mike said halfway through our game. "Are you coming to see me in the play next weekend?"

"Damn, I almost forgot," Felix said. "I'm supposed to be going out of town but I'll cancel."

Dwayne, Mike, and I were equally stunned. Usually Felix was all about Felix and wouldn't alter plans for anyone.

"You'd really do that for me?" Mike asked.

Felix threw the ball into his chest. "Of course. How long have we all been boys? You've been wanting to do this acting gig for a while and now it seems like you're about to get that big break. I wouldn't miss it for the world."

That much was true. Mike had made some waves in the industry but starring in the latest Strebor Entertainment play was as big as it got in the African-American community. This one was called *Curveballs* and Mike had one of the male leads. It was about a love triangle involving a female veterinarian, a famous baseball player and a homeless man. Mike was playing the pretty boy, the baseball player who'd been caught cheating on his fiancée after making it in the pros. She'd dumped him and sent him on his merry way. It was all good, the money, the fame, and the women, until he got hurt. Now he was coming back home, trying to win her back, but she wasn't having it. Instead, she was crazy over a homeless brother she'd met by accident. It was written by a *New York Times* bestselling author and Mike had let me peruse the script. It seemed pretty hot and I was looking forward to attending. I'd already asked Rayne to go with me.

"I'll definitely be there," I told Mike. "You know I've got your back."

Dwayne said, "And you can count me in as well. I already bought tickets for me, my folks, my grandparents, and my lady."

"Who's your lady?" Mike and Felix both asked in unison; nosy asses.

It had been awhile since Dwayne had considered a female "his lady." He wasn't a dog like Felix but he wasn't trying to get serious with anyone either. He'd date but rarely brought women around us for an introduction. We'd only hear fleeting tales of this woman and that woman. How good she was in bed; how her culinary skills were because Dwayne loved to eat. His momma was one of those old-fashioned Southern women who believed she had to have a full-course meal on the table every night.

We were all standing there, having paused the game, waiting for a response.

"Her name's Opal," he said. "Opal Reid."

"That name sounds familiar to me," Felix immediately chimed in. "She's not someone I used to bone, is she?"

While I knew Felix was joking—at least halfway—Dwayne didn't appreciate the question. "Fuck you, Felix! Do you ever think with anything other than your dick?"

Felix chuckled and looked up toward the right, like he was heavy in thought. "Honestly, no. I think about money but most of the time it's all about my dick."

I laughed then, remembering Arjay's comment about men only concentrating on money and pussy.

"What's so funny?" Dwayne asked, about to get militant with me. "That's the problem with you brothers. Life's about more than sex. Half the brothers in the jail are in there because they were trying to impress some hoochie; support them because they're too lazy to support themselves."

Mike chimed in on that one. "I disagree. Sure, some men have been stupid enough to let a woman talk them into a life of crime but a real man makes his own decisions. There isn't a pussy on the face of the earth that could make me sling dope or commit any type of crime."

"Amen to that," Felix said. "Those idiots are locked up because they fell for that easy money game. I love money but I work for my shit."

Dwayne went there then. "What about all the innocent brothers locked up?"

"Hold up," Mike said. "A minute ago you were preaching about how half the brothers in jail are in there because of women."

"Yeah," Dwayne replied, "and the other half are in there because they were railroaded."

"Whatever," I said in disgust. "Are we going to finish the game or what? I need to make tracks because I have something to do later."

"Your new girlfriend?" Felix asked.

"Yeah, what of it?" I replied.

"Don't get nasty, Yardley. I've apologized over and over about Roxie."

"And I've told you over and over again, Felix, you can have Roxie and she can have you."

"Yeah, yeah, yeah, I sit there and vibe with some of the brothers when I work the late shift and some of them are fucking brilliant. I'm telling you. They're in there writing novels, memoirs, getting their education, practicing jailhouse law, all of that." Dwayne was trying his best to change the subject back. "One young brother was valedictorian at his high school last year and now he's doing twenty to life for being in the wrong place at the wrong time."

"Let's just play," Felix said.

"Let's do this," I agreed.

We ended up working up a good sweat and decided to let bygones be bygones. Besides, I'd get to see Rayne later that night and she was all that mattered to me.

I got home around one that afternoon. I planned to grab a shower and a long nap before I headed to Rayne's place to pick her and her mother up. It was a bold move, inviting both Rayne and her alcoholic mother over my parents' house in Silver Spring for dinner. I wanted to spend the rest of my life with her so the cat was going to have to be let out the bag sooner or later. We'd all have to learn to be one big happy family.

When I entered the lobby of my building, I was taken aback when I spotted Sheila profiling on one of the leather guest chairs.

She hopped up and threw her arms around me. "I've been waiting for you, baby."

"Um, Sheila, what are you doing here?" I gently shoved her away from me.

"What do you think I'm doing here? I wanted to see you. Today's Saturday so I knew you'd be playing ball this morning. Some things never change."

"And other things do," I told her. "Listen, I——"

"Look at you, baby. Umph, umph, umph, still as fine as wine." She came closer and sniffed me. "Sweaty and all; just like old times. Remember when you used to come back on Saturdays, have me for lunch, and make love to me in the shower?"

"I remember a lot of things, Sheila, like you running off with your girlfriend Raven and leaving me a lousy note."

She pouted. "I made a mistake, Yardley. Can't you forgive me?"

"Forgiving isn't a problem for me."

"Great!" she exclaimed. "Then we can take up right where we left off."

"You're absolutely unbelievable!" I stated loudly, heading for the elevator so I could make an escape.

"Good idea. Let's go upstairs and make love right this second."

"Sheila, I'm not making love to you. I'm not even going to touch you." I pressed the up button and got out my access card for the penthouse. "Do you think I've been sitting around twiddling my thumbs since you jetted? Life goes on and I've moved on."

"Is she as pretty as me?" Sheila asked with much sarcasm in her tone.

"She's prettier than you," I said with a smirk. "Prettier, sexier, smarter, and everything else combined."

"That's some cold ass shit to say to me, Yardley! After all we were to each other."

"What we had was cool, while it lasted. You made the decision to end it and now I realize everything happens for a reason. We weren't meant to be together."

"Yes, we were," she insisted.

"No, not at all. I've found the person I'm supposed to be with. I've *finally* found her and I'm not fucking it up. You need to go out there in this great big world and find the man—or woman—you're supposed to be with, but I can't help you."

The elevator opened and I got on.

"Can't we talk this out?" Sheila asked.

"There's nothing to talk about."

I watched Sheila disappear behind the doors and prayed it was the last time I laid eyes on her. All I wanted, all I could envision, was a life with Rayne.

Twenty-six

Rayne

"Okay, I'll bite. I know what naps are but what the hell are baps?"

My mother had been hitting the bottle while I was at work and was being awfully loud as we sat in the waiting area of From Naps to Baps. She'd begged me to bring her with me to my weekly hair appointment. Against my better judgment, I'd decided to let her tag along. I felt sorry for her because she'd been hibernating in my apartment for a few days, feeling sorry for herself and only leaving out to make a "spirit run." Yardley had invited us both to dinner at his parents' home the previous Saturday, and it was a nightmare.

Mr. and Mrs. Brown were the kindest couple on the face of the earth and I saw where Yardley got his compassion from. I'd warned Momma not to show out but that was the equivalent of trying to teach a pig to wipe his snout with a napkin.

I'd given Momma one of my dress suits to wear because she

didn't have anything appropriate in her numerous bags. Yardley was driving an Infiniti that night. I didn't even realize he had a second car since he always picked me up in his two-seater Porsche. Momma ranted and raved the entire way to Silver Spring. I'd made her "dry out" and she was feenin' for some liquor.

When we arrived at the Browns' split-level home, Yardley used his key to let us in so he could sneak up on his parents, who were sitting in the family room watching *Jeopardy!* Mrs. Brown, a petite woman with a voice that sounded like it would belong to a woman twice her size, embraced both Momma and me as if she'd known us for decades. I immediately felt right at home.

His father was tall and it looked like he'd spit Yardley out; the resemblance was so uncanny. He was much more soft-spoken than his wife and I could imagine him teaching math. Mrs. Brown was a science teacher. They were the perfect match; two people who visibly loved their careers, their only child, and each other.

"So you're an only child also?" Mr. Brown asked me over the table as we dined on country-style steak, mashed potatoes with gravy, and string beans with homemade biscuits.

"Yes, I am," I replied.

"That's debatable," Momma blurted out, having taken Mr. Brown up on his offer for some dinner wine. She was up to glass four already and I was totally embarrassed.

"Debatable?" Mrs. Brown asked.

I glared at Momma across the table. She glared back and sucked her teeth.

"What do you mean by that, Arjay?" Mrs. Brown prodded.

"Being that I haven't a clue whose Rayne's daddy is, she could have fifty siblings for all I know. Surely if he pulled a fast one on me, then he's pulled fast ones on other women as well."

Yardley cleared his throat and took my hand, helping me to suppress the scream that was building up in my throat.

Mrs. Brown had this expression of disgust on her face. She glanced back and forth between Momma and me. I lowered my eyes to the table and refused to look back up until I could pull myself together.

"So, Son," his father asked, "how's the practice going?"

"It's coming along great, Dad. You have to stop by the office soon and see the renovations."

"Oh, they're done?" Mr. Brown pointed to the bowl of mashed potatoes. "Arjay, can you pass the potatoes, please?"

"Certainly, Corbett." Momma picked up the bowl and handed it to him. She lingered long enough to make eye contact with him and then touched his hand with her free one. "My, my, you have such soft hands."

No she wasn't! No she was not!

"Momma, can I speak to you for a moment? In the other room."

"We're in the middle of dinner, Rayne," Momma hissed at me. "We can talk any time."

Yardley leaned over and whispered in my ear, "It's okay, baby. Let it go."

"Corbett, how long have you and Agnes over here been married?" Momma asked, nodding her head toward Yardley's mother.

"We'll be married thirty-five years this spring," Mrs. Brown replied. "Have you ever been married?"

Momma smirked as if to say, "I wasn't talking to you!" She wanted Mr. Brown to answer.

"Humph, not me," Momma replied. "Never been married and never trying to be married. There are too many men on this planet for me to be tied down to one. Variety is the spice of life and I love my variety, don't I, baby?"

It dawned on me that she was addressing me. I didn't respond.

Momma continued, "You two come across as the swinging type. Do you ever swing, Corbett?"

Mr. Brown obviously knew what Momma meant but Yardley's mother didn't get it, so she asked, "Swing?"

I could tell Momma was getting vexed. She wasn't used to men snubbing her; even in front of their own wives.

"Swing as in fuck around, participate in orgies, get your freak on," Momma chastised.

"That's it!" I stood up, threw my napkin on the table, walked around to the other side and pulled Momma up by the elbow. "You're coming with me."

"But the party's just getting started, baby!"

I pushed Momma down into the basement and blessed her out with every word I could think of. She sat there, on the arm of a recliner, pretending like she was bored and picking specks of dirt out of her nails.

"Now you're going to take your ass back up there and apologize to Yardley's parents or else," I stated vehemently, ending my lecture.

"Or else what, Rayne? You gonna spank me?" Momma asked sarcastically.

"No, I'm not going to spank you, Momma; no more than you're ever going to spank me again." I got close enough to her to smell the wine on her breath. "If you don't make amends for your actions here tonight, I'm putting you on the first thing smoking back to Alabama and I'm never going to speak to you again."

Momma was shook. I had her. "Rayne, I was only having a little fun; trying to lighten the mood."

"You haven't lightened a damn thing, Momma. You've disrespected me, you've disrespected Yardley and his parents, and most importantly, you've disrespected yourself here tonight. I'm trying to build something real with this man, Momma. Something that will last. You will not ruin it for me."

Momma rolled her eyes and sat there in silence for a few minutes.

Yardley opened the door and peeked down at us. "Is everything all right, Rayne?"

"No," I said. "But you knew that already."

He came down the steps and put his arms around my waist from behind. I allowed my head to rest against his shoulder. I was so sick of Momma's antics. I'd left Alabama to get away from them and now she'd transported the shit across state lines.

Yardley kissed the top of my head. "It's okay, baby. I've explained things to my folks and they're cool. Let's head on back into town so I can get you home."

"How are your parents ever going to accept me, Yardley? Knowing where I come from, meeting Momma, how will they ever think I'm good enough for you?"

"Rayne," Momma suddenly said. "You're good enough for everybody. Don't ever forget that. My mistakes have been my mistakes. You shouldn't have to pay for them."

I glared into her gray eyes. "Then why must you act out in front of everyone I care about?"

"You're right, Rayne. I went too far tonight." She headed up the steps. "I'm gonna handle this. I'm gonna make things right for you, baby."

I was too humiliated to go back upstairs right away. I couldn't imagine what Momma was up there saying to Yardley's parents. As far as I was concerned, the damage had already been done.

Yardley embraced me and planted kisses on my fingertips, one at a time. "Rayne, I don't expect you to say anything back after I say what I'm about to say. You don't need to feel obligated."

"Obligated about what?" I asked, my interest piqued.

"I'm in love with you, Rayne Waters."

I exhaled. It was like a weight had been lifted off my heart.

"I love you, too, Yardley."

"Shh." He placed his index finger on my lips. "I told you that you don't have to feel obligated to return the feelings."

I took both of his hands into mine and gave him a peck on the lips. "I'm not returning the feelings out of obligation. I'm returning them because they're real."

Then our kiss began. Yardley pushed me back into the downstairs hall, out of range for someone to open the doors and see us from the stairs. We made out and got lost in time. I almost forgot we were in his parents' home.

"Rayne, you down there!" Momma yelled, disturbing our flow.

"Yes, Momma," I responded.

"Come on back up," she said.

When Yardley and I got back upstairs, it was like being abducted by aliens. Everything had changed. The three of them were sitting at the table eating sweet-potato pie and laughing. No further mention was made about my nameless father, his nameless other children, or group sex, and we all managed to get along for a few more hours.

When it was time to leave, Mrs. Brown pulled me aside. "Rayne, I want you to know that Corbett and I both think you are lovely."

"Thanks, Mrs. Brown. I appreciate that."

"Please, call me Agnes."

"Thanks, Agnes, for dinner and for making me feel comfortable in your home; despite what happened earlier."

"Your mother loves you, Rayne. She's a confused soul and she's led a rough life but that doesn't reflect on the love she feels for you."

"Wow, what did Momma say to you and your husband?" I asked in astonishment.

"She was open and honest; that's all. She's extremely proud of you, in case you didn't know that."

I was blown away. "Thanks for being so understanding. For the record, I'm nothing like my mother, Agnes. I care about your son a great deal and I do believe in monogamous relationships."

Agnes grinned. "No need to go there. I can see that you're a woman of integrity. Yardley's lucky to have you in his life. He's been hurt in the past but this isn't a dress rehearsal, so I'm glad he's found something unique with you."

"Unique!" I giggled. "That's a good word for it."

"I'm sure we'll be seeing more of you soon." She kissed me on the cheek. "Let me know when it's time to plan the wedding. Even though it's usually the bride's family who handles all the details, Yardley's my only child so I have to get in where I fit in."

Was she serious about a wedding?

"You think he'll marry me?" I asked, stunned.

"If you'll have him, I know he will." She let out a deep sigh and glanced at Yardley, who was helping Momma into the back seat of his car. "My son has never looked at a woman the way he looks at you. That's the same way Corbett looked at me when we started dating in 1968. The way he still looks at me and the way Yardley will be looking at you thirty-something years from now."

I was at a loss for words so I didn't respond. I hugged her and went to get into the car.

Sitting there in the beauty parlor, I was mulling Agnes's words over in my mind. Things were moving so swiftly. I wasn't sure if I was coming or going. Yardley hadn't mentioned the word "marriage" and I was hoping he wouldn't any time soon. I had a ton of insecurities I needed to sort through before I could be mentally stable enough to trust like that.

"Rayne!" Momma pushed me on the arm. "Are you going to answer me or what?"

"Momma, do you have to be so loud?" I asked, trying to shush her.

"I ain't loud, dammit!" she exclaimed. "I asked a simple fuckin' question."

I rolled my eyes and leaned in closer to her. "Baps are beautiful African princesses."

"Oh, well, your ass wasn't born in Africa and I sure as hell wasn't. My parents made me in the back of your granddad's 1957 Oldsmobile."

"I don't need to know all that, Momma." I glared at her. "How do you know where you were conceived anyway?"

"Your grandparents told me as much, stupid, before they kicked the bucket."

I couldn't believe Momma would talk about her parents' deaths so casually. I never got to know them before they were killed in a house fire. As for my father, Momma wasn't exaggerating at the Browns'. My mother never mentioned him and since the sixth grade, I'd never asked. Momma never knew which one of her lovers fathered me. If they had been airing the *Maury* show back then, she would've been one of the women featured on his paternity episodes. One of the ones that had to test a dozen men and still be pressing her luck that one of them was actually the father.

"Momma, do you see a hairstyle you like?" I asked, changing the subject by pointing to the hairstyle magazine she was holding in her lap. "I think that one would look good on you."

"That would make me look old as shit," she complained. "I need something that makes me look younger."

"Momma, that style would look great on you," I stated in disagreement. "But we can let Boom decide for you. She's great with hair."

"Boom?" she asked in disgust. "What kind of name is that?"

I spotted Boom eyeing us from across the room, pausing from finishing up the head of the sister in her chair. Her eyes narrowed and I thought, *Oh, boy! I hope the two of them don't rip each other's throats out!*

Suddenly, I was regretting bringing Momma. Certain personalities simply clash and I had the eerie feeling that Boom and Momma would end up exchanging words before the evening was over.

I was wrong. Boom and Momma were like twins; talking shit to one another and about practically everyone else in the shop, including me.

When Momma was sitting in Boom's chair getting the finishing touches put on her hair, she said, "Boom, you know Rayne has this new man whose dick must be golden. Has she told you about him?"

Boom looked at me and laughed as I sat in the chair across from them waiting my turn. I'd finished under the dryer and still had curlers in my head.

"Rayne, what man is this?"

"His name's Yardley, Boom," I answered.

"He's a chiropractor," Momma added. "That means he *cracks backs!*"

They both enjoyed a laugh at my expense.

"Conquesto's gonna be jealous as shit," Boom said. "He's still sweating you big time."

"What the hell is a Conquesto?" Momma asked.

"He's Boom's brother," I quickly replied, trying to key her in that she needed to chill on any negative remarks about Conquesto.

For once, Momma took the hint and switched up. "Yeah, that Yardley is a sexy motherfucker, too. So's his daddy but he's taken. Been married thirty-four years. Can you believe that shit?"

"No, hell no," Boom said. "I like to spread my goodies around from time to time. I got a lot of old broads that come in here who've been married since they invented hourglasses but not *moi*. My coochie's like a flower. It needs regular watering and fertilizing to keep it strong."

Momma giggled. "You're too much, Boom. I'm gonna have to get you down there to Alabama so you can hang out at the Eagle with me."

"Oh, Lord," I said. "Not the Eagle."

"What's the Eagle?" Boom asked.

"Trust me, Boom, it's not your type of spot. It's nothing more than a watering hole," I assured her.

"That's what I need," she said. "I've got a hole and it needs watering, like I just said."

"I know that's right," Momma agreed. "I'm telling you, that Alabama black snake is no joke. Some of the men down home will have you ready to move your ass and your shop down there."

"Humph, funny how I never met any of them when I lived there." I rolled my eyes and glanced at my watch. Yardley and I were going to catch a movie later that night and I didn't want to be late. "Can you two hens cut down on the clucking and move it along a little faster?"

Momma held her hand up, trying to shield me from her comment but speaking loud enough for half the salon to hear. "Don't mind her. She thinks she's a diva or some shit, now that she's all in love."

"I never told you I was in love with Yardley, Momma."

"You didn't have to tell me, baby. It's written all over your face. I don't know what the hell happened on Valentine's Day but it must've been all that and then some."

"Ooh, what did you do for Valentine's Day, Rayne?" Boom asked.

"We went out to dinner."

"And?"

"And then they fucked!" Momma yelled out. "They did some serious fucking!"

"Were you in the room, Momma?" I asked sarcastically.

"No, you deserted my ass in your shithole and you damn well know it."

"Damn, she called your place a shithole," Boom said.

Yo-Yo and Tamu joined her in a round of laughter.

"I don't live in anything remotely close to a shithole. Momma's mad because she expected me to drop everything and cater to her the second she hit town. Unexpectedly, I might add. I had no idea she was coming to visit and my plans were already made."

This new reality show was on the broken-down television. I decided to zone them out and see what it was all about. Boom, Momma, and the rest of the hens talked about the latest hoochie fashions, the latest players in the hip-hop arena, and of course about fucking while I watched the show. It was called *Raoul's Love Unions* and it was about women who were trying to hook up with midgets. I seemed to recall the same little fella having another show a few years back. *Raoul's Midget Gladiators,* I believed. It had done okay in ratings but left the air suddenly because one of the midgets got harmed during an obstacle course and sued the producers.

This blonde was on there talking about how she'd always had

this secret fantasy about making love with a midget. She hinted at the fact that his face would be in the perfect spot for "certain delightful activities." Some of the regular television stations might as well go ahead and go porno. Any person over the age of ten—possibly even eight—would know that she was referring to getting her pussy eaten.

I was shaking my head at the nonsense when my cell phone started chanting, "Incoming call!" I retrieved it from my purse, flipped it open and said, "This is Rayne."

"Rayne, this is Yardley."

"Hey, baby. We still going to the movies?"

"For sure. I was just calling to check on your progress."

"Things are coming along. Boom's finishing up with Momma and then it'll take her about fifteen minutes to yank the curlers out my hair and get it situated."

"Cool. I've missed you the last couple of days."

Now I was going to have to go home and change my panties yet again. He made me wet when he said things like that.

"I've missed you, too, Yardley."

Boom and Momma started snickering and I turned my back to them. I could see them in the reflection of the mirror, eyeing me and trying to read my lips once I lowered my voice.

I also turned the volume of the television up before I continued, "How was your day?"

"Long but prosperous. And yours at the bank?"

"Long and boring. Chance called in sick today so I was lonely."

"Is she okay?" Yardley asked.

"She's fine. She and Ricky went to go look at apartments and they didn't want to wait until the weekend. Most of the rental offices close by the time we get off from work."

"I see. Why do they want to move?"

"They're finally sick of living in an efficiency. Chance and

Ricky should've made that move a long time ago. They aren't too good with managing their finances though."

"Chance works in a bank and mismanages money?"

"I know. Mind-boggling, isn't it?"

He chuckled. "And then some. Well, I'll see you in a few, baby. I wanted to hear your voice—get my little fix—until later."

"Aw, that's so sweet."

"Not as sweet as you are to me, Rayne."

"By the way," I said, "that pain I was having before, it's back."

"Oh my, then we have to put you on a regular treatment schedule. I need to treat you at least three times a week before you can achieve any long-term improvement."

"Um, you want to crack my back three times a week?"

"Ooh, I heard that!" Boom yelled out. She looked down at Momma. "Arjay, you were right. Rayne's got it bad."

"I'll see you in a bit, Yardley," I said and hung up the phone quickly. "Do you think the two of you could be any nosier?"

Momma started chanting, "Crack that back! Crack that back!" Boom joined in and before you knew it, the entire salon was chanting and teasing me.

I concentrated back on the television. The blonde was on a dance floor at some club with miniature furniture and decorations, shaking her flat booty to Nelly's "It's Getting Hot in Herre" and bending down so she could swing her hair in the midget's face.

I grinned, not because the show was funny. I couldn't wait to get my *back cracked!*

There's nothing in this world so sweet as love,
And next to love the sweetest thing is hate.
—Henry Wadsworth Longfellow

Twenty-seven

Yardley

The Warner Theater was packed—orchestra section, balconies, box seats, and all—for the premiere of *Curveballs*. Dwayne had an entire row on lockdown. His lady friend, Opal, was on the conservative side but was pretty and rather quiet. I think she may have felt uncomfortable being put on display in front of so many of his family members at one time. He wasn't lying when he said he was representing for Mike. It had been ages since I'd seen Dwayne's parents and grandparents but they were all present. Mike's mother, a widow, was beaming with delight in her front row seat. Rayne and I were in the seats directly behind her. My parents were going to come the following week before the show left to tour in New York, Philadelphia, Atlanta, Detroit, Chicago, and numerous other venues. I'd attempted to get Arjay a ticket to come with us—against all of my common sense—but *fortunately* they were sold out. I'd made an attempt and that saved me from being an asshole in her eyes. She asked Rayne to bring her a program back so she could read about it.

The evening also marked the first time the fellas met Rayne. Dwayne and I managed to steal a few moments in the lobby before the play started.

"That Rayne is gorgeous, man. I can see why you were sweating her all that time," Dwayne said.

I'd filled him in on a little history on the phone a few days earlier. He was amazed that I'd had the patience to restrain myself from asking her out while I was pining for her. It was silly, reflecting back on the entire thing. If I'd asked Rayne out in the beginning and she'd shot me down, it would've been the way the cookie crumbled. Thank goodness I'd finally found the nerve to approach her.

"Yes, Rayne is gorgeous, but she's much more than that. Opal's lovely as well." I tapped him on the arm. "You seem extremely happy, man."

"I am, Yardley. I think she might be the one."

"This must be the year of finding the ones because Rayne's definitely the one for me."

Dwayne laughed. "This must mean that we're finally growing up, huh?"

There was a commotion at the entrance. Felix entered with two half-naked women; one on each arm. They both could've just finished shooting the latest female-degrading music video, or stepped off the stage at the Skylark Lounge over on New York Avenue.

All the men were staring and the women were gawking at the scantily clad females with disdain.

"Some of us have grown up," I told Dwayne, "and some of us never will."

Dwayne crossed his arms and shook his head. "Now why would that fool step up in here with those hoochies?"

"That's easy, man. Felix wants all the attention. This night is supposed to be about Mike, but he can't handle it. I'm glad he canceled his traveling plans to come, but he should've brought Mona and called it a day."

"Oh, is he still seeing that chick?"

"Felix will always be seeing Mona as long as Mona lets him troll for pussy at will. I don't get it. Then again, maybe I do. Some women don't feel desired unless they're mistreated. Backwards ass logic, but it makes sense to them," I said, thinking about the purple-eyed skank cousin of Mona's who'd asked me to keep her.

Felix made his way over to us and I was ready to dodge back inside. "Hey, my brothers. How long before the show starts?"

"Hey, Felix." Dwayne peeped at his watch. "There's only about five minutes left before curtain call."

"Then I'm right on time," Felix said. One of the women cleared her throat, reminding him that they were clinging to him. "Oh, Dwayne and Yardley, I'd like you to meet Vivacious and Miracle."

Humph, stage names if I'd ever heard any.

"It's nice to meet you," I said, forcing a smile. Dwayne didn't open his mouth. He was searching the lobby; probably to make sure Opal wasn't watching him anywhere near the two women with stilettos on that made them virtually the same height as all of us.

Rayne snuck up behind me and put her arms around my waist. "You ready to take our seats?"

"Sure, baby."

"Hello there," Felix said loudly, being all too obvious by trying to get an eagle's eye view of Rayne's body; even though she was braced up behind me. "I'm Felix."

"I'm Rayne."

"It's a pleasure to finally make your acquaintance, Miss Rayne. You've got my boy's nose wide open." Felix licked his lips. "You must be something extra special to take Yardley off the market for good, and so swiftly at that."

Rayne giggled. I sensed she could decipher his bullshit.

"Felix, don't even think about it," I told him.

He let go of both the chicks, like they were suddenly contagious. "Man, why do you have to go there tonight? I was only speaking to her. Don't be so insecure."

"Felix, first of all——" I started in.

"Yardley has no reason to feel insecure," Rayne chimed in. "There's not a man born who could distract me from him. He's compassionate, thoughtful, and he knows how to crack my back."

The two women giggled while Felix and Dwayne both stood there with their mouths hanging open.

Rayne let go of my waist and took my hand. "Come on, baby. Let's go sit down before they stop letting people in."

Curveballs was funny, heart-warming, and an instant hit. The cast got a standing ovation at the end and Mike was practically attacked out in the lobby when he and the other two main leads came out to sign programs and press photos. The women were all over his pretty ass.

There was a cast party later on that night at Foreplay, a trendy private club in Northwest; not too far from my office. Rayne and I decided to pop our heads in since Mike had insisted we come through. Rayne was complaining of a headache so she excused herself to the ladies room. When she hadn't returned a few moments later, I went downstairs where the restrooms were located to check on her.

I was about to knock on the ladies room door when it swung open. Roxie came out. When she spotted me, she started grinning—more like smirking. I could see Rayne standing in front of the vanity and glaring at me in the mirror.

"Hello, baby," she said. "Your slut and I were just getting a few things straightened out."

"How dare you call her a slut?" I lashed out at her. "You fucked my best friend, on my damn balcony, and you're calling someone else a slut."

Roxie smacked her lips and pushed me out the way. "Whatever, Yardley. It's only a matter of time before you come running back to me. Once you realize what you gave up, you'll be kissing my ass to get me back."

"What are you doing here?" I asked. "Are you stalking me, Roxie?"

"No, I'm not stalking you. I don't have to since you'll ultimately be stalking me. I'm an event planner, in case you've forgotten. I organized this party so I have every right to be here."

She let the door close behind her. I could no longer see Rayne.

"You don't have a right to go into the bathroom and talk shit to my woman. That's for damn sure!"

Roxie pushed past me and headed for the stairs. "I have to get back to work. See you next month, next week, or maybe even tomorrow. I think Miss Thang got the message so I suspect the two of you are done. See you in my bedroom, Boo!"

"When they start manufacturing Pintos again, bitch!"

Before I could turn around, I heard the bathroom door reopen. "Yardley, can we please leave now?"

Rayne had obviously been crying. She'd attempted to cover the evidence by refreshing her makeup but her eyes were red.

"We're definitely leaving now; right this second."

I took her hand and led her upstairs and straight out the front door without saying our goodbyes to the fellas and their dates.

I decided to take Rayne to my office. We walked since it was merely a few blocks away. We needed to talk.

After I'd given her a brief tour of my suite—something she would've undoubtedly been more interested in under different circumstances—we settled in my private office.

She was standing in the middle of the floor, staring at a chart of the human spine on my wall. "Can I ask you a question?"

"You can ask me whatever you like."

"Do you ever have any doubts about us?"

"No, never," I replied. "Do you?"

"No."

"Then why ask me that?"

"I was simply curious."

I sighed and walked up behind her. "Rayne, if this is going to last we have to be completely open with one another."

"I totally agree."

I ran my fingers down her back. "Then talk to me. Look at me instead of that stupid ass chart and tell me what's on your mind."

"Yardley, the situation with Roxie earlier tonight made be extremely uncomfortable."

"I know it did and I'm sorry that you had to be subjected to her nonsense."

Rayne finally turned to me. "Are you sure it was nonsense?"

I laughed uneasily. "I don't understand what you're implying, Rayne."

"She said that you're still emotionally attached to her. She said that you're only using me as a substitute to soothe your pain. She said—"

"She said?" I lashed out in anger. I took her saddened face in my hands. "Listen to me, baby. Roxie can't tell you what I'm feeling. Only I can do that and I'm telling you that I adore you. I want this relationship between us to work. I was as leery as you in the beginning. Hell, I've been hurt just like you have. Maybe even worse between the jobs Sheila and Roxie did on me back to back. We're not going to compare heartbreaks though. They're in my past. You're my present and my future."

Rayne bit her bottom lip. I drew it into my mouth and bit it gently also.

"You bring out so many deep emotions in me, Yardley. It's almost scary."

"Don't be afraid, Rayne. I meant what I said to you in my parents' home. I'm in love with you and I'm prepared to spend the rest of my life proving it to you. Can't you see that Roxie was jealous? I didn't hear the bullshit she laid on you in the bathroom but she was completely delusional when she was speaking to me in the hall."

"She's obsessed with you."

I backed Rayne up against the wall, knelt down, and buried my nose in her belly button through her silk blouse. "And I'm obsessed with you, Rayne Waters." I pushed her skirt up over her hips. "Damn, I can smell it calling me."

She had on these satin black thongs and thigh-high black silk stockings. I wanted her so badly.

"You think seducing me will get my mind off what happened tonight?" she whispered.

"Shhh, Rayne." I lowered my head as I pulled the thongs down and lifted each one of her feet so she could step out of them. I licked the front of her pussy. "Um, you taste so good; so sweet. Put your leg on my shoulder."

Rayne lifted her left leg and placed it over my right shoulder. "Anything else?"

"Yes."

"What?"

"Play with your nipples for me."

Rayne unbuttoned her blouse and let it cascade from her shoulders, down around her waist where the wall caught it from behind. She lowered her bra straps just far enough for her breasts to extend beyond the cups. I watched her from below, fingering her pussy while she ran her manicured fingertips over her nipples. They were hard; like diamonds.

She raised her left breast up so she could flick her tongue over the nipple. She moaned as I licked the lips of her pussy. She rubbed the back of my head with her free hand as I buried my tongue inside her; searching for her essence.

"You keep this up and you're going to spoil me," she whispered.

I stopped long enough to say, "Good."

"It's so quiet here; so peaceful."

"Only at night," I said. "Turn around."

"Why?"

"Just do it."

Rayne took her leg off my shoulder and faced the wall. "What are you about to do to me?"

"You'll see." I changed my mind about what I wanted to do the second I saw her scrumptious ass in the dim lighting from the X-ray wall; the only light I had on in the room. "Come here," I said, as I pulled her by the waist over to my desk. "Bend over."

She giggled. "You're getting awfully demanding." She turned around and pecked me on the lips. "But I like it."

She leaned over the desk and I scooted my ergonomic chair up right behind her. Her pussy was dripping wet. I took some of her onto my fingers and smeared it on her ass cheeks. Then I started eating her out from behind.

"Did you not have dinner tonight?" she asked jokingly after about ten minutes.

I unbuckled my pants, still pleasing her. By the time Rayne exploded on my tongue, I was primed and ready. I'd been stroking myself to hardness. I'd even managed to get a condom out my pocket and slip it on. Swiftly, I rose up so I could stick my dick right in.

"Oooh, my dick," Rayne whispered as I invaded her walls.

"Did you miss him?"

"Um, hmm."

"Can you tell he missed you, too?" I asked as we caught a rhythm with our strokes.

"Yes!" she exclaimed as I pulled her back more onto me by yanking her hair.

I'd always had this fantasy about making love in my office but in the years I'd been practicing, it had never happened. I was glad because now it meant the only memories of it would be with my wife. Rayne would be my wife. I didn't know how and when it would happen, but it would. I didn't want to scare her off by blurting my thoughts out right then. All in good time.

After my desk, I took Rayne in another room and laid her on the rolling table, where these small balls vibrated up and down her spine while I made love to her yet again. We fell asleep on that table; me and my future wife.

Twenty-eight

"Chance, what's the emergency?" I asked, having answered my phone on Saturday morning to her voice yelling, "You've got to get over here!"

"There's no emergency," Chance responded. "I want you to come over and see my new place. Is that an issue? I mean, you are my best friend and shit."

I plopped down on my sofa, relieved that there was indeed no true emergency. "Aw, vicious, aren't we?"

"I'm saying though. Just because you got a man now doesn't mean we can't hang out, does it?"

The sarcasm in her voice was as thick as lard. It had been a while since Chance and I had spent time together outside of the bank. That had never happened before. No matter who we were dating or how serious we were with them, Chance and I always hung out. Things were different now. I was caught up in Yardley.

"No, we can still do things," I told her. "I've been wanting the four of us to do something together anyway. You've seen Yardley hundreds of times but haven't really gotten to know him."

"This much is true, chica. That's because you've been hogging Mr. Wonderful all to yourself."

We both giggled into the phone. I bit into my saltine crackers and took a sip of sparkling water. Hell of a breakfast.

"So how about this? Yardley and I can come over tonight and help you and Ricky unpack." Chance didn't respond for a few seconds. "You there?"

"I'm here." She paused. "Actually, can you come by yourself?"

"Why?"

"Ricky's going out tonight and I thought we could spend some girlfriend time together."

I hesitated and then said, "Okay, that's cool. Yardley and I didn't have any concrete plans anyway."

"Great!"

"You want me to bring something to eat? We haven't had any Horace and Dickey's for awhile."

"You bring that over here and both of us will be laid out on the sofa."

We both laughed again. Horace and Dickey's was this carry-out on 12th Street in Northeast that always had a line down the block. They had the best fried fish and the macaroni and cheese was "saying something."

"You have a point. We do pig out on it," I admitted.

"That's because it's some good ass fish."

I needed to get off the phone and do some laundry, which I hated even contemplating doing. "Let me run, Chance."

"See you around eight?"

"I'll be there."

"With some salads?"

I paused. I was feeling the fried fish and macaroni and cheese idea more. I caved in. "Sure, with some salads."

I called Yardley on his cell phone to see what he was doing. He was out shopping with his mother for an anniversary gift for his dad. They were celebrating their thirty-fifth and Yardley was also helping his mother plan a surprise party. I'd gone with her to scout out locations and she'd booked the Atrium at Treetop in New Carrollton.

Yardley asked if I wanted to meet them at Blvd. at the Cap Center, a new outdoor shopping center that had recently opened up in Largo. As with all new shopping spots, it would be over-crowded and therefore, I didn't need to be anywhere near it. I hated crowds and preferred to shop right before stores closed and mostly in out of the way places.

I told Yardley that I'd catch up with him later on, but informed him that I would be spending the evening alone with Chance. He thought it was a good idea and said he might see if the fellas wanted to come over to the penthouse and play poker. They'd given up basketball on Saturdays for a while until the weather warmed up.

I spent the afternoon cleaning up my place. I hadn't really had a chance to do it since Momma had headed back to Alabama; *reluctantly.* She was hinting at possibly moving to D.C. and I was open and honest with her. I loved Momma but she and I could never live together again; or even in the same city, for that matter. She was too *animated* for me and I didn't want us to end up hating each other after we'd finally been able to hash some of our drama out.

She was still teetering between going and staying when Truck called and sweet-talked her into coming back to be with him. I couldn't figure the two of them out but it wasn't for me to under-stand. Truck knew Momma slept around and I suspected Truck was getting his groove on with other women as well. What was the point of having a long-term relationship if it wasn't exclusive?

I'd seen Roxie—that bitch—again once, coming out of a restaurant in Georgetown. She was with a date and I know she spotted me. I started to go up to her and bless her out in front of him. That would've served her right. I decided against it; grateful that she'd apparently moved on. That night at Foreplay, in the ladies room, I wanted to rip Roxie a new asshole.

I was finished tinkling and was standing at the sink washing my hands when she came in the bathroom.

"Good evening," I said, always one to address strangers when only two of us are present in the room.

She stood there and glared at me.

"Do I know you?" I asked.

"My name's Roxie!" She threw her hands on her hips as I recognized the name. There couldn't have been two of them. "You know who I am, don't you?"

I sighed, preparing myself for looming drama. "Yes, I know who you are. You're Yardley's ex."

"So he's told you about me?"

"He and I have both *briefly* discussed our pasts. Everybody has one."

"Did he tell you how long he chased after me?"

"Yardley told me that he had a crush on you in high school, that you lost touch for a long time, and then reunited for a bit. No big deal," I stated nonchalantly as I applied a fresh coat of lipstick in the mirror.

"Oh, it was a big fucking deal!" She came up closer behind me. "Yardley has always been and will forever be *my man!*"

"Is he aware of that?"

I laughed as another sister came into the restroom and entered a stall.

"You think you're cute, don't you?" she asked me.

I shrugged. "I'm not ugly."

"But you're fat!"

That comment stung. I wasn't fat but I hated skinny little women who said shit like that.

The other sister finished up and came out to wash her hands. She lingered a little longer than she needed to; trying to be nosy, no doubt.

I turned my neck to the right to glare at her, making her aware that she needed to bounce. For that matter, I should've stormed out right then. I wanted a piece of the bitch, though, so I stayed and waited for the other one to leave.

Once she was gone, I turned to face Roxie.

"I'm not fat. God didn't intend for me to be skin and bones like you. It's true that society has played up this anorexic image of what's considered sexy but the fact of the matter is that more sisters look like me than you."

She inched closer to me. "Your point?"

"My point is that none of us seem to be lacking in the relationship department. I know more miserable petite women than I know large ones. Think on that."

"This is a cute conversation," Roxie said, "but it's irrelevant."

"You brought it up."

"Yardley's using you, trying to get over me on the rebound, but he'll never get over me."

"Being that he's here with me, it appears he already has."

"Did Yardley ever tell you his nickname for me?"

I laughed uneasily, quite sure I didn't want her to reveal it.

"He used to call me his *dick slayer*."

"Cute name. Kind of like the nickname I have for his penis; *my dick,*" I came back at her. I turned to the mirror and straightened my hair.

Roxie pushed me on the back and headed for the door. I started to whip her little ass but wasn't about to get into a brawl on a night that was so special to Yardley and his friends.

I heard Roxie say, "Hello, baby. Your slut and I were just getting a few things straightened out."

Yardley was standing outside the door. I glared at him in the mirror's reflection; even though I knew what Roxie had said to me wasn't his fault.

"How dare you call her a slut?" he lashed out at her. "You fucked my best friend, on my damn balcony, and you're calling someone else a slut."

Roxie smacked her lips and pushed him out the way. "Whatever, Yardley. It's only a matter of time before you come running back to me. Once you realize what you gave up, you'll be kissing my ass to get me back."

"What are you doing here?" he asked. "Are you stalking me, Roxie?"

"No, I'm not stalking you. I don't have to since you'll ultimately be stalking me. I'm an event planner, in case you've forgotten. I organized this party so I have every right to be here."

I could hear their muffled conversation through the door. It was then that I realized there were tears flowing down my face. How could I have let that bitch get to me? I wiped them away with some facial tissues off the counter and straightened out my blouse and skirt.

As I opened the door to exit, I heard Yardley yelling, "When they start manufacturing Pintos again, bitch!"

He turned around and I asked, "Yardley, can we please leave now?"

We ended up going to his office. I'd never been there and had been looking forward to seeing it; being that he was at my job regularly. It was a beautiful suite. We had a talk about what had happened and he assured me that he was only into me. Then he proved it by making love to me; right there. He had this table with these balls that roll up and down your spine. He worked his dick inside me as those balls worked me from underneath. I hadn't done it yet but I definitely planned to order one of those massage chairs from The Sharper Image catalog. They were expensive but after that experience, I wanted Yardley and me to be able to perform that kind of magic in my apartment without having to go to his office. It was the shit.

I bought two chicken caesar salads from Chicken Out Rotisserie and headed to Chance's apartment around eight. She'd moved from Adams Morgan to Connecticut Avenue; within walking distance from the National Zoo. I hadn't been to the zoo in ages and that was a shame because I loved animals. So many people who live in big cities never take advantage of the local museums and attractions. Washington, D.C., was one of the biggest draws for tourists—even after the 9/11 terrorist attacks. Yet, I rarely went to check out anything. I was going to mention it to Yardley. He'd been living there his entire life—with the exception of attending NCCU—and I was willing to bet he hadn't been to a museum or the zoo in years.

Chance and Ricky had leased a two-bedroom. It was a high-rent district, much like Georgetown where I lived, but you got what you paid for. The lobby had a lot of character, with antique leather furniture and marble floors.

I pushed the button for the elevator and cursed because I realized I'd forgotten to ask for extra dressing for my salad. Most restaurants skimp people on dressing for carryout orders. They need to invent some larger condiment cups or make sure they give everyone at least two per salad. I was hoping Chance had some black cherry soda. It was strange. Black cherry was my favorite flavor but I never purchased it. I only drank it when I went to visit Chance, which meant I hadn't had one in a while.

I was excited that she and I would be able to do some bonding. I had so much to tell her; mostly about me and Yardley. Things were getting serious—as if they didn't start out on a serious note—and I had the feeling he was ready to take things to the next level already. I wasn't sure if I was emotionally prepared to go there.

I definitely wasn't emotionally prepared for what I saw when Chance's door swung up after I rang the bell.

"Hello, Rayne!"

There he was; after all those years.

"Hello, Ruiz. What a surprise," I stated with much discomfort. "I wasn't expecting to see you here."

He flashed that cinematic smile at me that I hadn't forgotten. "That's because I'm supposed to be a surprise."

Then I said something totally ridiculous. I looked at the bag in my hands. "But I didn't bring you a salad."

He laughed and moved aside, taking the bag from me. "Come on in." He set the bag in the dining room. "Chance is in the shower. She'll be out in a few. She was hot and sweaty from unpacking these boxes all day."

"Have you been helping her?"

"For the most part, she wouldn't let me. She was acting like she had some top secret shit or something."

I giggled because I knew Chance was afraid that her older brother would happen upon some of her sex toys. As unorganized as she was, I was sure she hadn't bothered to label any boxes. What would you label something like that anyway? *Anal Beads and Dildos?*

"You're beautiful, Rayne."

I found myself blushing. "Thanks for noticing."

"I've always noticed." He came closer to me and rubbed his thumb down my arm. "Remember that night we spent together?"

"How could I ever forget the night you took my virginity and then pushed me to the curb?"

The smile dissipated from his face. "It wasn't that way, Rayne."

"Humph, well, that's the way I viewed it."

He pointed at the sofa. "Why don't we sit down?"

I sat and asked, "So, when's the big day? The second big day, that is."

Ruiz shrugged. "What big day?"

"Aren't you getting remarried?"

He picked up a beer that had been sitting on the coffee table and took a swig. "Nah, not anymore. She called it off."

"Why?"

He shrugged again. "Who knows? She was a psychotic bitch anyway. That's all I seem to get caught up with. My first wife was a slut and this one was sick. I need to reevaluate my criteria when it comes to women." He put his hands on my thigh. "Or possibly revisit the past."

I couldn't believe it. After all that time, his mere touch still made me weak.

I moved farther away from him on the sofa. "What's taking Chance so long?"

"You know she washes her hair every time she takes a shower." He moved down also; closing the gap. "Relax, Rayne. I won't bite."

"I'm seeing someone, Ruiz," I told him. "It's serious."

He glanced down at my legs. "Can't be too serious; the way

you're moving your leg back and forth. Stroking that clit because I excite you, huh?"

Damn, he was right! I immediately froze my leg.

"Ruiz, I'm flattered that you still find me attractive, but I'm involved."

"And?"

"And I plan to see where things can go with him."

"What if I want to see where things can go with us?"

"That can't happen."

Ruiz pulled me toward him by the neck. "What can't happen?"

Before I knew it, we were kissing. Next thing I knew, I was laying on Chance's couch, with Ruiz on top of me, his hands under my sweater fondling my breasts. It was getting intense; I was rubbing his dick through his jeans and he was rock hard. If Chance hadn't come in the room and cleared her throat loudly, we may have ended up fucking right there.

"Ahem, what the hell is this?" Chance asked as we both got up and tried to straighten up our clothes.

"Hey, Chance, I'm here," I said, giggling with embarrassment.

"Ruiz, you said you wanted to see Rayne; not jump her damn bones in my crib."

"I brought some salads," I told her.

The three of us stood there, in the middle of the floor, in complete silence for a few seconds.

"You know what," I added. "I suddenly remembered that I need to run an errand before all the stores close." I headed for the door. "I'll call you a little later, Chance."

Normally, Chance would have talked mad shit and cursed me out in Spanish for making plans with her and then canceling them. She let me off the hook for once because she realized the situation was out of hand.

I got on the elevator and panicked. What had I done? All that time I'd been worried about Yardley caving into his past and there I was, within a matter of minutes, about to fuck Ruiz again after all those years. What if Will came back sniffing around me? Or Bryant? Would I be weak enough to fuck them too?

I arrived home around ten and took a long, hot bath. I felt so unclean; even though I hadn't actually slept with Ruiz. I'd called Yardley from my car, asking if I could see him. He said his friends had come over but he could either kick them out or leave them there and come to me. I assured him that I would be okay, but I think he sensed something in my voice; hopefully not the guilt I was feeling.

Chance had been blowing up my cell phone but I didn't take her calls. There were three messages on my home voice mail. One from Chance, asking me what the hell was *really* going on between me and her brother. The second one was from Ruiz, saying he had pressed redial on Chance's phone because she refused to give him my number. He wanted to know if I would consider seeing him again before he left in a couple of days. He claimed he wanted to talk but he wanted much more than that and we both knew it. Ruiz and I could go absolutely nowhere and I wasn't about to lead him on in any way. The final call was from Basil, wanting to know why he and I weren't hanging out anymore. I did miss chilling with him but Basil couldn't fit in my life at that moment with everything else going on. I was planning to start attending church on the regular again. I had kind of fallen from grace but intended to ask Yardley to start going with me; at least every other Sunday.

By midnight, I was starving. The latest version of *The Texas Chainsaw Massacre* had just finished playing on cable. It was truly gross and I wondered how many times they planned to remake the same film. What was really sick is that the storyline was partially based on fact, which made it even more disturbing to watch.

I could've kicked myself for not stopping by Horace and Dickey's anyway. Since I wasn't going to be helping Chance do any work, I could've easily thrown down on that bomb ass fish and passed out. To top it off, I'd left my damn salad and I had extra caesar dressing at home that I could've hooked it up with.

I was in the kitchen settling for a bowl of Frosted Flakes— since cereal is a quick fix 24/7—when I heard a knock at my door. I grabbed a knife out the block on my counter. There had been a serial rapist in the district recently and I wasn't expecting anyone.

I took baby steps toward the door and yelled, "Who is it?"

"It's the back cracker!"

An instant smile covered my face. I put the knife down on the table in my foyer and opened the door. "Hey, baby!" I leapt into Yardley's arms and locked my ankles around his waist. I was only wearing a Dallas Cowboys T-shirt and no panties. "I thought you had company?"

"I did. I kicked them out."

We shared a passionate kiss.

"You didn't have to do that," I told him as he carried me into my bedroom.

"No, but I wanted to. I'd rather spend all my free time with you anyway." He laid me down and buried his head in my neck. "You look better, you smell better . . ." He licked my earlobe. "And you taste better."

"Does that mean you taste your friends?" I teased.

"What do you think?"

"Hmm, I don't know. We women have to pay special attention to certain comments men make; since the word is out about the undercover bisexuals."

Yardley frowned. "Not a damn thing funny about that."

I giggled. "It is to me. You never know. Your boy Felix, the player, might be putting on a serious front."

Yardley couldn't help but laugh. "Now that would be wild, but I've known Felix all his life and if they locked him up in prison for the rest of it, he'd fuck imaginary pussy before he touched a dick other than his own."

"So did you come over here to talk or give me some dick action?" I asked jokingly.

"Oh, I'll give you some dick action, alright." He started pulling my T-shirt over my head. "But not with this ugly ass shirt on, traitor."

Yardley took off all his clothes and started licking every inch of me. As I gazed at him licking and sucking every inch of my body, his dick throbbing and glistening in the moonlight coming in through my bedroom window, I still felt a twinge of guilt about what had happened between Ruiz and me earlier at Chance's. There was simply no comparison. I'd been a fool. Everything about Yardley. His touch. His tongue. His dick. Everything was nature-made just for me.

There are two ways to live your life.
One is as though nothing is a miracle.
The other is as though everything is a miracle.
—Albert Einstein

Twenty-nine

I wanted everything to be absolutely perfect for my parents' thirty-fifth wedding anniversary. The weather was beautiful; life was beautiful. Rayne was beautiful.

We were all gathered at the Atrium at Treetop for the surprise party Rayne and I had helped Mom plan for Dad. The florist had really come through with breathtaking floral arrangements and Mom had never seemed happier. My parents had completely accepted Rayne and Mom had even kept in contact with Arjay; checking on her via phone to make sure she was okay. It's funny how mutual love of a person can make two completely opposite people closer. Such was the case with Mom and Arjay. In fact, Rayne had a surprise coming her way also. I'd arranged to fly her mother up for the party. I was putting her up at the Hilton, though. I didn't want Rayne to feel uncomfortable with her mother in her place. I started to plan for Rayne to stay with me, but didn't want to seem presumptuous; even though we were spending most nights together anyway. There were times when it felt like Rayne wanted to be alone.

Rayne was helping Mom get dressed and I was waiting outside for Dad to pull up. Uncle Clifton, his brother, was bringing him by the building on the pretense that I was considering opening a second chiropractic clinic in Maryland. The atrium was on the roof of an office building.

When they pulled up, Dad was waving. I waved back and then waited for them to park and walk toward me.

"Nice building, Son," Dad said, giving me a stiff handshake. "Thanks for making me feel special by including me in your decision."

Out the corner of my eye, I spotted one of his co-workers pulling up in a Ford pickup. I embraced my father and then used my hand to wave his friend off. He did a U-turn and headed back up the street. We'd been adamant about telling people to come early enough to already be hiding in the building when Dad and Uncle Clifton got there. That's the tricky thing about surprise parties; rarely are they truly a surprise.

"Dad, I wouldn't think of taking such a big step without you." I let him go. "I've consulted you about every major decision in my life. College, career, my first office location, and now this."

"Hey there, boy," Uncle Clifton said, shaking my hand. "Long time, no see."

I punched him tightly on the shoulder. "You're supposed to be coming by my office so I can X-ray your neck."

"I don't need a damn X-ray to tell me that I'm an old buzzard."

"You're only old when you believe it," I said.

"Let's get on in here and see this space, Son," Dad said. "I'm trying to get back in time to see *Jeopardy!*"

I laughed. "The highlight of your Saturday night."

"Each and every one, Son."

I led them into the building and pushed the elevator button. "There's one more thing I'd like to consult with you about, Dad." I glanced at Uncle Clifton, wishing Dad and I were alone at the moment. "I'll talk to you about it later."

Dad shook his head. "No need. I only have one comment. You need to hurry up and marry that woman before you let her get away."

I was dumbfounded. "How did you know I was talking about Rayne?"

"Because she's become your entire world, Son. A blind man could see that."

"This is probably the shortest life-altering discussion we've ever had, but thanks, Dad."

He chortled. "You're welcome."

When we go to the top floor, I said, "I hope you like it."

The elevator doors opened and everyone yelled, "Surprise!"

Rayne was standing there, beaming and hugging her mother. She seemed pleased and I was relieved. Dad was shocked and moved faster than I'd ever seen him move to embrace Mom. Their official anniversary wasn't for another couple of days and he was planning to take her to the Shenandoah mountains for a romantic getaway. He had no idea that I'd arranged to fly them to Paris, France, instead. School had let out for the summer so they were free to go away for a couple of weeks as opposed to a few days.

Everyone had a great time at the party. The caterer had really done her thing. The roast beef was tender, the chicken marsala was mouthwatering, and the seafood primavera was delicious. Chance and Ricky came in closer to the end of the event, when everyone was on the dance floor grooving to the band's music. I really liked them. Over the past couple of months, Rayne and I had spent a lot of time over their place and vice versa. We'd gone to the zoo the weekend before and had a picnic on the lawn. It had been ages since I'd been on a picnic; one of the simpler things in life that's often overlooked. We were all planning on attending some of the summertime concerts at the Carter Baron Amphitheater in Rock Creek Park.

Dad was trying to get everyone's attention to make an announcement. Perfect. I'd been waiting for Chance and Ricky to arrive before I made an announcement of my own.

"Excuse me, everyone," Dad said, motioning with his hand for the band to cut the music. Once they stopped, he continued. "I wanted to thank everyone for coming out here this evening to help my lovely wife Agnes and I celebrate thirty-five glorious years of marriage. In 1969, a feisty young lady made me commit myself to her for life and I've never regretted it for a single moment."

Mom looked like she was on the brink of tears. I was standing off to the side, holding Rayne around the waist from behind. She whispered, "That's so sweet. They're so in love." I kissed her on the cheek. "The party has turned out perfect."

"Yes, it has," I agreed.

"I'd planned on presenting Agnes with this little token of my appreciation when I took her away in a few days. Now I understand that all those plans have changed so I better go ahead and give it to her now." He beckoned my mother toward him with his finger. "Come here, woman of my dreams."

Mom blushed, gave Arjay a hug, and switched to her man with much pride and pep in her step.

He took her by the hand, embraced her, and then they shared a long, passionate kiss. I'd never seen my parents go for it like that; rather less in front of a crowd. There had to be at least two hundred friends and relatives present.

"Baby, years ago, thirty-five years ago to be exact, you made me the happiest man on earth. Now I just want to make you the happiest woman on earth."

"You already have, Corbett. You already have."

"Well, maybe this will make you even happier." He pulled a black velvet box out his pocket. "When we first got married, I couldn't afford to buy you the ring you wanted. Hell, I couldn't even afford a real diamond, so you settled for a simple wedding band." He lifted her hand and kissed the band. "And you've worn it all this time. Now it's time to replace it with what you deserved back then."

Mom threw her hand over her mouth as Dad opened the box. "Oh, my, Corbett! What have you done?"

"The right thing," Dad responded, popping the box open and exposing a three-carat diamond ring.

Mom was shaking so uncontrollably that he almost couldn't get the ring on her finger. He managed and they started kissing again.

I hugged Rayne tighter. I closed my eyes, took in a deep breath, and then let her go. "I'll be right back."

I walked over to my parents and embraced them both. The band looked like they were about to start back up but I motioned for them not to.

"I'd like to add something," I said. "As the only child of these two wonderful people here, I must say that I couldn't have asked for more loving and supportive parents. They've nurtured me and guided me throughout my life. While it hasn't always been easy for any of us, we've managed to make it this far."

I glanced at Rayne. She was so gorgeous, standing there in a royal blue flowing dress. "Many of you have met the new lady in my life, some of you have gotten to know her pretty well, but I want *everyone* to officially meet her now. Rayne, can you come here for a second?"

Rayne was hesitating and I saw Chance push her out in the middle of the floor. Rayne brushed her off and started taking tiny steps toward me and my parents. When she got close enough to hear my whispers, I said, "Don't worry. None of them bite."

I heard Dad laugh behind me.

I grasped her hand in mine and faced the crowd. Felix, Dwayne, and Mike had all snuck in at some point. Dwayne was with Opal; Felix and Mike were going solo. They were all staring, along with the rest of the crowd.

"Everyone, this is Rayne Waters. Rayne, this is everyone."

She laughed nervously as they applauded.

"Why are they clapping?" she asked in astonishment. "I haven't done anything."

"Oh yes, you have," I told her. When the applause ended, I said, "Rayne asked me why you were applauding us. She doesn't feel like she's done anything to deserve it. The fact is that she's done everything; she's changed my entire life. Before I met Rayne, I'd given up on finding true love. Every turn only meant more pain for me; more disappointment. But she's changed all that." I gazed into her eyes and spoke directly to her. "You've changed all that."

I reached into my coat pocket and took out an identical black box to the one Dad had pulled out of his. I'd spotted the perfect ring for her—five carats on a platinum band—the day Dad had selected the one for Mom.

Rayne gasped and so did half the room when I lowered myself onto my right knee. "Listen to me, baby. I know it seems like all of this happened fast. In many ways, it did. But I love you. I've loved you all my life; even before I met you."

She ran her fingers across my cheek. "I love you, too, Yardley."

"I know you do, and that's why I want you to marry me. I don't want to live my life without you."

She started crying. "I don't know what to say."

"Say yes." I took the ring out the box and slipped it on her finger. "Say that you'll be my wife, the mother of my children. Say we'll grow old together and make a ton of memories to tell our grandchildren."

Arjay came closer to us and said, "Say yes, baby."

Rayne glared at her. "Momma?"

"You know I'm the last person in the world who believes in marriage. It's not for me, but it is for you. I see that now. He's different, Rayne. He's rare, and you better grab him while you can."

I looked at Arjay and laughed, still kneeling. "You heard her. I'm rare."

"You are rare." Rayne clamped her eyes shut for a moment. Her entire body was trembling. "You're rare, Yardley, but I'm not."

"What are you saying?"

She pulled her hand away from me, took the ring off, and placed it back in my palm. "I'm saying that you don't deserve this. I'm not good enough for you."

I jumped up. "You are good enough for me."

Rayne shook her head violently. Chance started walking up behind her. She warded her off. "Please, Chance. Let me do this."

Chance stood there with this hopeless expression on her face; one that probably mirrored my own.

"I'm so embarrassed. I wish you wouldn't have asked me this in front of everyone," Rayne said as tears started flowing freely down both of her cheeks. "I can't marry you, Yardley. When it comes down to it, I'm simply not good enough."

Rayne took off for the door. Arjay ran after her. I was right on their tail. "Son!" I heard my dad yell behind me. "Give her some time to think."

I looked at him and Mom, who was also crying. This had ruined their day; a day I'd hoped to become two celebrations.

"I have to go to her, Dad. I have to make her understand."

"You can't make a woman understand something she's incapable of understanding."

I was halfway to the door when Felix yanked me by the arm. "Man, she's one fish in a sea of millions. Fuck that bitch if she doesn't want you."

I punched Felix right in the mouth. He was stunned as blood trickled down his chin.

"You and I are no longer friends. Don't let me see you again."

I ran down the stairwell instead of waiting for the elevator. By the time I got outside, they were gone.

Thirty

"I know you don't want to talk, but we have to."

Momma was rubbing my back while I laid on my bed. I kept seeing the painful expression on Yardley's face when I'd turned him down. It would haunt me for the rest of my days.

"Momma, please just leave me alone," I said, lashing out at her in anger.

"No, I won't. This is all my fault."

I sat up. "How do you figure that?"

"Your real problem isn't with Yardley. It's with me." She clasped her hands together and sighed. "I'm the reason you have so many trust issues with men."

"No, men are the reason I have so many trust issues with men," I stated adamantly. "But it's not even about that."

"Then what is it about?"

"I've realized something about myself lately, Momma."

"What's that, baby?"

"I meant what I said; about not being good enough for Yardley. I'm not good enough for him."

She stood and started pacing the bedroom floor. "You said that same shit months ago when I was here. I thought we'd straightened that out."

"I thought we did too, but . . ."

"But?"

I hesitated before replying, "We've never really had a candid conversation, Momma. Not a real one."

She smirked at me. "I'd like to think we've had at least one or two."

"Well, we haven't. We've beat around the bush, touched upon some subjects, but never truly let it all go."

"Then let's do that now."

I took a moment to analyze the situation. I'd been giving things a lot of thought lately and expressing my true feelings to my mother was vital to my sanity. That moment was as good a time as any.

"Remember the night I lost my virginity?"

The sarcasm reeked in her voice when she replied, "I remember the night you *denied* losing your virginity and then finally confessed."

I rolled my eyes at her. "It was Ruiz, Momma."

"Ruiz!" Momma damn near screamed. "That no-good bastard! He's just like his father! Fuckin' pussy hound!"

She needed to calm the hell down.

"Momma, do you want to hear this or not?"

Momma must've realized that I'd clam up if she didn't regain some composure. She did that and then sat down beside me. "Yes, I'm sorry. Go ahead, baby."

For some reason, I felt she needed to be familiar with the fact that, "Chance doesn't even know about this."

"Why not? You tell Chance everything."

"Well, I've never told her *this*. I'm sure she suspects that he and I have hooked at some point; especially recently."

"What happened recently? Isn't that fool married?" Momma asked with much disdain.

"He's divorced and he was supposed to get remarried, but he's not."

"And?"

"I'll get to the present, but first let me tell you about the past."

Momma sighed. "Okay."

"Chance and I had planned to go to the drive-in movies with Ruiz, but she got strep throat."

"I remember that. Wasn't that when she was kissing numerous boys at school?"

I was surprised Momma even knew about Chance getting caught ass out with those boys. She stayed drunk most of the time and didn't know if she was coming or going. "Yeah, that's what happened," I said.

"So you and Ruiz went alone?"

"Yeah. I'll never forget it. The movie was *New Jack City*."

Momma couldn't have cared less about the movie title. "And then you all did the nasty?"

"Yeah," I replied softly.

"In his car?"

"No, he took me over one of his friends' houses."

"I see."

She grew quiet, like she was waiting for me to continue. I did.

"When I gave myself to him that night, I thought it would be special to him. I thought we'd be together from that point on. I was so stupid."

She started rubbing my back again. "Rayne, everyone makes

mistakes. If I had a nickel for every one I've made, I'd be richer than Oprah."

I buried my face in my hands. "Momma, you've always drilled in my head how men only care about pussy and money. Somewhere along the way, it started making sense to me."

"Well, I stick by my word on that. Most men are like that but now I realize that there are exceptions. Exceptions like Yardley."

Yardley! What a mess I'd created!

"I do love him so, Momma."

"That's obvious."

"I'm not sure if I can be faithful to him," I blurted out. "In the long run, I mean."

Momma started getting hyper again. "That's bullshit. You've always been a good girl, Rayne. You're not the type that would cheat. That's my nature; not yours."

I flailed my arms in the air in frustration and then landed them on my thighs. "Momma, you don't know everything about me. Until a few minutes ago, you didn't know I'd been with Ruiz."

"Okay, I'll give you that one," she admitted. "Let me ask you this. Have you ever cheated on a man?"

Was she for real?

"Yes, Momma, I've cheated on a man." She looked like a deer caught in headlights. "Don't look so surprised. You always talked about the world of whoredom and all that shit. You always use the phrase 'like father, like son.' What about 'like mother, like daughter'?"

"Aw, I get it. You won't marry him because you're afraid you'll turn into me."

I jumped up and exclaimed, "I'm afraid I've already turned into you!" She scooted up to the edge of the sofa but didn't get up. I continued, "Ruiz was in town a couple of months ago and it was like we'd never been apart. That night we spent together seemed like it was the night before. He touched me and I was ready to sleep with him. We started making out on Chance's sofa and if we'd been someplace else—anyplace else—there's not a doubt in my mind that we would've done it."

"But you didn't do it, baby," Momma stated reassuringly.

"Not because I didn't want him."

"Rayne, it was a mistake. That was months ago and you and Yardley have been going strong ever since. That man worships the ground you walk on. He stood up in front of everyone he knows in the world today and asked you to be his wife."

"I understand that. No one has ever made me feel like him. I couldn't ask for anything more."

"Then what's the problem?"

I'd never been so confused in my entire life. I'd relived that day at Chance's apartment with Ruiz a thousand times. How easily I was prepared to give it up; even though Yardley was everything I desired. I never wanted to hurt Yardley. I'd been hurt enough myself over the years. In the beginning, I had fears that he'd end up cheating on me with Roxie or whoever. Then I started fearing my own actions. I was convinced it was better to break it off and hurt him, instead of dragging it out indefinitely until the inevitable happened.

"Even though I get excited just thinking about him, I still almost cheated," I told Momma.

"That's the same way your father made me feel."

Had she said what I thought she said?

"My father!" I glared at her. "You know who he is, don't you?"

"I've always known." Momma grabbed a toss pillow and clamped it to her chest. "I loved your father."

She'd had a relationship with someone.

I was suddenly livid. "Why'd you let me think I was some cum spot gone awry?"

"Because it was for the best, at the time."

"So who is he?" I demanded to know.

"He *was* Mathis Quiroga. Fine ass Mathis Quiroga," she said in a barely audible tone.

"Mathis Quiroga," I repeated. The name was familiar to me.

"Yes, *the* Mathis Quiroga."

It dawned on me where I knew the name from. "The boxer?"

Momma nodded. "The boxer."

Mathis Quiroga was destined to be the next middleweight boxing champion of the world. With a flawless record and the majority of his wins by knockout, at the time he reigned, there was nobody who could touch him in his weight class. All of Birmingham acted like they'd given birth to him themselves. They called him "The Birmingham Bomber" and all the local school kids learned about him in history classes when I was growing up. He'd been killed by a tragic blow to the temple by Dominic Ortega aka "Silver Bullet" during a bout in Nashville, Tennessee. I had no clue that Momma had ever known him, but I knew for sure she wasn't lying. Just hearing his name, the way it made me feel inside, was enough proof to me. He was my father.

"Did he know about me?" I asked.

"No, he was killed in the ring when I was three months pregnant. I hadn't told him yet because I was still trying to decide what to do. His family would've sworn I was trying to trap him since he was on the brink of becoming a champion. I guess I thought they'd convince him that I was using him and he'd dump me."

"But you two were an item?"

"Oh yeah, a heavy item."

"How come you never told me?"

"What was the point? He never knew about you and he was no good to you dead."

Momma was unbelievable.

"It would've helped to know that my father was an actual individual, instead of some nameless, faceless person," I said excitedly. She simply didn't get it.

"Rayne, I'm not as bad as you think I am and you're not as bad as you think you are." She stood, walked up behind me, and embraced me, laying her head on my shoulder. "I do love Truck but I've never gotten over Mathis. I've acted a fool because of it; I realize that. It was my way of coping with the pain."

I felt her tears streaking down my arm. "I'm so sorry, Momma."

"No, I'm the one who's sorry. I should've told him. He deserved to know. If I'd been woman enough to tell him—instead of being paralyzed by fear—things might've been different." I'd never heard her sound so weak; so defeated. "He might've fought harder if he knew he had a child on the way, or he might not have fought at all, which would've been even better."

"Is that the reason you drink so heavily, too?" I asked her, hoping to get everything out.

"Yes, it's the reason I do everything destructive."

Her sobs grew heavier and I turned to take her into my arms. I drifted her back over to the sofa so we could sit down. I cradled her for a moment while she let all of her emotions out. Before I knew it, I'd joined her. Her pain was my pain and I felt bad about everything negative I'd ever said or thought about her. She didn't need me to chastise her; she needed me to help her.

"You can get help, Momma, if you want to get help."

"I do, baby. I do want to live again; really live."

"I'll get you into a center, Momma. Right away. They'll make you all better."

"Thanks, Rayne."

"No, thank you." I lifted her face so I could stare in her eyes when I said, "I see everything so much clearer now."

"I lost my only chance at real happiness. Don't lose yours."

We sat there, holding one another, as I pondered her last statement.

Momma had managed to fall asleep in my bedroom. She was totally exhausted from all the tears shed; so was I. I was walking out the kitchen with a tall glass of water when a knock came at my door. I knew who it was before I opened it.

Yardley was a disheveled mess. His eyes were red; a perfect match for mine. Before I could open my mouth, he started rambling.

"I've been wandering the streets outside your building for the past two hours, debating about coming up here. Part of me is angry. I can't understand how you could do this to me. All I've ever tried to do is love you. All I want to do is love you forever."

I bit my bottom lip, but hesitated to say anything. I couldn't find the words I was searching for.

"If I've done something wrong, please tell me and I'll fix it."

He put his hand to my face and rubbed my cheek, then my hair.

"Whatever you want, whatever you need, I'll give it to you."

I threw my arms around his neck and whispered, "Yes."

"Yes?" he asked with a nervous chuckle.

"That's the answer you wanted to hear earlier, right?" I kissed him on the cheek and spoke it directly in his ear the next time. "Yes."

A wide grin spread across my face, then his.

"Yes," I said for a third time, and pulled him into my place.

Less than an hour later, we were in the room he'd booked for Momma at the Hilton, and my engagement ring was on my finger.

Thirty-one

Rayne
August 2004

"How's my girl, Arjay?" Boom asked me as she put the finishing touches on my hair once again.

"She's fine, Boom."

From Naps to Baps was packed. Sisters weren't joking about looking good. The summer was coming to an end so they would have to give up the miniskirts, bikinis, and shorts riding up the cracks of their asses before too long.

Boom placed her hands on my shoulders. "I'm still planning on getting down there to see her. I wanna check out some of that Alabama black snake firsthand."

Yo-Yo spoke up. "Don't forget me, Boom. I'm going with you."

"Me, too," Tamu said.

I was thinking if the main stylist, the manicurist, and the shampoo girl all left town at once, it would put a serious wrench in the business.

"Damn, who's going to run From Naps to Baps while all of you are down South getting your backs blown out?" I asked.

I could hear Tamu's lips smacking clear across the room. "Shit, with all the drama we have to put up with up in here, we all need a fuckin' vacation."

"Word up!" Yo-Yo exclaimed.

"Momma's not home right now anyway. She'll be back in a few weeks," I informed Boom.

"Cool, I'll give her a call then."

"She'd like that."

I drowned them out for a few moments while they started talking shit about this homosexual brother who had opened up a salon around the corner from Boom. She wasn't feeling that at all, and I wouldn't have been surprised if she was already devising plans to sabotage his business. She'd never be stupid enough to talk about that out in the open though. Calling him names was one thing; revealing actual covert operations was another thing altogether. Either way, I wouldn't have put it past her.

I was thinking about Momma. She was in a treatment center in Atlanta that specialized in not only rehabilitation, but they offered serious psychological counseling as well. Not the basic stuff they had at most centers; really intense counseling. I was hoping that Momma could face her demons, get over my father, and move on with her life. I'd told Yardley and Chance about my dad. It felt funny to even be able to refer to someone as that; even though I never got the chance to know him.

I zoned back into the conversation in the shop when Tamu asked, "Rayne, when are you getting hitched? Have you set a date?"

"November," I responded. "Early November."

Jada, another regular Thursday customer, said, "I still can't believe your ass is gettin' married; leaving all the rest of us heifers single to wrestle over the pitbulls."

Yo-Yo said, "Humph, there are a couple of poodles out there you can tame before they become vicious."

Boom took the comb she was using on me and started swinging it from left to right in the air. "Shit! Ain't no poodles nowhere 'round here. Not unless they've got a little sugar in their bowls."

"Boom, I want you to start thinking about a special hairstyle for my wedding day." I didn't even comment on what they were saying. I'd found my man; they were on their own. "You know I love the way you hook me up every Thursday, but I want to walk down the aisle and blow Yardley's mind."

Boom said, "I've always got your back, girl."

"When do we get to meet Mr. Magnificent?" Tamu asked.

Yo-Yo stopped folding towels over by the bank of sinks for a few seconds. "Yeah, I'm dying to see what he looks like. I bet he's megafine."

I laughed. "Megafine? Is that a new word?"

"Girl, megafine means a man can make you cream all over yourself by just looking at you," Yo-Yo answered.

"Damn, that is fine," Jada commented. "I'd like to see something that fucking fine."

Boom suddenly froze in her tracks and stared at the door. "Speaking of which!"

I glanced at the door in time to see Yardley saying, "Hello, ladies."

Yo-Yo came running to the front. "Hey there."

"What's up, baby?" Jada asked him.

"Can we help you?" Boom inquired. Her voice had become noticeably softer.

"No, you can't help him." I got up from her chair and reached in my pocket for the money I already had counted out and prepared to give her. I handed it to Boom, then went to Yardley and slipped my arm underneath his elbow. "Boom, Yo-Yo, Tamu, ladies, I'd like you to meet my fiancé, Yardley Brown."

"Oh, my goodness!" Boom yelled out as a collective sigh echoed through the salon. "No wonder you didn't want to be bothered with Conquesto."

Yardley looked down at me. "Conquesto."

"Long story," I told him. "Tell you later."

Tamu must've hovered over the floor because I didn't see her coming. Miraculously, she was standing a foot from us when she'd been in the back of the salon a minute ago. She reached out and shook Yardley's free hand. "So you're the brother who swept Miss Rayne off her feet."

Yardley let my hand fall so he could entwine his fingers with mine. "It was more like her sweeping me off my feet."

"Aw, she rocked your world, huh?" Tamu asked, winking at him.

He winked back. "She rocks it every chance she gets."

"Quit. You're embarrassing me," I said, pulling Yardley toward the door. "Thanks again for everything, Boom."

"See you next week, Rayne."

As we were exiting, we heard Tamu say, "Girlllllll, that man is so fine, I'd lick motor oil off his ass."

After the door had closed behind us, we both laughed.

"Looks like you're a hit."

"Come here and give me a kiss." Yardley drew me to him and laid one on me. "You look beautiful."

"And you look handsome."

I'd intentionally asked Yardley to pick me up from the salon that night so the sisters could see a little eye candy. I was proud of him, and wanted them to see what fineness he possessed. I didn't plan to invite them all to the wedding, just Boom, but I didn't want them to miss out on getting to meet him. I'd driven my car home after work and caught a cab to get there.

"Have you decided what you want for dinner?" he asked.

I looked at the digital clock on the building across the street. It was well after nine. "It's kind of late, so something light."

"What about Chinese? That goes in and an hour later, it's gone."

"Sounds good. I'd love some chicken lo mein."

"How's your mother?" he asked.

"I spoke to her today. She's hanging in there."

"Great!"

"I also talked to her counselor for a few minutes."

"And?"

"He said every day's a struggle for Momma. She's not used to having her time regulated and being told what to do." That was an understatement if I'd ever heard one. I could picture Momma down there raising holy hell when someone told her to get up at 7 A.M. for breakfast. She probably hadn't seen the sunrise in a decade. The discipline was good for her; she needed it.

"Well, at the end of the day, she'll be much better off."

"Let's hope so," I said. "The next thing I need to do is get her a better job. The one she has is depressing."

"Any thoughts?"

"Yes, a few. I spoke to a friend of mine from college who runs an accounting firm in Birmingham. Momma can't crunch numbers but my friend, Brook, said she might be able to use her for filing or mild typing."

"That's cool."

"If that doesn't work out, Brook knows a lot of business owners, through networking, who might be able to help out."

We'd made it down the street to Yardley's car. As he unlocked

the door, he said, "Mom wants to know when you want to go se-
lect a china pattern."

"I don't even see why we need china; neither one of us cooks
on a regular basis." The fact of the matter was that I didn't cook at
all. That's why I kept every carryout menu imaginable in my
kitchen drawer.

"And when we do, we use paper plates," Yardley said, speaking of the few times when he'd prepared dinner for me. They
were simple meals—once it was Hamburger Helper—but he was
still a step ahead of me.

"I know that's right," I said in agreement.

"Make Mom happy. She's relishing helping you plan the wedding. This is her only shot at it since I'm an only child." He closed
the door for me after I'd gotten into the passenger side. As he
walked around the car to get in, my heart sank. I was planning my
wedding and Momma wasn't around. After he'd climbed in beside me, he said, "I'm sorry, baby. I know you wish Arjay could
help plan it, too."

"It's okay," I lied. "She'll be out in time for the wedding. That's
all that matters."

"Have you picked out your wedding dress yet?" he asked as he
started the car.

"Yes, I finally decided on one."

"What does it look like?"

I giggled. "Let's try 'none of your business.' "

"Cute."

"If I tell you what the dress looks like, it'll ruin the surprise.
The point is that I'm supposed to blow you away the day of the
wedding so you'll never forget how I appeared walking down the
aisle; even fifty years from now; when I'm old, gray, and my tits
are down on my knees."

"Fifty years from now, you'll be just as beautiful to me as you are today."

"Remember you said that shit when it's time for me to get dentures."

"Hey, eventually I'll probably become impotent. Will you still love me then?"

"Sure. Think about it. We've got Viagra now. Imagine what kind of shit they'll invent by then."

We both laughed.

"Well, right now I don't need any Viagra." He took my hand and placed it in his lap. His dick was hard. "You feel that?"

"How could I miss it?"

"Still want dinner?"

I started rubbing him. "No, I only want you."

"Your place or mine?"

"Mine."

"We need to decide where we're going to live."

"Your penthouse is a hell of a lot bigger than my apartment."

"I know, but I'm thinking we need to go house hunting."

I was stunned. "House hunting?"

"Yeah, I plan to have you knocked up by the spring so we're going to need more space. Plus, children don't need to be in high-rises; especially not on the penthouse level."

Damn, he was ready to have kids already! I tried to envision myself pregnant, with a bad back, and carrying thirty or forty extra pounds on my poor knees. I sure hoped they had cute maternity clothes. I'd never bothered to check into it.

"Earth to Rayne! Earth to Rayne!"

"Sorry, I was tripping off that knocked up by spring comment."

"We're not getting any younger."

"True. I guess I'm ready for kids, but you're taking the night shift. You know how I love to get my sleep."

I was serious about that comment. I didn't play when it came to getting my beauty rest; I never had. If I didn't sleep but four or five hours a night, I slept like a rock when I did. The odds of me hearing a baby crying in another room—nursery monitor or not—were slim to none.

"I'll take all the shifts, if I have to. I can't wait to see what you and I will look like blended into one."

"Should be an interesting combination."

"You still have that chocolate whipped cream in the fridge?" Yardley asked as we headed for my place.

"Yeah. Why?"

"Just contemplating the possibilities."

He reached over and started rubbing my clit through my pants while I continued to fondle him.

"Contemplate away," I whispered. "Contemplate away."

Thirty-two

There's nothing like birthday sex. Rayne and I brought my thirtieth one in with a bang. We spent the evening before addressing our wedding invitations. Two months from the wedding and counting, so it was time to send them out. I could tell she was getting frustrated with the wedding plans. Not because she didn't want a nice wedding. The details were overwhelming her. Mom wanted a seating chart for the reception and Rayne was already stressing over who to sit beside who. She didn't want anyone to be offended if they weren't close enough to the head table. It was such a big deal that many of my relatives were already requesting tablemates and they hadn't even been officially invited yet.

We finally finished them about eleven that Wednesday night. Both of us had to work the next day but we were determined to follow the wedding planner timeline and get them out two months beforehand.

"Whew, that was a job and a half," Rayne said, yawning and stretching as she got up off my living room floor. "I'm about ready to turn in."

"Aw, you can't go to sleep now. In exactly one hour, I'll be thirty."

"So you were born at midnight?" Rayne joked.

I laughed. "Actually, I've never known what time of day I was born. I'm not even sure if it was morning, noon, or night. I'll have to ask Mom."

"I've never understood why people always celebrate birthdays right on the second; especially adults. Kids are usually asleep."

"Adults are glad to make it to another year."

"Maybe that's it." Rayne shook her head. "Damn, thirty. Next year it'll be my turn."

"But you don't look a day over twenty."

She grinned at me. "Flattery will get you everywhere."

"Will it get me some birthday booty?"

She got back down on the floor, pushed me down, and straddled me. "Birthday booty. Is that different from ordinary booty? From daily booty?"

I reached around her with both hands and caressed her ass. "I don't know. Why don't we wait about forty-seven more minutes and find out."

"Why wait forty-seven more minutes?" She lifted my shirt and started pinching my nipples. "We can get started now and, by the time midnight rolls around, we can be rumpling the sheets."

"Sounds like a winner to me."

She kissed me on the lips and climbed off me. "I'm going to run us a bath. Come join me in ten minutes."

"I'll be there."

Rayne disappeared into my bedroom and the phone rang, as if on cue.

"Hello. This better be important," I said, not even knowing who it was.

"Hey, man. It's me, Felix."

It had been several months since I'd spoken to Felix. I was pissed at him when he'd called Rayne out of her name at my parents' anniversary party. He was the last person that needed to be commenting about anything.

"Yardley, you there?"

"I'm here."

"I'm a bit early but I wanted to wish you a happy birthday tomorrow," he said.

"I'm surprised you remembered."

I sat down on my sofa as an uncomfortable silence ensued.

Felix sighed on the other end of the phone. "Of course, I remembered. Are you forgetting that the boys and I gave you a party for your sixteenth birthday? I remembered your birthday then and I remember it now."

"Well, thanks for the well wishes."

"Yardley, I realize that I fucked up royally—more than once—but I've always regarded you as my closest friend. Mike and Dwayne are cool with me, but you and I have always been tighter than tight."

I couldn't help it. I had to say what was on my mind. "Is that what was going through your mind when you and Roxie disrespected me in my own home?"

"We can rehash that shit over and over and it will still turn out the same way every time."

"True," I agreed. I decided that was the last time I'd ever bring that up; to Felix or anyone else. Roxie was a dropped issue. She'd finally given up her pursuit and determination to have me run back to her. The shit wasn't going to happen. "We won't mention that again."

"I do need to apologize for what happened at your parents' party. That remark I made."

"Yes, you do need to apologize for that. That's for damn sure."

I wasn't that hot under the collar, but I refused to even consider being his friend unless he made amends for that.

"I apologize, man. I really do, and if I ever get the opportunity to apologize to Rayne, I will."

Felix was one of my closest friends. I didn't understand his ass but I did love him like a brother. I thought about Belford. I'd been thinking about him a lot lately; about all the things he never got to do. It was time to either accept Felix as Felix or let him go forever.

"Felix, Rayne didn't even hear your comment, but you can apologize to Rayne at our wedding. It's in two months."

"You're inviting me?"

"Yes, I'm inviting you." I paused. "I can't have you stand up for me, man. I'm not prepared for that yet. But I'd appreciate it if you'd be there."

"I'll be there, man."

The situation was getting too emotional for me. "Listen, I need to run. Rayne's waiting for me."

"Okay, cool, man. I'll call you again tomorrow. What are you doing for your birthday anyway?"

"Rayne's actually cooking for me. This will be the first time."

"She's never cooked for you?" Felix asked in astonishment.

"No, never."

"You mean she hooked you without having to get to your stomach? That shit would never happen with Dwayne."

We both chuckled.

"Yes, that's exactly what she did. I've cooked for her a few times, though."

"I bet those were some science experiments."

"Ha, ha, ha, very funny." I heard the bath faucet turn off,

which meant the water was ready. "Thanks for calling, Felix. I'm glad we were able to be civil."

"Me, too. Does this mean you're going to start coming out on the courts on Saturday mornings so I can whip your ass?"

I'd stopped showing up for the weekly games when Felix and I had the big fallout. Dwayne, Mike, and I would hit some happy hours from time to time, but it was never the same.

"I'll be there this Saturday. You better be prepared because I'm going to make up for lost time."

Felix laughed. "See you then, but I'm going to still holler at you tomorrow."

"Peace," I said and hung up the phone.

I addressed one last invitation, to Felix, before I cut out the lights in the living room area and went to join Rayne.

She was in the tub, posing like a Nubian princess—*my Nubian princess*—when I came in. I'd taken off all my clothes in the bedroom and put on the latest Jill Scott CD. It was smooth as silk; just like Rayne's skin.

"I took the liberty of bringing a bottle of champagne in with me," I told her as I pulled it from behind my back.

She seemed mesmerized by my dick. She didn't take her eyes off it.

"See something you like?"

She finally looked up at me. "I'm sorry. I was hypnotized there for a second."

"It's not like you haven't seen it before."

"Oh, I've seen it," she said. "Shit, I own it."

"Damn, next thing you know I'll be sporting a ball and chain."

"Don't worry. They make them with leather accessories now. They complement anything."

I got into the garden tub, facing her. She started giving me a foot job. She rubbed my balls with her big toe and I grabbed her foot.

"What's wrong?" she asked and giggled. "You're not ticklish down there, are you?"

"You know the answer to that."

"What I don't know the answer to is why you brought a bottle of champagne in here and no flutes."

"Who needs flutes when I have toes?"

I lifted the foot I was holding and poured about an ounce of the champagne on them. Then I sucked each toe one at a time. Rayne slid her back farther down in the tub and started moaning. Once I'd sucked the other set of manicured toes, I poured a little on her calves and licked them also.

"Damn, it feels like my birthday instead of yours," Rayne whispered softly.

I stopped and started giving her a foot massage. "You're the only present I need. You can just wrap yourself up in a big bow and let me unwrap you."

"Stand up," she instructed. "I want to taste some of that champagne."

I stood up and flinched when she got on her knees, picked up the bottle of champagne and poured some on my dick. It was freezing.

"Aw, don't worry. I'll warm it up."

Rayne drew me into her mouth and warmed me up indeed. Her lips felt so soft and succulent, wrapped around my dick. I helped guide her head back and forth as she devoured me for the next ten minutes or so; until I couldn't take it any more and climaxed.

We cleansed each other with shea butter soap and then toweled each other off. We ended up in my bed, on crisp white sheets, enjoying the sex we'd learned to master. Rayne had masturbated in front of me on several occasions. She wanted me to witness what turned her on. She realized that brothers aren't psychic so I'd watched and I memorized "her spots." She'd lie there, in front of me, and play with her nipples with one hand; her clit with the other. She'd tell me what she was fantasizing about, describing every little detail. Then she'd cum. It was an amazing thing to watch a woman cumming by her own hard work. Men jack off all the time, so we know what we look like, with the scrunched up faces and the "oh shit!" comments. Watching Rayne please herself pleased me and ultimately, allowed me to truly please her.

At midnight, she sang "Happy Birthday" to me while I was deep inside her. After each line, she'd tongue kiss me, so it took her a few minutes to get through it. I didn't mind a bit.

I fell asleep inside her.

Damn! Happy, happy birthday to me!

You only live once, but if you work it right, once is enough.
                                                                    —Joe Lewis

Thirty-three

Rayne
October 2004

I hated it when the weather lived up to my name. It had been gorgeous all day but, as usual, come quitting time it was overcast. Within ten minutes, about the length of time it had taken me to get my car from the parking garage and pull out into traffic, it was a torrential downpour.

Just when I thought things couldn't get any worse, there was a six-car pileup on Massachusetts Avenue, which meant I had to take an alternate—slower route—home. Why couldn't people learn not to act a fool during bad weather? Getting into an accident won't get them home any sooner; that's for sure.

The smaller side streets only had one lane going each way and during rush hour, it was a nightmare. I decided to calm down. After all, I was a month away from marrying Yardley and I'd never been happier. As the wipers danced back and forth on my window, I daydreamed about what our children would look like.

We'd already discussed names. Our firstborn son would be

named Yardley, Jr., and if there were a second son, his name would be Yavier. If we were blessed with a daughter, her name would be Yasmin. I was really feeling *Y* names because I was feeling Yardley so damn much.

Yardley. It suddenly dawned on me that I'd promised to cook him dinner. I was planning to make Cajun fried catfish and had forgotten to pick up flour the night before when I'd purchased the fillets. Luckily there was a small market on P Street; two blocks away from where I was inching along in traffic.

There was no parking along P Street during peak hours but I lucked out a second time by finding a space around the corner from the store. I planned to be in and out of there with a quickness. I had on a new pair of high-heeled pumps and my feet were killing me. Besides, I wanted to be home early enough to take a bath, or at least a shower, before Yardley got there around eight. With all the licking and sucking that went on during our lengthy lovemaking sessions, I always liked my coochie to be fresh.

I'd barely gotten out of my car when my cell phone started ringing. I hoped it was Yardley. I missed him and simply wanted to hear his voice. I cringed when I looked at the caller ID and realized it was Momma. As I pushed the talk button, I promised myself that I wouldn't allow her to disrupt my flow of happiness.

I was trying to clutch my purse under one arm and juggle my phone and opened umbrella with the other. I was getting soaked.

"Hello, Momma."

"Hey, baby," she said anxiously. "I need to talk to you about something important."

"Can this wait, Momma?" I asked, realizing that she was likely to start rubbing her stress onto me.

"No, this can't wait!" she snapped. "I'm about to lose my home!"

I rolled my eyes up to the clouds. "Again?"

"Yes, Miss Smarty Pants! Again!"

Momma had gotten out of rehab and gone right back to drinking. I was so disappointed, but realized that it was a lost cause to expect her to reinvent herself after all that time. It was like that day in my apartment, when we'd revealed and supposedly released all our pain and built-up frustration, had never happened. It was like I'd never sent her to Atlanta to get help.

My friend Brook had hired Momma to help out in her accounting office, but called me less than a week after she'd started to tell me that she was showing up for work drunk. Under those circumstances, Brook couldn't keep Momma on, or recommend her to someone else. I'd assured Brook that I understood. I loved my mother but she'd have to take a backseat to what I was trying to build with Yardley.

"Let me guess. You expect me to send you some money?" I asked her.

"Uh-huh, I damn sure do," she stated demandingly.

"Momma, I'm in the process of making final plans for my wedding. A very expensive wedding, I might add."

I could hear her hissing through the phone. "Rayne, no one told your fast ass to plan some fancy wedding you can't afford."

I was pissed then. *How dare she come at me like that?* Then again, being that it was Momma, *how dare she not?*

"Oh, I can afford my wedding. I simply can't afford to do that and keep playing parent to you, too."

"What the fuck did you say to me?" she asked with venom in her voice. "You better watch your tone, young lady, when you speak to me. If it wasn't for me, your ass would've been a cum spot on my waterbed back in the day."

I was in front of the store but didn't want to go inside so people could overhear my responses to her.

"Listen, I'll call you back in a few minutes, Momma."

"But what about me and my problems, Rayne? I realize I may not be the greatest mother in the world, but I did the best I could by you, baby. I really did. Now I need you to do right by me. You owe me."

"I know you did the best you could, Momma. And yes, I do owe everything I am to you," I said, not agreeing with her but realizing she probably—in her mind—believed every word of it.

We were both silent for a brief moment. She was obviously waiting for me to hold true to form and give in. Eventually, I did.

"Don't worry about a thing, Momma," I said reluctantly. "I'll take care of everything, like I always do."

Instead of saying thanks, she held true to form. "Don't you need to know how much money to send?"

"I'm about to run in this store. I'll call you back in a few minutes."

"But, Rayne, I need—"

"Momma, give me three lousy minutes. I'll get right back to you."

"Promise?"

I took a deep breath and sighed. "Promise."

"Okay, baby."

I hung up before she could change her mind and start rambling again. What was she going to do if something happened to me? If I lost my job or something and couldn't keep sending her funds on the drop of a dime.

There were only a handful of people in the store. I was thankful that no one was at the register waiting to be rung up. I was going to locate the flour and haul ass. Like the majority of small markets, all of the items were overpriced to pay for convenience.

I made my way to the rear of the store, grabbed a two-pound sack of flour and headed back toward the front. I was rifling through my purse for a five-dollar bill and not paying attention when I bumped into another patron; a young white man.

"Excuse me," I said, walking around him. He didn't reply.

I was less than four feet from the counter when I froze. There was another young white man pointing a rather large gun toward the Middle Eastern man behind the register.

"Freeze, old man!" he yelled at the merchant. "We don't want any trouble! Give us all the cash in the register and we'll leave! Don't fuck around, so we can all go home tonight!"

"What are you? A fucking crackhead?" the man shouted back at him with an accent.

I practically drowned him out. *Did he say "we" and "us"?*

I scanned from side to side, trying to figure out who else could've been with him. There was a Puerto Rican woman holding an infant in the health-care aisle. One second after I'd ruled her out as his accomplice, I felt the cold metal on my temple and an arm grab me around my waist.

"Don't move, bitch, or you're dead!"

I whispered, "Shit," as everything dropped to the floor out of my hands.

He was trembling as much as me and so was his partner at the counter. I had a feeling that they were crackheads or some type of drug addicts.

"Don't fucking move!" he screamed so loudly in my ear that I felt like my eardrum might explode.

"I'm about to get married," I heard myself saying.

"Who gives a fuck?" He tightened his grip around my waist and started gyrating his hips behind me, rubbing his dick against my ass. "You know what? Now that I'm checking you out, you look like a sweet little piece of ass. Want me to take you in the back room and do you?"

His friend started chuckling. "Do her right here, Donny. I wanna see, and save some for me."

"Listen to me," I said. "You're not going to rape me because I won't allow it. You came here for money, right? Simply take the money and leave."

The one at the counter eyed me with disdain. "Bitch, if we wanna fuck you, we will. Who the fuck do you think you are?"

I don't know why but I still felt like I could talk some sense into them. "I'm a woman who is in love for the first time in her life—truly in love—and I want to live. I want to get married in a month, grow old together, and have beautiful children to carry on our names. I want to have a nice home, go to work every day, and come home to my family. I want to travel around the world with my husband and kids. I'm a woman who wants to love life. Don't you love life?"

"Does it look like we love life, bitch?" the one behind me yelled and pressed the muzzle of his gun harder onto my temple. "On second thought, man, this whore is psychotic. Let's get the money and get the fuck out of here. I need a fix, man."

The woman holding the infant started crying and clutching her baby to her chest. The man behind the counter started fidgeting with the cash register. Good, he could simply give them the money so they could leave and we'd all be safe.

My heart dropped in my chest when I saw a glimmer of metal in his other hand that had been reaching under the counter. *You idiot,* I thought as everything seemed to move in slow motion. *Now I won't be able to keep my promise to Momma!*

As the first of many shots rang out, only one word left my mouth. "Yardley!"

Thirty-four

Yardley

As I sat there, listening to Chance deliver Rayne's eulogy, I found it difficult to even breathe. This wasn't fair. I heard someone weeping in the pew behind me and glanced to see an older woman drying her tears with a handkerchief. I'd never seen the woman but she was visibly distraught; probably depressed about the horrific situation like everyone else.

"Yardley, did you want to say something?" I heard Chance speak the words but they didn't register until she repeated them. "Yardley, would you like to say something?"

Chance was standing in the pulpit, holding out her hand to me. I stood up slowly, willing my knees not to give up underneath me. Mom and Dad were flanking me on both sides in the pew and the safety net was suddenly invisible as I somehow managed to make it up there and face everyone.

Many of the faces I recognized and many I didn't. They'd run the story about Rayne's murder on all the local television stations but had no leads on finding her killer. Obviously a young punk who had no value for life; especially his own. I would've given anything to get my hands on him at that moment and would've given even more to get Rayne back. I'm sure the poor man who'd lost his wife and child in the same massacre felt the same way. Their double funeral had been the day before.

Many strangers had come to pay their respects to the beautiful young woman who had lost her life for no reason. The young woman who'd finalized her wedding chart and the menu with the caterer mere hours before she was gunned down like an animal.

"Do you need me to stay up here with you?" Chance whispered.

"No, I'll be fine."

As Chance descended the steps to take a seat, I found myself staring at Rayne's casket. It was now closed but the memories of her wake both haunted me and gave me pause to reflect on her beauty. It was her mother's idea to bury Rayne in her wedding dress. At first, I was opposed but then both she and Chance convinced me that it was what Rayne would've desired. That dress meant so much to her; she'd put forth so much time and effort to find the perfect one. Perfect it was; like she was to me.

Chance sat next to Rayne's mother and placed her arm around her. The death of her only child had devastated her. She was merely a shell of the woman she once was. I'd made all of the funeral arrangements because I knew she could never handle them.

I cleared my throat, made a fist with my right hand, and pressed it down on the podium in anger. "This isn't supposed to be happening," I said, speaking softly at first into the microphone. "I'd like to thank everyone for coming here today. It sounds crazy to say that because a month from now, I would've been standing up in a banquet hall not far from here, at my wedding reception, thanking everyone for coming to witness my marriage to the woman I love."

I paused and looked at all my boys, sitting there together in the third pew, with tears in all of their eyes. We'd been through so much together since our youth; in the heat of the moment, they were always there for me. This was no exception.

"I do love Rayne," I continued. "And even though she is gone, in the physical sense, she'll always exist right here." I placed my left hand over my chest. "Right here, in my heart. Rayne loved her life and everyone and everything in it. She had her ups and downs, her disappointments, but she kept everything in the right perspective. She . . ." I searched for the right word for a second. "She *appreciated* life; even when it let her down."

Rayne's mother started flailing her arms in the air and screamed, "I'm so sorry, baby! I'm so sorry I wasn't a better momma!"

Chance managed to calm her. At least she knew that she'd been the cause of much pain in Rayne's life.

"More than anything in this world, I wanted to be Rayne's husband. I wanted to be the father of her children. I wanted to watch her age, get gray hair and wrinkles, get dentures, walk with a cane; whatever life held in store for her. To me, she would've always been lovely; no matter what." I stared at her coffin again, the white ivory one with brass handles and a huge arrangement of pink roses. "But God had other plans for Rayne. For whatever the reasons, He had her venture into that store the other day, and now she's with Him."

I grasped onto the podium with both hands because I felt like I might collapse. "Everyone, each and every one of you, need to *appreciate* your lives. Don't let a single day pass without telling someone you love them. Better yet, don't simply be about words.

Show someone that you love them; be it an effortless gesture or even a hug or kiss. Let them know that they're loved. Rayne and I wasted a lot of time; before and after we became a couple. We wasted a lot of time in the beginning thinking that we were both tied down with someone else. We wasted a lot of time getting caught up in other people's problems and letting them cause us problems in return. I wish that she and I could get all that time back. I wish that we could start over. I would've spoken to her the first day I laid eyes on her in the bank. I would've asked her to share a cup of coffee or a couple of bagels." I found myself grinning as I recalled Rayne pretending to meet me in the bagel store instead of on her job. "Life truly is short; whether you live ten years or a hundred. Sooner or later, it's taken away. Live it so you have no regrets when your time comes."

I daydreamed during the entire repast in the church meeting hall. People came up to me constantly expressing their regrets. But they all seemed to blend together for me. Chance tried to force-feed me but I refused. I doubted that I'd ever have a real appetite again. Nothing would ever be the same for me. Food wouldn't taste the same. The sun wouldn't shine the same. My practice meant nothing to me. My life meant nothing to me. All I could think about was Rayne Waters. The way she smiled. The way she smelled. The way she tripped over her own feet all the time. The devilish grin she gave me when she was up to something sneaky. The way she screamed out my name when we made love.

"Earth to Yardley."

I glanced beside me to see Rayne's mother sitting there. She placed her hand on my arm.

"How are you holding up?" I asked her.

Arjay shrugged. "As well as can be expected. I'm gonna miss my baby girl so much."

"That makes two of us."

She looked across the room where Chance was being held up against a wall by Ricky. Chance's eyes were practically swollen shut. Her parents had come into town for the funeral and they were standing nearby; probably feeling helpless as far as coming to her aid. My parents had sat beside me during the service and the interment at the cemetery. Now they were busy, working the room, expressing their gratitude to everyone for their support.

"Chance is gonna really have a hard time," Arjay said. "They've been best friends for so long."

"Rayne loved Chance like a sister," I agreed. "There was nothing they wouldn't do for each other."

Felix and the rest of my crew were sitting at a table together, whispering quietly among themselves. I knew they'd try to cheer me up, in some way, but no matter what plan they conspired to pull off, it wouldn't work.

"Arjay, do you think Rayne is watching over us now?"

She grinned. "I certainly hope so. I sure need someone to watch over me. I wish I'd been a better mother."

I suddenly felt sorry for the woman who'd once been so determined to cause havoc in my relationship with Rayne. The one Rayne had tried to help by sending her to a rehabilitation clinic, only to have her turn right back to alcohol.

"Were you the best mother you knew how to be?"

"Yes, I did the best I could."

"Then, let it go. Don't blame yourself for anything. This is the fault of one person, one idiot, who I hope is caught before he destroys someone else's life."

"Still no leads, huh?" she asked.

"None that I've heard of. I can tell you this much. If they do catch him and he somehow manages to get off lightly, I'll kill him with my bare hands."

She didn't respond; only stared at me. "Yardley, promise me one thing."

"What's that?"

"Promise me that you'll love again."

I let out a heavy sigh. "That's one promise I definitely can't make. I could never love someone else the way I loved Rayne. She was the one; the only one."

"But you have so much to give to a woman."

"There's nothing another woman can do for me. Not now; not ever."

After everyone else was long gone, I went back to the cemetery to stand over Rayne's grave. The diggers hadn't finished covering up her remains. I looked down in the hole where a few of us had sprinkled dirt earlier and finally released all the tears from their prison.

I got down on my knees as storm clouds began gathering above the funeral home tent.

"Rayne, I don't know why you were taken away from me but I know that my love for you will never die. You've taken the biggest part of me with you; my heart. When you look at that diamond on your finger while you're in heaven, remember. Remember our love. Remember everything we were; everything we could've been. For I will always, always, remember you."

Epilogue
Charlotte, North Carolina
Two Years Later

"Doctor Brown!" I could hear someone shouting my name but couldn't see them through all the congestion at the baggage claim area in the Charlotte airport. "Doctor Yardley Brown!"

A tall, leggy woman pushed her way through the people waiting patiently for their bags at turnstile C. She was dark-skinned with her hair pushed back in a bun and wore glasses.

"Looking for me?" I asked her when I realized she was standing there glaring at me.

She looked down at a page torn out of a magazine—medical journal to be exact—and back up at me. "I guess this is you in the picture but you look different," she commented.

I held out my hand. "May I see that?" She handed it to me and it was a picture of me from several years earlier. I barely recognized myself. It was an article I'd written as part of my educational requirements. I chuckled. "I was much younger in this photo."

She smiled, exposing a perfect set of teeth. "Well, none of us are cheating time." She offered her hand for a shake. "I'm Doctor Solitaire Baker-Reynolds; an associate of Doctor Thompson's."

I shook her hand. "Doctor Yardley Brown, but you knew that much already."

We both laughed.

"Welcome to North Carolina. First time here?"

"Not at all. Most African-Americans have deep roots in the south; especially North Carolina. In my case, I attended college here. North Carolina Central."

"True. At least the ones on the East Coast. Have you gotten your bags already?" she asked.

I pointed to the garment bag at my feet. "Yes, I'm all set."

We walked to the parking garage in almost complete silence. It was strange because our initial words had been so lighthearted and friendly. She was driving a Volkswagen Touareg and I tossed my bag into the back.

We were out of the garage and getting on the highway when I couldn't take the quiet any longer. She didn't have on the radio or anything and you could've heard a squirrel run under the SUV.

"So, Doctor Solitaire Baker-Reynolds, that sure is a long name. I take it that you're married."

I'd seen the wedding ring on her finger so I already knew the answer; between that and the hyphenated surname. At least, I thought I did.

"Actually, I'm a widow. My husband was killed in an auto accident during my pregnancy."

"Oh, I'm so sorry to hear that."

She gave me a sideways glance. "You have nothing to be sorry for. It wasn't your fault."

I let out a laugh and instantly regretted the implications of it. "I'm sorry; about the laugh, that is. It's just that I understand where you're coming from. I've spoken those same words so many times over the last couple of years."

"Really?"

"Yes." I took a deep breath, debating about whether I even felt like discussing Rayne. It was still so painful for me. "My fiancée, Rayne, was murdered shortly before our wedding date."

"Oh, my God! That's horrible!"

"Yes, it was horrible."

There was a pause while we both gathered our thoughts. Certainly, her loss was as devastating as mine, so we were two souls left behind.

"You said you were pregnant when your husband was killed?" I asked her.

"Yes. I have a little boy, named Jeremy after his father."

"How old?"

"He's nine, going on ninety. He thinks he's going to be the next Bill Gates."

"Hey, there's nothing wrong with aspiring toward a goal like that. There could be much worse things."

"True, but try having a nine-year-old asking you for all of your receipts and duplicate checks so he can keep track of them on his accounting software."

I chuckled. "That is pretty funny."

"He's a mess but he gives me reason to live."

"Well, it's always great to have a reason to live."

We chatted for the rest of the way to Doctor Thompson's

Sports and Medicine Clinic in downtown Charlotte. He'd flown me into town in hopes of convincing me to take a position there. While I'd lived in the D.C. area the majority of my life, things had never been the same for me since Rayne's death. Felix, Dwayne, and Mike tried to hook me up with women right and left. They couldn't understand that replacing Rayne wasn't as easy as one, two, three. For me, there was no replacement.

Doctor Thompson, whom I'd met several years earlier, did still look exactly the same. The lucky ones never seem to age. He was in his midfifties and had more than twenty thousand patients on the record for his clinic. There were three other doctors working there, including Solitaire, and he felt it time to add a fourth.

He greeted me with a bear hug and led me into his office, after thanking Solitaire for giving me a ride. After we took seats, he gave me his best speech.

"Yardley, we could really use you down in these parts. Business is booming and Charlotte is becoming a progressive city; it's growing by leaps and bounds."

"Yes, I know. The news has spread up North and I've heard of a lot of people moving this way, down to Charlotte and on down to Atlanta."

"Charlotte's great, but I'll always be a Giants fan," he said with a grin.

"That's right," I said. "You're originally from New York."

He laughed. "How could you forget? My accent still hasn't left me after all these years. I get many jokes about it from Southerners whose accents are just as humorous to me."

"Well, I hope that I don't develop a drawl. I managed to get through college without one."

He got serious and stared at me. "So, you're considering it?"

"In all honesty, starting over might be the change that I need," I admitted. "I guess you heard what happened."

"Yes, and I'm truly sorry."

I started to tell him that he had nothing to be sorry about but remembered my earlier conversation with Solitaire. Instead, I said, "Thanks."

"How about I give you a tour? That's always a good place to start."

"Fine by me."

"And don't forget that the cost of living is lower down here; an added bonus."

"You sure are laying it on thick," I stated jokingly.

"Got to give it a hundred percent effort."

Doctor Thompson gave me a lot to think about that afternoon. He dropped me off at the Marriott and invited me to dinner. I accepted and decided to catch a quick nap before he came back for me.

I laid down, closed my eyes, and dreamed of Rayne. I woke up to a knock on the door three hours later. Expecting it to be Doctor Thompson, I didn't bother to put on my shirt.

"I apologize. I overslept. Give me a few——"

Solitaire stood in the doorway, looking much different than earlier. Her hair was cascading down her shoulders and she had on a shapely black dress with open-toe high heels.

"He asked me to come pick you up," she stated uneasily, staring at my bare chest. "I hope you don't mind."

"No . . . No, come on in." I moved aside so she could enter. "I didn't realize you were joining us for dinner."

"Well, I certainly hope you're not disappointed." "He thought it would be a good idea, since we mi so closely together in the near future."

"Are the other doctors coming as well?"

"Strangely enough, no, not to my knowledge." She giggled. "Maybe he expects me to try to persuade you in some way."

She sat down on the bed and I rushed into the bathroom, where I had to confront what I physically couldn't control. Solitaire Baker-Reynolds had sexually excited me. But it was more than that. What was it?

To be continued in:
Solitaire: Afterburn 2

Wasting Time
A Commentary by Zane

I know right now a lot of my readers are wondering why I chose to kill Rayne Waters off in the novel; something I have never done to a main character in my previous works. The answer is simple: I wanted to show how precious life is and how important it is to live every single day to the fullest while you still have an opportunity.

When it comes right down to it, this novel was about one thing: wasting time. Too many of us waste time on insignificant things that, ultimately, do not matter. At the end of our lives, are we really going to care about trifling behavior of our friends and relatives? Are we really going to care about how much our clothes cost and what material possessions we owned? Are we really going to entertain the kind of shallow thoughts so many people do on a daily basis? Who looks better? Who makes more money? Who this and who that?

I loved the Rayne character for many reasons. She was full of life, compassionate, and she was a sister who had her head on straight. But she also had demons she was battling within herself because of her mother's promiscuity. It was hard for me to kill her off but the fact remains that some of us do die young. Rayne will never see her thirtieth birthday, much like a beautiful cousin of mine who died the same year that I lost my firstborn daughter, who never really had a chance to live at all. Rayne and Yardley both wasted a lot of time on people who could not love them the way they deserved to be loved; as many of us do.

For all the sisters and brothers out here currently wasting time, please stop. I am not just talking relationships that obviously are headed in the wrong direction. I am talking about those of you who have given up on your hopes and aspirations; deciding to settle for whatever comes your way. You have to learn to be proactive and not reactive. Life waits for no one and this is the only chance you will ever get to make a difference.

If you are not happy with your job, don't quit—you still have bills to pay—but start to get your game plan together to do something that will make you happy. You do not have to remain in a dismal situation—no matter what others may tell you. Trust me when I say that there are many dream stealers and reality stealers lurking around you. Eight out of ten of them will say something negative or attempt to dissuade you when you discuss your life goals with them. Ignore them. Let them go. Surround yourself with positive people who have positive thoughts and you will be amazed at how quickly things will change.

In my life, God has closed a lot of doors in my face because He knew I was headed in the wrong direction. The good part is that He opened the right doors and steered me that way. If your gut feeling tells you that you are headed in the wrong direction, turn around before it is too late.

Many readers have asked me how do I come up with my stories. I always say the same thing. Yes, I have always been blessed with a vivid imagination but more importantly, I am one of those people who truly loves life. I take something positive away from every experience; good ones and bad ones. Everything happens for a reason. The main thing is to bring closure to anything that you begin. I love creating characters because I love human nature; how we act, how we love, how we show our emotions. I am extremely observant and it brings me joy to see people happy. It saddens me to see people in stress; especially my sisters. For one period of about six months last year, everywhere I seemed to go, sisters were being hostile to one another. Whether I was in a department store or a restaurant or just walking down the street, I would see women fussing; even though they did not know one another. I reasoned that it could not be because they disliked one another since most of them did not even know each other's names. We are just a society of "superwomen" dealing with too much stress. Stress can do a lot of things to you—none of them good—to both your physical and emotional being. Do not let it defeat you.

No matter how bad things seem, they could always be worse. It amazes me to see people worried sick over a flat tire or a broken nail, when there are other people living with disabilities who cherish every single moment they have on this earth. Earlier this year, I lost a dear friend who had been sick his entire life. He was not supposed to live past his tenth birthday but he almost made it to thirty also. The one thing about Kevin was that he never complained, even though he was always in severe pain, he never once complained. Even though he was in and out of the hospital throughout the years, he never complained. I only wished he had lived long enough to attend the Prince concert I had purchased tickets for him to go see. The concert was in August, but he was gone in July. His parents attended the concert in his place.

My brother went out to a party when he was nineteen years old and never came back. My daughter lived exactly five months and five days. As I sit here typing this, my Aunt Jennie has just died on the very day I completed this novel. We all must remember:

Life is like a coin.
You can spend it any way you wish,
but you can spend it only once.
    —Author Unknown